"EVERY

M

"Everything, hn er got his dander up a an who's leaving the mountain in two weeks?"

Mary lifted her tear-stained face. "The professor—Jude—he wants an annul . . . annulment."

Grossmuder May laughed. "So he plans not to touch ye, does he? Well, then, I say your job is to turn this wedding into a marriage . . . and I don't mean only the bedding; that's the least of it in some ways. A marriage is about the physical body, eh? But also the spirit, the mind, and the heart."

"It's not that easy, though."

Grossmuder grunted and lowered herself onto the bunk. "*Nee*, it won't be. He's afar off, I think, from loving that way—anyone, not only you. But if you keep to what you know to be true, true of the Lord and true to the mountain, you'll be all right, child, no matter where you go."

The Amish Bride OF ICE MOUNTAIN

KELLY LONG

ZEBRA BOOKS
KENSINGTON PUBLISHING CORP.
http://www.kensingtonbooks.com

ZEBRA BOOKS are published by

Kensington Publishing Corp.
119 West 40th Street
New York, NY 10018

All Kensington titles, imprints, and distributed lines are available at special quantity discounts for bulk purchases for sales promotion, premiums, fund-raising, educational, or institutional use.

Special book excerpts or customized printings can also be created to fit specific needs. For details, write or phone the office of the Kensington Special Sales Manager: Attn.: Special Sales Department. Kensington Publishing Corp., 119 West 40th Street, New York, NY 10018. Phone: 1-800-221-2647.

Zebra and the Z logo Reg. U.S. Pat. & TM Off.

First Printing: November 2014
ISBN-13: 978-1-4201-3544-2
ISBN-10: 1-4201-3544-9

First Electronic Edition: November 2014
eISBN-13: 978-1-4201-3545-9
eISBN-10: 1-4201-3545-7

10 9 8 7 6 5 4 3 2 1

Printed in the United States of America

To my father,
Gilbert Lee Stout,
his doctor,
William McCauley,
and to my daughter,
Grace—
who created one of
the most valuable
characters in the book—
BEAR.

Prologue

Coudersport, Pennsylvania, 1894

The miner wielded the pickax with ruthless precision, pausing only now and then to wipe his brow in the high summer heat. He was sure that he was mining the spot the Cattaraugus Indian had indicated as the source of the silver ore he possessed. The rocks and dirt gave, and then he was through. The shine flashed against his eyes with a blast of cool air. He leaned into the hole, staring in amazement, as his dreams of silver gave way to a palatial display of summer ice . . .

Chapter One

Ice Mountain, Pennsylvania, Present Day

Associate Professor of Amish Studies Jude Lyons squeezed his eyes shut in the bright light of the summer sun and pretended he hadn't heard what the girl said.

But the word rang indelibly through his mind . . . *dishonored.* He opened his eyes and stared down off the wooden porch step into the serious young face of the Amish girl, Mary King. Her dark hair was neatly coiled beneath her *kapp,* displaying only a straight, white part. Her hazel eyes were soulful, mournful, and the pale skin of her throat was even whiter than he remembered.

Say something, you idiot, his brain chided him. But he couldn't seem to get past the heated imagery that flashed through his memory—the day had been hot, the blueberry patch more than cool. And maybe he'd known somehow that their relationship would build to that sudden torrential burn of intense moments, but he stupidly hadn't considered the consequences. And he certainly hadn't imagined that Mary's older brother, Joseph, might have been observing from the forest.

Jude never usually let himself go physically, not even with his fiancée. The blood thrummed in his ears—Carol . . . what would he say to Carol about this? But of course he was overreacting. He needn't mention making out with Mary at all . . .

"My *daed* and *bruders* will be along shortly—to make sure you do the right thing."

Her melodic voice was calm, rich with decades of dialectal purity, but he blinked at her words.

"What?"

"I expect they'll take a while to rouse the bishop. He likes to sleep, you know."

He likes to sleep . . . Jude took a shaky step down to the flagstone nearest her and her small bare feet.

"Mary, I'm sorry. It was all a mistake . . . I'm due to be married in the fall. Are you sure Joseph saw . . ." He let his eyes drop with irreverence to her shoulders, as if she'd bear the imprints of his fingertips somehow, but there was nothing visible between the covering of her apron and dress.

"You know you were the first man who ever kissed me like that or touched—"

"I know. I know," he broke in hastily, not wanting her to verify what he remembered all too well. Her innocence had been as palpable as his own heartbeat, her novice mouth returning his kisses with a tentative response that had made his throat burn.

"*Dat* wasn't happy, what with you being an outsider and all, but he's willing to settle seeing that you're *schmart* in the head."

Jude thought of the endless hours of study, sleepless nights upon nights, now his doctorate work, and his almost-completed book about the Amish of Ice Mountain, Pennsylvania. He had plans of returning home and breaking away from his father's successful business and wealthy lifestyle and becoming a professor of Amish studies. He told himself that there was no way he was going to be coerced into "doing the right thing" for kissing a willing girl in the broad light of day. But he should have known better. If there was anything that he'd learned from his study of this people, it was their inherent sense of old-fashioned honor. The Mountain Amish were also about a hundred years farther behind the times than other *Amisch*, both in values and circumstances, and he was in the middle of nowhere with not a single soul to speak in his defense.

He scrambled in desperation for an answer, an angle . . . "Mary, your dad isn't going to want you to leave the mountain, and you'd have to if I . . . if we did anything hasty. You know I'm supposed to go back to Atlanta in two weeks."

"Metro Atlanta." She emphasized what he knew she had heard him say from time to time.

"Never mind," he muttered, but then another thought came to him. He peered into her eyes. "Mary, how old are you?" *And why in heaven's name have I not asked that before—*

"Eighteen—nineteen in October."

"Well, that's something . . ." She wasn't underage by his world's standards at least. At least—what the devil was he thinking? He owed her nothing. "I'm twenty-six," he offered in spite of himself.

"Way past marrying age," she observed.

"Yeah." *From your world's view.*

She glanced behind her as instinctively, he knew, as a doe. "Here they come."

Jude was suddenly more than nervous. He wanted to sink into the ground, dissolve, or at least run as the four men broke from the line of trees, their faces set like stone. And then he felt everything go black . . .

Mary watched him fall to the ground with dismay. She hurried to kneel by his side, feeling his head; she'd heard a thud when he fell. Sure enough, as her careful fingers combed through his short, neat dark blond hair, she came upon a fast-swelling goose egg at the back of his skull.

She frowned, wishing *Grossmuder* May was there with her poultices. Then she carefully picked up his spectacles from the ground, glad that they hadn't broken.

"Weak as water."

Mary looked up as her *fater*'s voice boomed out, filled with scorn.

"I gave him the news, *Fater*, but you know he has an illness of the blood that can cause him to become light in the head."

"Ach, the *buwe* wilted like a rose when you told him; some husband he's bound to make. Haul him up . . . Edward, Joseph."

Mary leaned aside as her two older *bruders* caught Professor Lyons's arms. "Be careful," she urged as they half dragged him to his feet, supporting him on either side.

Mary got up and hurried to move so she could look up into his handsome face. His head lolled from side to side, his blue eyes closed behind thick lashes.

"Let's git on with it," her *dat* said, glancing at Bishop Umble.

"But he's not awake yet," Mary protested, looking into the wise old bishop's wizened face.

"Ah, but he was awake enough a day ago, eh, Mary?" her father barked. "It makes *nee* difference if he's out of his head or not. He'll do what needs doing."

Mary flushed at her father's brash words, true though they were.

Bishop Umble cleared his throat. "Your *fater* is right in this matter, Mary. We cannot allow such things on this mountain . . . a man dallying with an innocent maid. This must be set right."

The professor groaned and Mary pressed her hand to his warm cheek. She felt like she was touching some wild, beautiful thing that had come to rest in her world for a moment and would soon be gone. She knew she didn't match him, couldn't understand him, but she wanted him, wanted to keep him and care for him . . . like a wounded eagle.

And then the bishop began to speak in High German, saying with quiet, sacred reverence the words that would bind her to the *Englischer* for all time.

Jude heard the old language as if through a long funnel and recognized its import. He tried to open his eyes. He wanted to throw up and his head felt as if it had been hewn in two. He knew his sugar must be very low, but he still managed to speak. "No."

He felt rough hands shake him a bit from side to side and he thought of the clamor of iron bells in an old church tower. He tried again. "I said no. I do not con—consent."

"I—I would . . . Thrash him, *buwes*!" The thunderous voice could only be Abner King's—Mary King's father. He wanted to wince away from the blows that he knew were coming but couldn't seem to lift his eyelids.

Then he heard Mary's voice and felt the soft press of her back against his chest. "*Nee, Fater.* You will not hurt him . . . I—I don't want him like this, not with force. He-he didn't force me, I-I wanted . . . I mean . . . I've told you we were only kissing."

Jude got his eyes open with grim thankfulness for the tight grips on his arms. He caught the scent of Mary's hair beneath his chin and spoke with gaining strength.

"Look, *Herr* King . . . Bishop. We kissed some, true, and I . . ."

Mary was thrust aside to be replaced with the blunt, reddened face of her father. "Don't say it, scoundrel. Joseph here filled the picture in real clear. Do you think I'll allow you to shame her like that?"

Jude swallowed at the pounding violence in the words and shook his head. "I never meant to do any harm."

"I'll tell you what you'll do, you—you . . . You'll marry her or give up them notes you've been takin' these past months. Always working on your book—well, there'll be no book if there's no marriage. Consider it a fair dowry."

Jude heard the pain lacing the outcry and the threat, and his head swam. He didn't want this . . . he'd come to know and respect these people. But losing what he considered to be his life's work so far—the notes for the book on Ice Mountain—was not an option.

Jude felt the grip on his right arm ratchet up.

"I say we beat him into agreeing," Joseph King growled.

"*Nee,*" Bishop Umble said. "There'll be none of that. You know that violence is not an option for us. Abner, *buwes*—I'm surprised at you."

"But it's my girl!" Mary's father cried.

Jude nodded though the effort cost him. "It's still another two weeks until I leave. Let me and Mary have time to—decide."

"You already decided," Abner growled. "Yesterday."

Jude lifted his chin, and the older man apparently took it as a challenge.

"Burn his cabin and all that writing, *buwes.* Now."

Jude staggered when he was released and Bishop

Umble caught his shoulder. "Joseph . . . Edward. Stop this instant!"

Jude saw one of Mary's brothers strike a match against a booted heel and his world spun into crystalline clarity.

"I'll marry her."

Mary bit her bottom lip as the bishop finished the old words that bound the professor to her for the rest of this earthly life. She didn't like the trapping her *fater* did during the winter, and somehow, this wedding seemed equally bad in a way. She noticed that the professor didn't look at her but was focused on snatching back the pile of yellow notebook paper that Joseph had held out as extra reinforcement. He'd also pulled some hard candy from his jeans pocket and was sucking it. She knew it had something to do with his blood.

"Bring the broom," her father bawled out and Mary jumped. She'd forgotten the broom and its meaning.

Edward brought a broomstick forward, and he and Joseph bent to hold it level about a foot off the ground.

"What's this?" the professor asked, his voice laced with sudden interest. Mary understood his shift of mood. She'd helped him with his work all summer, and whenever he came across something "unique," as he called it, about her people, he furiously wrote it down in one of the yellow tablets. Now he pulled a pencil nub from the pocket of his blue jeans and started to write on the back of one of the pages he'd secured from Joseph. Mary handed him his spectacles and he slipped them on with an absent word of thanks, then went back to his words.

"Stop yer foolishness and writing," her father ordered in a voice that made Mary cringe. She couldn't understand her *daed*'s contempt for the professor even though he acknowledged that the younger man was *schmart.* It was something to think about. But now her heart beat with growing excitement. Somehow, the broom made everything seem more real.

"Hold hands with my girl and jump the broom together," her *dat* instructed. "And don't fall—or it'll be worse luck than what you're startin' off with."

The professor neatly folded his papers and put them in his back pocket, then reached for Mary's hand.

"Why are we doing this?" he asked.

Her *daed* snorted.

"You jump over the broom together to symbolize moving from life alone to a life together," the bishop explained.

"So there's no religious significance?"

Mary knew the professor might ask about religious doings but that he didn't believe in *Gott.* He'd told her that one day. And she knew it was wrong, though she couldn't help being drawn to him all the same.

"*Nee,* no religion," her *fater* snapped. "Now jump."

* * *

Jude gazed down at Mary's hand in his. One part of him kept murmuring *annulment . . . annulment*, while the other, that part his grandfather had nurtured and taught, wondered if he could really do it to her. He knew she had intense curiosity about the outside world and understood how keenly her mind worked. It might be an interesting last few chapters in the book to see how a Mountain Amish girl would fare in the world of the wealthy of Atlanta, and then he could always bring her home and leave. She might hate him for a while, but then she'd forget and marry someone else from her own people . . . He ignored the strange prick of disquiet that accompanied this idea.

He felt her tighten her grip in his, her hand small and trusting, and realized that she'd caught hold of her skirts. She bent her knees and he did the same, hoping that Joseph and Edward wouldn't raise the broom. And then they were jumping over the long stick in fluid unison to land in the moss on the other side. He let her warm hand go.

"An excellent jump." The bishop clapped. "There—see, Abner, things are bound to be right now."

Jude's new father-in-law grunted while Joseph and Edward rose from holding the broom.

"We'll leave." Bishop Umble spoke with authority and Jude ducked his head away from the solemnity in the man's wise eyes. It was almost as if the *Amisch* leader could see his less-than-honorable plans, and Jude had the passing thought that he might have felt better if Joseph had taken a swing at him.

"I'll stay on a bit and take care of his head," Mary said.

"That, and nothing else, Mary. You'll be home in time to fix supper," Abner warned.

The bishop laughed and clapped Abner on his broad shoulder. "I'm afraid that you can't have it both ways, Abner. The girl's his wife now. She takes care of him and gets his supper now. And 'anything else' is up to them."

His new father-in-law blustered, then seemed to realize that he'd forced himself out of a cook, and Jude had to suppress a smile. He knew how hard Mary worked and he'd be glad to give her a break from it all for a while. He slung his arm around her shoulders and grinned at his new brothers-in-law.

"Well, boys, it looks like you two will be taking up Mary's place and chores."

"*Ach*, but maybe I should . . ." Mary began and Jude tightened his hold on her with deliberation.

"You should care for our cabin, sweetheart. At least for the next two weeks—until we leave the mountain."

Then everyone looked sober and he regretted his loose tongue, though he'd spoken the truth.

"Be well, daughter," Abner mumbled and started off. Her two brothers followed and Bishop Umble paused to gaze up at Jude.

"You'll be good to the girl?"

"Yes, sir. I give my word." Jude felt the other man weighing his words. Then he nodded and also turned to go, and the men disappeared into the tree line once more.

Jude would have moved his arm but Mary turned in to the line of his body, pressing against his hip and burying her face in his white shirt.

"Mary . . . Mary," he whispered, thinking she might be sad, but then she lifted her head to smile at him with her beautiful mouth.

"What would you like for supper, Professor?"

You . . . Jude's mind recoiled from the unbidden thought as if he'd held his hand to white-hot coals. He cleared his throat. "Anything will be fine."

"All right, Professor."

He stepped away from her. "Call me Jude."

Her smile grew and he blinked.

"All right. Jude."

Chapter Two

She had been inside his cabin before, but now she felt an intimacy about the ordered stacks of books and papers that lined his makeshift desk of plywood on two sawhorses. She stared at his neat handwriting until the letters and words made a blend of twining thread, swirling out into a lifetime of possibility. She jumped when he touched her arm.

"Well, little friend, we seem to have gotten ourselves into quite a situation." His deep voice sounded tired.

"Is your head still hurting?" Her eyes swept the simple single bunk made up with white sheets and a green sleeping bag he must have somehow gotten past the bishop. She knew that his coming to Ice Mountain was conditional upon his living with strict adherence to all the ways of the people. He'd told her how warm the strange fabric of the sleeping bag was at night, and more than once during a summer storm, she had longed for the covering as she shivered in her own bed under threadbare quilts.

He must have seen her staring at the bed because he cleared his throat and stepped away from her.

"I need more sugar."

She watched him unwrap some candies and pop them into his mouth. He turned to hold one out to her but she shook her head. He sighed. "I have the type of hypoglycemia that is not diabetes—it's rare." He must have known she didn't understand, and he shook his head. "Yesterday, Mary . . . Look, I want to talk about it."

She fingered a knot on the bedpost and thought of the warmth of the tanned skin of his throat beneath her fingertips. He'd smelled like summer and pine and something strange and wonderful in its unfamiliarity and she'd . . . "What is there to talk about?"

He dropped down onto the stool in front of his makeshift desk and sighed. "I shouldn't have touched you—kissed you like that."

She swallowed. "So why did you, then?"

His eyes swept her body from head to toe and he half smiled. "You're beautiful—inside and out. You deserve a lot more than a selfish writer who doesn't share your ways."

"You want to take it back, then—the kissing?"

"I'm not going to lie to you, Mary. I've tried to be honest with you all summer. You've been my friend, taught me so much about your people—you deserve the truth now. I know how curious you are about the outside world. I could give you a chance to see it, experience it. And then that wedding we had . . ."

Something was wrong, she could tell from the

way his blue eyes dropped to the rough hardwood floor. "All right." She felt she should speak with caution, having the same instinct that she did when a bear was along the path ahead when she went herb picking.

"Well, you could come to Atlanta—Metro Atlanta— with me, as my wife, of course—but we wouldn't . . . we couldn't . . ." He paused, struggling, and awareness dawned in her mind.

"We wouldn't lie together?"

"Right," he exhaled with a quick smile. "Then we could get an annulment in a few months, an end to the marriage, and you could come back here afterward and . . ."

"Wait . . . *sei se gut.*" Her voice shook a bit and she paused to steady herself. "We . . . we jumped the broom."

He stood up and came to bend close to her face. She could see the heavy fall of his lashes and smell the butterscotch-candy sweetness of his breath. She wanted to sob aloud.

"Mary, come on. We can't . . . you can't leave this mountain, these people, forever. What about Isaac Mast? Hmm?"

She felt her face flame in embarrassment at the thought of the pimply faced youth who dogged her footsteps. "Isaac is a boy."

He smiled and brushed a finger down her hot cheek. "All right. But, Mary, think about it. Freedom . . . excitement, a taste of what you want and then home again."

"Why?" she managed to say. "Why not leave me here in the first place? This is not right, a lie before

Gott." She bit her lip, knowing she'd said the wrong thing when he stiffened and pulled away.

"I forget your Amish roots, don't I?" he asked with a wry twist of his handsome lips.

"And I can never forget," she whispered. She clutched her hands in her apron, then jumped at a scratching sound on the door.

She met her husband's eyes and he shrugged. She hoped her *dat* hadn't decided to come back, then moved to open the door.

Jude rubbed at the lump on the back of his head and wanted to crawl under the desk when Mary opened the door to reveal *Grossmuder* May. The *Amisch* woman was older than time, had a toothless grin, and knew far too much gossip about the mountain community she helped take care of with her herbs and remedies. Mary's questions tore at him. Why couldn't he simply leave her here? Gather his notes and be gone during the night? But some sense of twisted honor held him, and now here was one of the eldest in the small mountain community—come to watch the debacle of his entrapment.

No doubt news of the impromptu wedding had spread, and May wanted to chat. He rose in deference to the old woman, who was revered as a healer, and waited for her to speak.

"Married, are ye?" she rasped, hobbling farther into the small space.

"Jah, Grossmuder," Mary said shyly.

Jude felt the weight of the raisin-dark eyes in the wrinkled face and stood his ground. May brushed past him to pull a small pouch from her apron pocket. "I've come to bless the marriage bed."

"What?" Jude was nonplussed and felt his cheeks grow hot in spite of himself when he glanced at Mary. His new wife looked distinctly uncomfortable. *My wife . . .*

"It's a custom . . . you can write it down," Mary said.

But for once, Jude had no desire to write as he watched *Grossmuder* May open her pouch. The air in the small cabin became permeated with the smells of lavender, rose petals, and other entrancing scents he couldn't identify as the old woman lavishly sprinkled his bunk with the contents of the dried herbal mixture.

"Now the *kinner* will come quick enough."

The old woman turned and Jude felt a chill go down his back—the children. He reminded himself that none of this was real—not the wedding nor the bed.

"I think I'll walk up to the meadow for a bit—clear my head." Jude gave Mary an awkward pat on the shoulder and nodded to May. He left, intent on the grass beneath his feet and the stretch of sky above him—blue and framing the tops of other mountains that were far, far from weddings and children.

Mary sank miserably down on the bunk despite the herbs beneath her skirt.

The old woman leaned on her cane and shook her head. "What is it, child?"

It didn't occur to Mary to do anything but tell the truth. *Grossmuder* May was as close to a *mamm* as she'd ever had. "Everything's wrong," Mary choked.

"Everything, hmm? You mean to say that Abner got his dander up and now you're married to a man who's leaving the mountain in two weeks?"

Mary lifted her tear-stained face. "The professor—Jude—he wants an anull . . . annulment."

Grossmuder May laughed. "So he plans not to touch ye, does he? Well, then, I say your job is to turn this wedding into a marriage . . . and I don't mean only the bedding; that's the least of it in some ways. A marriage is about the physical body, eh? But also the spirit, the mind, and the heart."

"It's not that easy, though."

Grossmuder grunted and lowered herself onto the bunk. "*Nee*, it won't be. He's afar off, I think, from loving that way—anyone, not only you. But if you keep to what you know to be true, true of the Lord and true to the mountain, you'll be all right, child, no matter where you go."

Mary nodded and leaned into the firm embrace of the older woman, feeling the seeds of hope begin to burgeon in her heart.

Grossmuder stroked Mary's warm cheek. "And don't forget, child, to make the rounds of the mountain before you leave. There'll be wedding presents for you aplenty."

Mary smiled, wondering what the professor would think of the coming gifts.

* * *

Jude flung himself down in the grassy meadow and drew an arm over his eyes. He realized that he probably had a minor concussion when the back of his neck throbbed without ceasing.

He drifted in and out of thought and decided that Mary might be more than a help to him if he was straightforward with her, maybe if he told her about Carol . . . He remembered the day he'd left home to come to Ice Mountain and almost had to laugh when the scene played across his mind . . .

"I hate that you're going," Carol said for the fourth time, and Jude resisted the urge to grit his teeth at the blonde lounging on his old bed. *Yeah, you hate me going because there's nothing you want more than to have me trussed up for a wedding that I am in no way prepared for* . . . He'd come back to his parents' mansion to pick up a few books he'd left behind when he'd moved, and Carol obviously couldn't resist another opportunity to hound him.

"It's three months, Caro—you can shop with my mother, go to the spa, all that. I'll be back." He waved a hand in dismissal and tried to concentrate on filling a hiking bag with some of the books. The rest could always be sent.

He was doing his doctorate work in Amish studies, and he knew that Carol Sutherfield had been waiting a long time to see him properly brought to the altar. He'd been drinking one night three months before and had, on impulse, gone to the family safe and provided Caro with his grandmother's engagement ring and a proposal he could barely recall. *Stupid idiot* . . . But it had made both families more than happy because Carol and he had grown up together and were expected to marry as soon as age permitted. Still, this was his doing, and she sat on his old bed, both confident and petulant, her long legs curled catlike around the side of his bag as if she might keep him from going somehow.

"But, Jude, all I've listened to forever, it seems, is your ongoing, single-minded preaching about the Amish . . . the Amish in Lancaster, in Ohio, and now *Mountain Amish* in a place called Ice Mountain—I doubt they'll even have shoes."

"I don't preach," he said, reaching behind her knee to find the zip for the bag. *And you know it, Caro . . . I don't preach and I don't believe in God. It's simple. But you'll probably want the wedding in a church, where you can wear virginal white over your so-impure self . . .*

"You know what I mean." She rose off the bed on high black heels, still not tall enough to reach his mouth unless she balanced on tiptoe. He stepped away before she could wind her arms around his neck, and she teetered for a moment before regaining her footing.

"Jude, please."

Please what, Caro? Please touch you, go through the motions, make you feel what I never do, never will, with you? We'll settle down to quiet, horribly perfect domesticity . . . the Lyon in the cage . . . I am such an idiot. But there's no going back now. I'm committed and I always follow through . . .

"Three months. And you've got me, right, sweetheart?" He bent and swiped his lips across her carefully made-up cheek, then grabbed his bag.

"But we won't even be able to text or talk on the phone," she wailed as he started out of the room.

He'd turned around for a brief moment, giving her a wry smile. "Then write me letters, Caro. There's an *Amischer* who comes down off the mountain to pick up the mail every few days."

"I haven't written a letter in ages. Jude! You simply cannot go."

But I'm gone, Caro. Three months. No mansion, no money, no you . . . He started to grin as he jogged down the broad staircase.

He'd turned into the sunlit library and looked with affection at the old man in the wheelchair seated near the large windows.

"So, you're ready then, Jude?"

His grandfather's voice always reminded him of the gravelly sound of rocks in rough seas. Jude had put his hand on the frail shoulder and nodded. "Yes, sir."

"Ice Mountain, eh? I remember you begging for tales of the place when you were young . . . always drawn there for some reason."

He'd laughed. "It sounds mysterious, I guess . . . and the university believes that there is a lot to be learned about the Mountain Amish."

The old man coughed once and Jude patted his back with concern. "Grandfather . . . this three months . . . I'll miss you."

"Don't worry, boy. I'll not go far while you're gone and that Carol creature won't either, I wager. Can't understand why you don't wriggle out of that mess."

"Have to keep up with my duties, right?"

"Duties, bah! You should marry for love and love only, like I did with your grandmother . . . Amelia . . . she was so beautiful."

Jude saw the old blue eyes start to cloud and gave his grandfather a brief hug, then adjusted the lap robe around the front of the wheelchair. "I'll be back," he whispered.

Then he was through the foyer and nodding to the servant who opened the door.

"See you in three months, Bas."

"Yes, sir, Professor Lyons."

"And tell my parents good-bye for me, will you, Bas?" *Because I am not going to listen to their crap about what I'm about to do . . .*

"Yes, sir."

He threw his bag in the back of the blue Expedition that had been brought round and climbed inside. Then he turned the key and started the drive to freedom . . . to Ice Mountain.

He sighed into the soft wind, coming back to the present with a wry smile on his lips.

Chapter Three

After *Grossmuder* May left, Mary went to sit on the small stoop of the cabin. She realized she'd have to go back to her *daed*'s cabin because she had no clothes with her, or any of her small possessions. She tried to think over the difference between a wedding and a marriage and sought *Gott*'s help in silence, as was her habit.

Dearest Fater in heaven, surely you see everything as you've promised . . . our going out and our coming in. Ach, I have come into a new life today and do not know how to live it. What the prof—my husband wants seems wrong, but let me follow him with faith that I might be a light, Your light to him. And please forgive me for wanting him like this . . . Amen.

She rose, relieved in spirit, and turned her mind to the practical matter of what to have for supper. She had grabbed a pail to hunt for late huckleberries when someone came walking through the grass down the path near the cabin. She looked up, disappointed because she knew it was not her husband's step. *More likely Isaac Mast . . .* wunderbaar.

She fixed a smile on her face and waited until the boy ambled from the woods but felt surprise when Isaac seemed to stand taller and his booted steps turned to her. There was a suppressed aggression about him that made her nervous, and she swung the small pail back and forth.

"I heard the news. Expect the whole mountain's heard it by now," he spat.

She nodded with a calmness she didn't feel. "*Jah,* the professor and I are married. *Danki,* Isaac."

He caught her arm and pried the bucket from her fingers with an ungentle hand. She watched as he flung it far off into the weeds and caught the scent of alcohol on his breath.

"I didn't come for no sayin's of celebration, Mary. You know that. I figure if you was givin' yerself to one man, you'd do as well fer another." He took a step closer to her and she lifted her chin, reached up and flicked his straw *Amisch* hat off, trying to subdue the fear beginning to rise inside.

"Another man, Isaac? Where would he be? I see none here."

She wasn't prepared for the shaking he gave her and she felt her teeth rattle. Her heart began to pound.

"Ye're a witch, Mary. A temptress and a witch, jest like my *daed* says. And I'll show you what a real man is to be."

He caught her around the waist and she began to struggle in earnest, but he was strong from working the fields and managed to drag her into the cabin. He flung her down on the bunk and laughed as he bent over her to flick a sprig of lavender across her face.

"So, the old crone's blessed the bed already. Fair blessing on us, then, Mary, since you've no husband hereabouts."

She tried to scream, but he slapped her hard, then climbed atop her, holding her down with his greater weight.

"Isaac, stop . . . think," she tried to reason with him, but he was grabbing at her dress.

"*Ach*, I'm thinkin', Mary. I'm thinkin'."

She felt his hand pinch the inside of her thigh and she tried to bite his arm, but he slapped her again and she tasted blood.

"Now, jest lie still, Mary. Lie still and it'll go better for ya," he panted.

She squirmed against him and then they both froze when the click of a gun's hammer sounded clear and tight.

"Get up."

Mary couldn't breathe for a moment when she recognized her husband's voice. Isaac slowly began to crawl off her and Mary saw his hands go up as Jude held the revolver to the back of his head.

"I should kill you, Isaac Mast. Right here. Right now."

Mary twisted as a bead of sweat fell from Isaac's brow onto her face; she half sobbed.

"Mary, are you all right?" Jude's voice was different now, soft, concerned, caring.

"He—he didn't hurt me much, Jude. It's all right."

"If you had taken her, you'd be dead right now, Isaac Mast. So, this is what you're going to do—turn around and run. Run from this cabin. Run from this mountain and keep on running. I don't ever want to see your miserable face again. Do you understand?"

Isaac blubbered out a response and eased past Jude and the gun; then he took off running, his heavy boots clomping on the floor and out into the grass.

Jude drew a deep breath, uncocked the gun, then put it down on his desk. He turned and went with his heart pounding to the bunk. He dropped to his knees, then reached a shaky hand up to wipe the line of blood from his wife's mouth, cleaning his fingers on the edge of the white sheet. Then he cupped her bruised jaw in his hand. "Oh, Mary. If I'd have been a minute later . . ."

"I-I can't believe—Isaac. He—was so ugly, so mean."

"Drunk too. What did he say?"

She shook her head and he felt her tears slip through his fingers.

"Come on, sweetheart. You'll feel better to talk it out."

She swallowed as he traced the line of her throat down to rub her shoulder.

"He said . . . if I gave it away to you that I'd do it for any man."

"Fool," Jude said with calm deliberation. *I should have pounded the kid's head into the wall.*

"Why do people call . . . that . . . *it*?"

His eyes flew to her face and he floundered for a

moment, but then he got a grip on his sensibilities. She was asking a normal question, a question anyone who'd been assaulted might ask.

He moved to sit down on the bed next to her, gently threading a leaf of sage from her long hair, which had come undone in the onslaught.

Because men are crude idiots, English or Amish. "Mary, I'm sorry he said that to you. And sex, well, you're right . . . it's so much more than *it*, but people cheapen the idea, the feelings . . . I suppose that's what you'd call sin."

"It felt like sin when he was talking."

Should have strung him up right then. "Well, that's his problem, not yours. You're the most pure, wonderful girl I know—like spring water from the mountain."

"What about . . . well, you said you were engaged to marry. Shouldn't she be the most wonderful girl you know?"

Jude laughed. "No . . . yes, but no. In a way, you've saved me, sweet Mary, from a life of desperation."

"I don't understand."

"I'll explain sometime, but right now, I want to know if he hurt you anywhere else."

"*Nee*, I'm fine."

He thought she spoke too quickly and seemed to wince away from his hands.

"Please, Mary. I won't hurt you."

"I know that." The affirmation in her tone did something to his heart and he smiled.

"All right then."

She sighed and slipped off the bed to stand between his knees. She undid her apron, then sought the pins that held her dress in place. Jude knew a sudden regret for his words. Did she mean to simply undress in front of him? He cast his eyes to the log wall behind her, then gasped when he saw her exposed side. The skin between her fragile rib cage and the curve of her hip was badly bruised.

"Oh, Mary." He stood up and caught her close, moving her to the fall of sunlight near one of the two glass windows.

He slid his glasses down the bridge of his nose and peered closely at her side. Already, deep blue and purple blotches marred her white skin. Jude swallowed hard. Being in this proximity with her was more than hazardous to his senses, and he straightened fast.

"Anywhere else?" he asked, his voice hoarse. *Nowhere else. Please, nowhere else.*

She shook her head, holding her dress up, and he helped her lie back on the bunk.

"I'll get some cool cloths from the creek and you can stay here and have a bit of a rest, all right?"

"You won't leave then?"

Her voice sounded small and he could have cursed himself for seeming so calm. He'd been trying to reassure her and he'd probably come off as uncaring. He lifted one of her small, reddened hands from the bed and drew it to his mouth, kissing her carefully.

"I won't leave, Mary. I promise." He put her hand back to her side and forced himself to smile at her. His words echoed with anxious cadence in his mind. *I won't leave, won't leave, promise . . .*

* * *

Mary had known the occasional outburst of violence from her *bruders* fighting or arguing together but she'd never been assaulted, and her mind kept replaying Isaac's actions until she was so jumpy that a skittering chipmunk, moving from the windowsill to the desk, made her sit up in fear.

Jude came back into the cabin from the creek with a dripping pail of water and looked at her in alarm.

"What's the matter?"

She tried to smile. "A chippy . . . on your desk. It startled me."

"Oh . . . yeah, those little guys are all over. I've brought the water."

She lay back down but couldn't quite control the shaking of her hands as he knelt by the bed. She carefully arranged her dress so that her side was exposed and he wordlessly wrung out a wet cloth and pressed it with gentle hands against her.

"Feel good?"

She nodded, trying not to replay the images of Isaac hurting her in her mind.

Jude leaned over her, tenderly stroking her fast-swelling cheek. "Mary, I don't like the idea of leaving, but I do have all that I need for my book. We don't have to wait the two weeks. The only thing I haven't seen is that new beaver dam up the mountain stream."

"You mean . . . you want to leave sooner because Isaac might be here?"

"Yes, that and I'd like some distance to settle between our wedding and the gossip surrounding it. In another six months or so, you could come back without being so much as a blip on the radar."

"A—blip?"

"Sorry. Without causing too much notice."

She was silent for a moment, *Grossmuder* May's words tangling in her mind. What could she accomplish in so little time in his world? And yet, it also seemed like an eternity to be away from the mountain.

She drew a deep breath. "It's August now . . . I've told you, the mountain becomes near impassable sometimes as early as October, sometimes as late as March."

"Well, that should do us, sweetheart. What do you say?"

"I have to go to my *daed*'s to get my things and say good-bye."

"And I've got to pack up this pile of notes and books. We could hike out tomorrow afternoon, if you feel up to it. If not—we'll wait." He wrung out another ice-cold cloth and exchanged it for the one on her side.

"I'll be well. I'm sure of it."

"We'll see. Now, what do you want for supper?"

She frowned and struggled to rise. "I'll get it."

He pushed her back with a gentle hand. "Oh, no, Miss, er, Mrs. . . . it's on me. Tell me what you like . . . stew, stew, or stew?" He gave her a lopsided grin.

"I've never had a man bring me food. It—seems wrong somehow."

"Mary, I'm afraid you're going to find a lot of things 'wrong' or upside down in my world, but that doesn't mean that they're really wrong. It's okay to try new things."

"Then I'll have stew."

She was pleased at his answering smile and settled back in the bunk to watch him move about—a man, her husband, making supper for her. It was something worth watching.

Jude tried not to remember that the beautiful girl in his bed was his wife. She'd been through a forced marriage, a near rape, and the looming possibility of leaving her home, all in one day. She certainly didn't need to know that his mind felt pulled in a thousand directions where she was concerned. It wasn't something he could truly understand himself.

He supposed that if he were a praying man, today would have been the day for it. But no words would come from inside. He'd studied too much in college not to believe that organized religion was anything but a crutch . . . not that it wasn't a commendable crutch and not that the *Amisch* didn't handle it masterfully, but man would always be what he was with his baser nature at the forefront—like Isaac Mast. *Like me.*

He clanged the cast-iron lid of the stew pot and turned over his shoulder to apologize to Mary for the noise, only to find her fast asleep. Against his will, he was drawn to the side of the bunk in the waning light of day. He lit the kerosene lamp on the small, carved bedside table, then sat down on the edge of the bed.

There was no doubt his little friend of summer was truly a beautiful woman. She looked like a sleeping princess from a fairy tale and he smiled at the thought. He'd seen her shoot small game with a bow and deadly accuracy, making sure the animal did not suffer.

He suppressed a sigh and thumbed his way across the half-closed fingers of her hand, then peered closer at her palm. He realized with a sudden tearing sensation in his heart that she held a handful of the now-dried herbs and flowers that *Grossmuder* May had used to bless the bed. It was as if she'd still hoped . . . wanted . . . He shook his head and drew a single rose petal from her palm, then got up from the bed.

He went to his bookshelf and idly chose Dickens's *A Tale of Two Cities*. He opened to the first page: "It was the best of times . . ." Then he slid the rose petal carefully between the pages and closed the book. Who knew? It might make a great keepsake, a petal of memory long gone that he could share with his grandchildren. He glanced back to his bed . . . but not her grandchildren. Never hers.

Chapter Four

She was dreaming. *It was hot and her dress weighed heavy upon her. She was in the blueberry patch, seeking cool respite from the day. She recognized the professor coming toward her. He seemed shy but intent somehow. He reached out and caught her hand in his. Then he wet his lips; she bit hers. She'd wanted him to come to her like this for weeks, wanted his blue eyes to be intense and dark, wanted his body to rule where his mind did not. She knew it was sinful,* jah, *that he'd soon be gone, but then he dipped his head toward her. He placed her hand along his lean hip and rocked his weight forward. It seemed that her blood slowed between heartbeats as he inched closer and then his mouth was on hers, slow at first, then seeking. She put her hand up to the warmth of his throat and lifted her gaze to meet his eyes, only to stare into the sweating, distorted face of Isaac Mast. She screamed and tried to fight from his grasp, but he held her tight and she could not get away.*

Jude knocked his head on the bottom of the bunk when her scream woke him from a fitful sleep.

It was dark in the cabin and he'd been sleeping on the floor. Now he hopped to his feet and felt in desperation for Mary as she struggled on the bed.

"Mary, Mary, what is it?"

She trembled beneath his hands, her hair slipping through his fingers like ocean waves. He knew he was affected by her, never would have let himself make out with her in the first place if he wasn't, and he hated to see her upset. He put a knee on the bed and half turned from her, but she grasped at his arm.

"Mary, sweetheart. Let me turn up the lamp, okay?"

She continued to hold him, putting her mouth against the sleeve of his shirt, and he felt her teeth chatter. He fumbled with the lamp, got it going, then moved to sit beside her, drawing her into his arms. She was half-in, half-out of his sleeping bag and her eyes still held that stark look of somewhere between dreaming and waking. He kissed her instinctively on the forehead and she turned to meet his mouth with her own. He heard the strangled sound that came from his own throat as if far in the distance and slanted his head to deepen the kiss. *Comfort, you idiot. Comfort her.*

But when she twined her arms around his neck and clutched at his hair, he knew he needed to stop. *Must stop. Must.* He broke away with a painful gasp, his breathing ragged. "Mary, it's all right. It's all right. You were dreaming. That's all."

She whimpered and pushed closer to him, as if she were trying to burrow inside his shirt. "It—it was Isaac, not you. I thought we were kissing that day, but then it was him. *Ach,* Jude, I was so scared."

I'm scared too . . . scared to death. What am I going to do with a wife, an Amisch *wife who makes my arms ache and my mouth burn? Never touch her. Just never touch her.* He stiffened with resolve and tried to move from her.

"Please, Professor," she begged.

Please? Please what? What does she want me to do?

"Please sit here with me for a minute until I fall back to sleep. I want to sleep. I promise. I want it all to go away when I wake up."

"All of it?" he couldn't help asking.

"Mmm-hmm . . ." She laid her head on his shoulder and he resolved to sit for a minute or two, stiff and unresponsive.

The song of the first morning bird woke her and she realized that she was snuggled tight against the professor's side. His white shirt was half-undone and she ducked her head away from the glimpse of his tanned chest. His blue-jeaned legs were tangled around the sleeping bag and his breathing fell slow and even near her ear. She tried to remember how they had got this way, and then the horror of the nightmare came back to her. She remembered Jude holding her, and now as she adjusted her neck with the slightest movement, she found his blue eyes, languid and sleepy.

"Hello, beautiful," he whispered.

She felt herself flush at his words and he grinned, a secret, knowing smile that did something to her insides.

"Hello."

He blinked then, almost as if coming to himself, and he pulled away from her, rolling off the bunk.

He stood up and ran a hand through his hair, then grabbed his spectacles from the bedside table and hastily buttoned his shirt.

"You—uh—had a bad dream and I, um . . ."

"You slept by my side, Jude. Thank you."

He nodded. "Right. That's all right." He clapped his hands together. "Looks like the stew will be dried out, but how about some fresh scrambled eggs?"

"I really can get it for you," she said.

"No. I insist." He smiled at her, grabbed an old basket, and headed outside, leaving her deep in her thoughts.

"My girl, how's my girl?"

Jude looked up as the anxious voice of his new father-in-law cut across his thoughts.

Undoubtedly after the night's passing, the mountain's amazing and mysterious communication grapevine had brought news to Abner about Mary and Isaac Mast.

"Mary's fine." Jude set the basket on the grass and rose to his feet.

Abner passed a ham-like hand across his brow, tilting back his straw hat. "*Gut . . . gut.* I heard you ran Isaac Mast off the mountain—saved me the trouble."

"I thought you would take the matter up with the bishop first, but I wasn't in the mood to wait," Jude explained. "I should have let your community handle it maybe."

"*Nee,* we've looked aside many a time, given the

boy many chances over the years. He's started fires, run moonshine, everything, and now this . . ."

Jude felt surprise yet again at the ways of the *Amisch* of the Appalachians. They were so much more a morally driven people than some other cultures, balancing right and wrong, trying to find ways to help their young along but without overcoddling. If Abner said Mast had been given chances, it had been more than a few.

"Good." Jude gave his father-in-law an impassive stare. "An attempted rape—I hope he runs to the devil or I'll see him in prison where he belongs."

Abner nodded. "I guess I'll go back to the cabin, then; calm the *buwes.* They wanted to track Isaac down like a deer."

"I heard that, Abner King, and I tell you that my *buwe* had better come back soon and with no problems about it!"

Jude glanced at the wooded path and saw Mahlon Mast stomp toward them. The tall *Amisch* man was Isaac's *fater* and had never been receptive to Jude's presence on the mountain. Other members of the community described Mahlon as "overly conservative" and a family leader who kept his son and wife away from many community gatherings.

"That 'boy' is a grown man who nearly raped my wife," Jude said with an even calmness he wasn't feeling. The elder Mast had a wild look in his eyes, something driven and fervent, that must have transmitted itself to his son.

Mast gave Jude a hard poke in the chest. "You done married a witch; it's hexed ya are, and you can't see nor feel it."

Jude took a step nearer to the belligerent older man, only to have Abner King come in between them. "Mahlon Mast, I've knowed you since we was *buwes* and I know ye fear the hex of a witch, always have. But that's my girl ye're talkin' about, and a *gut* and honest woman she is. Beauty don't make no witch of a person, and mebbe ye're a mite jealous that yer own ain't that but homely."

Jude had to hide a grim smile. His new father-in-law could hit the mark when he wanted and Mahlon Mast struggled visibly to control his temper.

"Now, go on wi' ye," Abner growled, finishing the encounter and dismissing the other man. "Else *Derr Herr* may bring upon you all that you fear."

Mahlon's face took on a reddish hue as his eyes darted furtively about. Then he turned and stomped off back into the woods.

"That's a strange man," Jude observed.

"*Jah.* Always was. But it's nuthin' to trouble Mary about. I'll go on home now."

Jude cleared his throat and nodded. "Mary and I—we'll be over today for a visit."

"*Gut.*" Abner frowned up at him. "*Gut*, then."

Jude wanted to say something to the other man, something about what a wonderful daughter he'd raised, but found the words wouldn't come. So he waited until he was alone once more, then set about gathering the rest of the eggs for breakfast.

Chapter Five

Mary felt the cool earth of the worn path beneath her bare feet and soaked in the sensations of the bumps and roots, the pressed grass and the soft moss. Her husband followed her as they made their way to her home—her old home. She knew a clutch of anxiety in her chest as they approached the small, hardwood cabin. It was here that she'd been born and her mother had died, here that she'd grown, knowing every knot in the wood of the brief front porch, and here that she'd depart for other places, another home, for as long as she could hold her husband . . . She pushed away the thought. *Nee*—she must not worry about keeping him but about building a wedding into a marriage like *Grossmuder* May had said.

He caught her fingers in his warm hand as they came in view of the cabin. Mary sighed. The place appeared unkempt, unlike the rather pristine *Amisch* farms she'd read of in Lancaster, Pennsylvania. There were piles of scrap metal, wood, and various outbuildings scattered around the yard, but her mother's beautiful wild pink roses still clambered nearly halfway up the house, covering one railing and reaching for another. The roses redeemed the bland surroundings, and she knew that her *daed* had planted them when her mother had carried her—the mother she had never known but whom she had often spent hours trying to picture. It had made her wish, on more than one occasion, that the Amish believed in taking personal photographs and that those images would not be considered graven.

She felt Jude looking down at her as they walked into the clearing and she smiled up at him.

"You'll miss this," he said.

She shook her head. "Only the roses."

"Your mother's, right?"

"You have a *gut* memory. I didn't even think I mentioned my *mamm* much to you."

He pulled her to a slow stop and she felt herself tremble in expectation in spite of herself. Maybe he'd kiss her again . . .

Instead, his blue eyes were dark, serious. "Mary, I'm lots of things—maybe things you wouldn't like if you knew. But one good thing about me is that I remember details about the people I like."

She curled her fingers tighter into his hand and swallowed hard. "And do you—like me?"

He didn't smile but his eyes burned like blue flame. "I like you," he whispered. "Very much."

"*Ach,* I like you too," she couldn't help exclaiming, then blushed at her forwardness. Though this was the man she was married to, *nee,* wedded to—it was all very confusing.

He skimmed a long finger around the curve of

her jaw. "I like you, Mary. And I like you enough to remember the time you told me of your *mamm.* Do you recall the field of goldenrod?"

She nodded, feeling lulled by the timbre of his rich voice. She saw herself standing on the verge of the bright field they'd entered during one of his note-taking rambles about the mountain. A slight summer breeze had soothed the back of her warm neck and she'd watched him wade into the yielding plants, a sea of color against his lean waist.

He was so beautiful . . . Gott *made him so beautiful.* She hadn't wanted to intrude on his pollinated swim until he turned to her and laughed, arms extended. "Come on in, Mary."

She'd put a cautious foot against the first green stem, feeling it give with ease. Then she concentrated, head down, on each step forward.

"Mary, this is beautiful. What's wrong?"

She'd swallowed, trying to stuff down the fragmented thoughts that sprang to life inside her. "Nothing's wrong."

He still smiled. "Mary. I've known you for two months now. Tell me."

"I'll sound strange," she muttered, stretching her fingertips to the golden-yellow flower nearest her.

"I like strange."

She nodded. She could believe that . . . "I—well, I feel as though my mother had been here once . . . I don't know. I feel her."

He came toward her, his handsome brow arched in thought. "I know your mother died, but you've never said when or how. Is she buried near here?"

"*Nee* . . . nothing like that. She died giving me

life—it's that simple." She crossed her arms in front of her chest and hugged herself protectively.

"Oh, no, sweet Mary. There's nothing simple about that." His voice had dropped and he stood in front of her, only three stalks between them.

She'd wet her lips and stared down at his large work boots, tamping down the plants.

"Mary," he whispered. "Her death wasn't your fault, your doing. And if you can feel some sense of her here, then be happy that whatever nothingness rules this world saw fit to give it to you."

"Nothingness?" She tasted the strange word on her tongue and felt sad.

He'd shrugged and reached to brush at a stray tendril of her hair with the back of his hand.

"It doesn't matter . . . but you do."

Mary blinked out of her reverie and realized they stood poised on the damp grass surrounding her cabin home. She looked up at Jude and felt his eyes, kind but questioning, and she had to look away.

"So, she's yours now, is she?"

Jude swallowed the words that Abner King's statement riled up in him. He didn't want a confrontation on Mary's last visit home, and he didn't want to discuss the activities, or lack thereof, of his wedding night with his grim father-in-law.

"Mary is her own . . . not mine to possess." *Though I'd like to . . . every inch of her; our hands clasped together, little breathy sounds coming from her mouth with the taste of summer, me coming apart and . . . Am I out of my mind? What the devil is wrong with me? Restraint, you idiot. Restraint.*

Abner regarded him with a dry look. "Uh-huh."

Jude felt himself flush and turned away from the other man, looking around the main cabin room to distract himself.

"Please, *Daed*, we're going tomorrow. I don't want any fighting." Mary pressed her skirts against herself in a pleading gesture.

"Tomorrow?" her father exploded. "I thought to have these last two weeks with my girl—especially after what happened with Isaac Mast."

Jude drew a deep breath. "I'm sorry—I wish there was something else to do, but I believe time will be a healing factor in this . . . what happened."

Abner stepped in front of him in the cramped space of the cabin's kitchen. "You remember, *schmart* man, that you owe my daughter a life of time, a life of love."

Jude grimaced inwardly. *A life of time for a few kisses; hardly a fair exchange where I come from, but still . . .*

"All right. All right." Abner waved his thick hands. "Me and the *buwes* have a wedding present for y'uns at any rate. Joseph, bring it over."

Joe King was tall and lanky and shouldered past Jude with a less-than-obvious bump, then returned to place a small box in Mary's hands.

"*Ach, Dat,* I can't," she whispered.

Jude peered over her shoulder as she opened the box and an intricate carved scene of the mountain slowly slid upward, then clicked into place.

"That's amazing." Jude was sincere in his praise.

The woodworking craftsmanship of the Mountain Amish was unsurpassed.

"It was carved by my *grossdaudi* when I was a very little girl," Mary said. "It belongs to *Dat*."

"And now to you—both of you." Abner pulled a blue hankie from his pocket and blew. "I want you to remember the mountain. It's in ya, daughter. But now you'll have a *gut* reminder."

Mary moved to kiss her father and Jude hung back as her *bruders* somehow encircled her. He felt a distinct lack of being part of the family but figured it was pretty much what he deserved . . . *Annulment. Annulment.*

But then Mary moved and drew him close and he was surrounded by the reality of brotherhood, something he'd read about but had never known. He told himself he was being ridiculous when he had to clear his throat, but decided to enjoy this rare moment of life anyway.

Inside her small room, Mary took a moment to sit down on her single bed and let her fingers play over the stitching in the Nine Patch quilt she'd pieced when she was ten—three blocks over and three blocks down. So easy. It was soothing to touch the threads and to remember a time when knowing what to do meant simply obeying. Now that she would leave the mountain, she'd have to make her own decisions, and she wondered what the outside world would truly bring.

A soft knock on the door interrupted her thoughts. "*Kumme* in."

Jude had to duck his head a bit to fit into the doorway but was then able to rise to his full height with only inches to spare against the beamed ceiling.

"Hi," he said. "Am I disturbing you?"

She shook her head, though it was strange to see him in the intimacy of the center of her girlhood. She appreciated that he kept his eyes on her and didn't appear to be looking around the room.

"Your *dat* wanted me to bring this satchel in to you." He handed her a heavy, handled bag with faded brown flowers on its outside. "Do you want to pack alone?"

"*Nee.*" She rose and gestured to the bed. "Please sit down. I'll be quick."

The small bed creaked under his tall weight and Mary turned to the shelf that held the store of procured books she'd read and reread over and over again throughout the years. Her hand hovered over the titles, then she chose her Bible, her mother's cookbook, and *Wuthering Heights.*

"Bring everything you want," he urged. "I can fit some in my backpack."

"This is enough for books. I've other things." She moved to the carved wooden chest on the floor beneath the deep-set window and felt his eyes on her. She knelt down and opened the cherrywood lid, smelling the cedar shavings that she kept inside to protect against moths.

All of the sewing and quilting that she'd done since childhood in preparation for her marriage filled the chest. She was plunged into memories as she lifted pieces and thought of the women of the community who'd helped her over the years in learning the sewing and quilting arts.

She was fingering the scalloped edge of a pillowcase, not certain what to pack because she was setting up an unknown household, when she felt the professor's touch on her arm as he knelt next to her. She felt surrounded by his presence, his scent, and her pulses began to race.

"I—I don't know what to bring," she confessed.

"You've made all of these things?" he whispered. "For the time you would have your own home?"

"Jah." She wondered at the disquiet in his voice and knew uncertainty in her heart once more.

Jude brushed his fingers against the snowy white fabric, matched with perfect white stitching, and wondered how he'd gotten to this place in his life. How could he rob this innocent girl of her hope chest and all that it represented? He felt a deep pain in his chest. He was a fraud.

"Mary, I . . ."

She turned to face him, her knees between his thighs. "It is all right, Jude. We are married. I understand that you—you do not belong here and I go willingly with you to see a glimpse of the world, your world. I can come back to this chest with those memories."

He watched her lift her fine chin with a brave air and felt his throat throb. He reached his hand to her warm neck and, against his will, leaned forward, losing himself in the sincerity and truth in her eyes. Everything seemed to hang suspended in the pool of sunlight that encircled them from the window. He felt things slip away—time, remorse, what he should do . . . He touched his mouth to her forehead, as close to sacred as he could understand, trying to tell her how much he admired her courage. Then he allowed his lips to brush hers. Once . . . twice . . . like sips of water to a dying man.

He wasn't prepared for her response or the onslaught of sensation that tore through his belly when she began to kiss him back. *Think,* his mind screamed, but it didn't seem to matter. She pressed light fingertips against his chest and he deepened the kiss, hearing his own ragged breathing like a roaring in his ears.

"Mary?" Her father rattled the latch on the door and Jude felt himself crash back to earth with brutal force.

He gasped, nearly sick with desire, and grabbed the pillowcase she still clutched. "Bring it," he managed between breaths. "For the love of God, bring anything you want."

Chapter Six

Mary slanted a glance at her husband through veiled lashes. They'd left her *dat*'s and were making quick rounds of the community. The news had spread that she and the professor were leaving the next day. He now sat on Rachel Miller's best ladder-back chair with seven cats balanced in all manner of repose about him—and he looked happy. Of course, he knew the oddities of Rachel's house from his note-taking that summer, but the quirky *Amisch* woman was in rare form and a reminiscing frame of mind.

"Sorry you've got to see my underwears on the line, Professor. Didn't have time to get 'em down before you was comin'."

"You're always a perfect lady, Rachel. I didn't even notice."

"Well, there. I've been thinkin' as to what wedding gift would suit the two of you." She rattled a teacup in its saucer.

"We're fine, really." Jude laughed, pulling a roly-poly tabby kitten off his head.

Mary realized that the professor had no idea that he was verging on being offensive to the older woman by turning aside a wedding gift. They'd never really gotten to explore the wedding culture of her people that summer.

"Y'un's ain't fine. I think I'll give you that cat adanglin' from yer shoulder, Jude Lyons."

Mary could see the protest forming on his lips and sweetly broke into the conversation. "That would be lovely, Rachel, but we're leaving for Atlanta soon, and I'm afraid a kitten would not do so well on such a long ride." *And I probably won't either . . . I've never ridden anywhere but by wagon or sled.*

"That may be," Rachel considered, stroking a rather obvious chin hair. "I know—I'll give ye some fancy *fraktur* I did back when I was a young girl. Wait right here."

"I don't want to take her things," Jude whispered, leaning across the small distance between them and handing Mary a kitten.

Mary shook her head. "You'll hurt her feelings. We have to. We can—I could give it back after—I mean . . ." She paused, confused, trying to hold on to her resolve to make the wedding a marriage.

She saw his eyes darken and his face flush, and he leaned even closer to her, parting his lips as if to speak, when Rachel reappeared. Jude drew back with a faint sigh as the older Amish woman sat back down opposite them.

"Here now . . . some *fraktur* work. A mite fanciful but it suited me once." She unrolled an age-tinted scroll of paper. "It's a mermaid. What'd ya think?"

She held up the bright and intricate design for them to see.

"Ach," Mary exclaimed in delight. "It's beautiful—I mean, she's beautiful."

Rachel wore a pleased smile. "Yep. *Danki.*"

Jude had reached out to touch the edge of the colorful, fine-lined drawing, allowing a black cat to use his arm as a ledge. "I'm surprised to see such fancy work, Miss Rachel. I thought *fraktur* was done only to adorn birth and marriage certificates. I would have imagined that drawings as *wunderbaar* as this would be frowned upon among the *Amisch.*"

"Ha," Rachel snorted. "Maybe down the road a ways, but not up here so much. Ain't you learned that, *buwe*?"

Jude laughed, hauling the black cat back in. "I've learned some but maybe not enough."

He flashed an I've-got-a-secret grin at Mary and she couldn't control the blush that stained her cheeks. He was so quicksilver in his moods; she had trouble keeping up with him. But she couldn't deny that there was something exciting about it all.

Rachel crowed with delight at his words. "All men—be they *Amisch* or *Englisch*—got somethin' to learn. You remember that." She swung her gaze to Mary.

"I'll remember," Mary murmured, but she couldn't help feeling that she would be at a distinct disadvantage when it came to teaching her husband anything much. Still, it was God Who was the Great Teacher, and that was what mattered most of all.

Rachel put down her teacup and leaned back to

rock, handing Jude the intricate drawing. "I'll tell you both the tale of the mermaid *fraktur—if* you can tell me, young man, what I used to get the colors there in that picture. They didn't come from no store neither."

Mary smiled as Jude adjusted his glasses. She knew how dyes were made from natural items but wondered if her husband's studies included such things.

"Okaaay," he began. "Let's see. Lavender on the scrolling. I'd say grape juice."

"Meebee some would," Rachel sniffed. "But I used violet blossoms and a touch of lemon juice. Try again."

"Blue for the water . . . how about blueberries?"

Mary clapped a bit and he smiled but Rachel shook her head. "Nope. Red cabbage leaves, boiled."

"All right. Green . . . some kind of chlorophyll," he mused.

Rachel snorted. "Fancy word for just plain green you're usin'—what kind of plant?"

"Spinach," Mary cried, then popped a hand over her mouth at the older woman's sour look.

"I know you know, miss . . . let him try."

"I've got this one," he said. "Brown . . . black walnut shells."

Rachel nodded with approval. "Now you earned the story."

"Danki." Jude nodded and Mary felt proud that his pronunciation was perfect. She watched him gather two cats close on his lap and tilt his head

back in anticipation. She knew that he loved a *gut* story.

Rachel put a hand to her cheek and pressed in a dimple where back molars used to be as she gathered her thoughts. Mary felt a little thrill of enjoyment as well; there was a lot to learn about people, even in as small a community as her own.

"My man's dead," Rachel began. "Ya both knowed that. But my boy, my baby, he died way back when I was a young thing. I nursed him through the pneumonia, but it hung on like. He was two when he went on—Peter wuz his name." She cleared her throat and gestured with a bony finger to the drawing in Jude's hand. "I might've gone out of my mind back then but for the story that *fraktur* tells. *Derr Herr* brought back an old love when He took my baby, an old love . . ." She paused, her blue-gray eyes musing, and Mary heard the cats purr as they surrendered to her husband's clever fingers around their ears. She thought then how hard it would be to ever lose him, to let him go . . .

"Jah," Rachel went on. "The bishop and some others thought I took to being a hex when Peter died. It was winter and I wuz leavin' our bed at night to go walkin' in the snow by the light of the moon. It got to be that they thought I was out a gatherin' herbs to bring my *buwe* back—as if I'd want that when he'd have known the joy of heaven. My man followed me once, thought mebbe I had it in mind to run off with another fella. Ha! *Nee,* it wasn't that. Can ya guess, either of ya, what I'd found?"

Mary shook her head, trying to think while Jude pursed his lips.

"I give up," he admitted finally.

Rachel clapped her aged hands on her knees. "I found the swimmin' hole where I used to go as a girl. Now, mind, it was winter and I had to take a hatchet to break the ice, but that icy water cleared my soul somehow and my heart. There's nuthin' like swimmin' in the suit you wuz born in during the dead of winter and findin' life again, I can tell you both that. And when my man found me, he pulled me outta the water with my hair streamin' all around us and he carried me home to bed. I did that *fraktur* later on that spring, kind of to remind me of the swimmin' that brought me back to livin'."

Mary watched Jude's throat work and he shook his head. "We—I can't take this, Rachel. The mermaid—it's you."

"So what if it is, *buwe*? I can tell you, you need it now more than I do. So blessings on it and on you both."

Mary watched as the old woman closed her eyes and continued to rock; it was a signal of dismissal and she helped unload the cats from Jude, then touched his shoulder with a gentle hand. He seemed to shake himself as he rose, then surprised her by bending close and kissing Rachel's wrinkled cheek. Then Mary watched him roll the *fraktur* and tuck it under his arm.

She savored the feel of his hand on hers as they left the quiet cabin in tender silence.

After a few more stops, Jude decided it was time to go to the Kauffman's or "the Store," as it was known on the mountain. He'd made friends with

Ben Kauffman, someone his own age, but married with a full beard and five children. Ben had welcomed him to talks around the store counter and it had meant a lot, both in terms of research and, more importantly, friendship.

They mounted the steps of the long, clapboard building, and Jude knew he'd always remember the mingling smells of propane, leather, spices, and old wood, as the floor creaked comfortably beneath his feet. He'd first compared Kauffman's to Walmart in his notes, citing the availability of anything and everything imaginable that the community might need, but he now understood the place to be the unofficial town hall—where Amish men gathered to talk and exchange hunting and fishing stories and where women spoke in happy twos or threes around the fabric and thread corner.

Bishop Umble turned from a small group of men to greet them. "*Ach*, the new couple. Ben's heard that you're leaving and he has something for you, Jude, in the back."

Jude looked askance at Mary, who seemed to understand that a surprise for him was in the making, but she merely smiled and slipped off to greet some other women, leaving Jude to walk alone to the back room behind the store. Here the smell of leather was at its most intense and Ben Kauffman at his happiest as he made and repaired boots by hand.

"Hiya!" Ben got up from the old-fashioned cobbler's work bench and greeted him with a wide smile and a hearty handshake. "I heard about the wedding and that you're leaving tomorrow."

"All true." Jude smiled as the *Amisch* man offered him a black licorice whip from a tall glass jar. He chewed the candy with true enjoyment while Ben stood, hands on hips, his large leather work apron stretching from his shirt collar to his knees.

"Well, those truths kept me up late last night, my friend." Ben laughed.

Jude stopped chewing. "Why? Were you worried about the wedding?"

"*Nee*, not that—though weddings bring about their own share of worries. *Nee*, I had to finish your leaving-the-mountain gift."

"What? You do not have to give me anything. Your friendship has been all the gift I want."

"*Ach*, well . . ." Ben stalked back to a shelf behind the work bench, pulled down a brown cardboard box, and brought it over.

Jude let the licorice dangle from his lips as Ben placed the box in his hands. Jude could sense the air of expectancy emanating from his friend and put the box on a counter to lift the lid. Inside was a pair of the finest work boots he'd ever seen, and he felt genuine bewilderment as he stared at the gift.

"Ben, I don't know what to say."

"Don't say nothing. Try them on. I had to guess on sizing a bit, even though Mary smuggled me one of your boots a while back to measure. But these boots I make will last a lifetime, or at least until you send them back for repairs."

Jude felt a lump in his throat as he laid the

licorice on the counter and touched the supple leather. He hadn't cried over a gift since the Christmas he'd turned nine, when his grandfather had given him a microscope, which his father had disparaged. Now here he was, in a backwoods *Amisch* general store, and he felt so close to the boy he'd been—wanting to see other worlds through a glass. But now his experience was authentic and not some removed study. Another human being had given up sleep to work with his hands to make him a lasting gift.

"Try them," Ben urged and Jude broke from his reverie to slip out of the boots he'd used all summer and into the wonderful strength and comfort of the pair Ben had made.

"They're wonderful, Ben. Truly."

Ben looked pleased. "You've got solid leather there, even an all-leather shank, so you won't have any of the rust you can get with a steel shank. And the leather guarantees you twice the support of the ones you were wearin'. Mine's got a vamp that won't stretch, and the eyelets are solid brass—again, no rust. And, well, I might as well tell ya, I prayed that *Derr Herr* would guide your steps as you and Mary walk through this world together."

Jude shook his head and moved forward to embrace the *Amisch* man. "You're a gifted artisan, Ben. Again, I thank you." *How can I tell him about Mary and me? How can I hurt him when I bring her back? How can he pray for me when I've never mentioned God . . .*

Ben took a hankie and blew, then stroked his beard and cleared his throat. "Extra support will help wherever you work, except I bet you can't be no professor in boots like those."

Jude laughed. "I can wear whatever I want to teach, and you can be sure that these boots are going to the university."

"That's fine, then." Ben clapped his hands as one of his younger sons ran through the shop. "Hey, Samuel, come and say *sayn dich schpaydah* to Mr. Jude here."

Jude had to concentrate on the little boy's good-bye to keep from hugging Ben again. He knew that he'd cherish his friend's gift forever.

Chapter Seven

Jude shifted the bundles in his arms as they walked back toward his cabin. They'd collected two quilts, beeswax candlesticks, honey off the comb, and a small medicine chest of herbs, as well as Rachel Miller's *fraktur* and a hand-carved wooden spoon. He felt dishonest in some ways, taking the wedding gifts offered with so much pride from the community. He especially felt bad in the comfort of Ben's boots, but he didn't know how else to go along. He wondered how Mary would feel, walking about, taking the things back once he'd returned her to the mountain the following spring. Somehow, the idea was sounding less and less palatable to him, and he knew that he had to talk with her—especially after the kiss in her bedroom that afternoon. Then he thought about the coming night and wondered if he could manage the single bunk one last time . . .

"So, quite a haul, hmmm?" he asked, indicating the bundle in his arms with his chin.

"For a sudden wedding, you mean?" Her voice

sounded tired, and he wondered, for the first time, whether she had desired this wedding. After all, she'd been as forced as he had, perhaps even more so.

He cleared his throat as they mounted the three wooden steps of his cabin, then leaned against the door instead of opening it.

"Hey, Mary?"

She looked up at him, her eyes like twin pools. *A man could drown there and be happy . . .*

"What is it, Professor?"

"Jude," he corrected her absently. "Hey, about this wedding and coming back here. I've been thinking that it's not the fairest thing to you, and I think that we'd better plan on maybe—you not coming. I mean . . ." She put a soft hand on his chest, right above the pile of stuff, and his breath caught.

"Jude . . . we're married. I told you today—I will see the world, as you call it. We'll—we will go day by day, and when you tire of it all"—she straightened her spine—"I can come back. *Derr Herr* commands us not to worry about tomorrow anyway."

He grimaced in spite of himself and she moved her hand from his chest. "Right. All right." He pushed open the cabin door and piled the stuff on the table while the wooden spoon clattered to the floor in the cool dimness.

Mary skimmed the bunk with grateful eyes. She'd spread the wedding presents out the better to see them. Her people were so generous, though she knew that the professor was generous too. He was kind and giving with words and affirmations, whereas it was the tendency of the men she'd grown up with to be sparse in their language. *But, ach, how I love to hear him talk. His voice is rich and commanding, yet can caress like the waters of a summer stream . . .*

She shivered in delight at the thought, then nearly jumped when she heard him speak.

"What are you thinking of?" He'd come to stand behind her and she fancied she could feel the press of his long legs against the back of her skirt. His scent, too, twisted in her senses—something manly and woodsy and caught with sunshine. She turned to stare up at him.

"The gifts are *wunderbaar.*"

"They are—that's true."

"I suppose I should clean off the bunk, though. It's getting late."

He nodded but she sensed a restlessness in him.

"Mary, uh, look . . . last night I ended up sleeping beside you. You were afraid, but I—sometimes it's difficult for a man to lie near a woman without—He starts to dream, maybe, and it becomes painful not to . . ." He broke off in frustration and she tilted her head in thought.

"Did you lie with your fiancée?" She could have clapped her hand over her mouth at her wayward tongue. "I—mean. Forgive me. That's not for me to know . . ."

He was frowning but still managed to look impossibly handsome. She blushed and dropped her gaze. She heard him exhale slowly, then felt his warm fingers cup her chin as he raised her head.

"Mary, look at me. Forget Carol for now. I'm trying to tell you that I don't think I can sleep with you without it being difficult, that's all. I was going to suggest that you sleep in the bunk and I lie on the floor."

"*Ach,*" she whispered, feeling foolish. But his words niggled at her brain. *He didn't give me a straight answer, so maybe he's kissed many girls . . . And how do I compare, especially as the one whose family trapped him into a wedding?*

She struggled to control her thoughts and realized she didn't want to admit that the bunk still frightened her a bit when she thought of Isaac. "Maybe I could have the floor?"

He smiled then and reached his hand from her chin to slide to the back of her neck, beneath her *kapp.* "Are you afraid, sweetheart? Mast is gone. He's a coward."

She swallowed and nodded. "I know."

"But you're still frightened? I guess I can't blame you for that." He skimmed his fingers down her shoulder. "All right. We'll share the bunk tonight, Mrs. Lyons, and then we'll figure something else out."

She heard the resignation in his voice but there was something else there too—something young and free, and she wished she heard him like that more often. *One more night . . .*

Jude reread the paragraph of notes for the third time as he listened to his wife's gentle turning in the bunk. He knew it was late but had kept the candle guttering in hopes that she'd be asleep before he eased himself beside her. He finally gave up and blew out the light, then fumbled briefly in the darkness toward the bed. He put a cautious hand down and came into contact with the side of her breast, jumping back as if he'd been scalded.

"Sorry," he muttered, feeling foolish. He heard the sheets and sleeping bag rustle and knew instinctively that she'd pressed herself as far against the wall as she could get. *All the better, Lyons. What did you expect?*

He could smell her sweet, delicate scent, like soft mint and lavender, and drifted off uneasily, one hand clamped to the outside edge of the bunk. He awakened to the unmistakable sound of something scratching against the door and sighed.

When he'd first taken up residence in the woods alone, he'd had to grow used to midnight visits—anything from an opossum to a buck scraping its velvet off on his porch rail. So he now eased from the bed and stumbled through the play of moonlight from the window to open the door. He peered down in the half light to find what looked like a black wolf staring up at him with gleaming golden eyes and a fierce grimace. The overwhelming smell of skunk spray completed the assault to his senses. He shut the door.

"What is it, Jude?"

Without his glasses, he could make out the fuzzy outline of Mary leaning up on one elbow on the bunk.

"I know I sound ridiculous, but are there wolves

on this mountain?" He felt his heart begin to pound in delayed reaction at the prospect.

"What?"

She scooted out of bed and padded across the floor to brush past him.

"Hey, don't," he cried when she pulled the latch. But then the door was open and she was on her knees, her arms flung around the great neck of the animal as she sobbed aloud.

"Mary, what . . . ?"

"*Ach*, Jude. *Derr Herr* knew. He knew I needed Bear and He sent him back to me right before we left. Now Bear can come too."

"Bear? It's a wolf, and how can that scary-looking thing travel with us?"

Mary swiveled on her knees and grabbed his hand. "Here. Make a fist."

"Why? I'm not touching that . . ."

But he curled his fingers inward in obedience and let her lead his hand under the vicious-looking wolf's mouth. Jude caught his breath and waited for the bite. But all he felt was a damp tongue as the animal tasted his skin.

He took a step closer, looking down in confusion. "Bear?" he questioned.

"*Jah*, he's been missing since last winter. I thought maybe hunters or a trap had taken him. My *dat* got him for me a few years ago as company when I went walking. I haven't seen him in months. He must have been sprayed by a skunk recently. *Ach*, Jude, isn't he *wunderbaar*?"

Yeah, wonderful . . . "Is it—is he a wolf?"

She laughed—a gentle sound that broke through

the night and brought him fully awake. "Nee . . . *ach*, maybe a wee bit wolf, but dog mostly. It's amazing that he traced my scent here." She got to her feet and swiped away her happy tears. "We've got to get the skunk smell off him if he's going to sleep near the cabin. Can you go milk the goat while I pick a few tomatoes?"

"What?"

"The milk, you know, mixed with tomato juice, it cuts the smell." She lit the kerosene lantern as she spoke, and Jude couldn't help but make out her slender silhouette beneath her nightdress, even without his glasses. He decided a midnight goat milking had to be better than the torture of seeing the gentle shadows of her body and grabbed a pail by the door and the lantern.

But when he moved to sidle past the smelly wolf dog, it growled. Jude turned to look down at Mary in frustration.

"Ignore him," she advised airily, taking up another light. "Let's go."

Jude followed the white of her nightgown and the bulk of the beast until they turned into the kitchen garden. "I'll meet you back at the cabin," she called.

"Right." He stubbed his socked toe against a rock on the path and limped into the small pen that housed the goat, and nearby, the chickens. Mary's brothers had promised to come over in the morning and collect the animals he'd kept, and he had to admit he'd miss them—or at least the idea of them. Rose, the goat, had never been an easy milker, and being disturbed in the middle of the night didn't seem to improve her mood any. As it was, Jude got a few firm kicks for his pail of milk and went back to the cabin half cursing the arrival of the dog under his breath.

When he got to the porch, he found that Mary had the dog overfilling an old tub and was squeezing tomatoes into its thick fur. The light from her lamp illuminated her small bare feet, and Jude forgot the goat pains in the pleasure of her nearness, handing over the milk.

Bear seemed quite amenable to being drenched, but Jude couldn't tell much difference in the strength of the skunk smell and longed once more for the length of the bunk. But Mary was a bundle of happy midnight energy at rediscovering her pet, and he didn't have the heart to discourage her.

"Now, we'll leave this on him all night and I'll give him a creek bath in the morning before we go. He'll be right as rain." She gave Jude a broad smile in the light of the lamp and made a gesture to the dog. "Go and lie down now, Bear."

To Jude's chagrin, the huge animal made its docile way out of the tub to one side of the porch and collapsed in a dark heap.

"*Ach*, I am so glad." Mary turned and stretched to kiss Jude on the cheek. "You'll see, he will be a great friend to you too."

Jude nodded and tried to silence his doubts as he helped her empty the tub. Then he followed her wearily back to bed, grateful that at least he was too tired now to worry about touching her.

Chapter Eight

"Do you mind if we stop at the Ice Mine before we head out?" Jude asked the next morning as they hiked the moss-covered trail down the mountain with the still-pungent Bear in the lead.

Mary glanced round at him for a moment. "I was going to suggest the same thing."

He smiled. "It was the first place we met, really."

"I know."

Jude indulged in the memory as he watched his footing, balancing his backpack and her satchel.

Three months before, when the mountain air had filled his lungs with sweetness and promise, he'd slid a yellow notepad from his backpack and grabbed a pen. He'd sketched out his first impressions of Mary as he'd walked behind her. He'd had to focus, he remembered ruefully, on something other than the enticing sway of her hips beneath her blue dress and apron strings. *Should have known better*. . . And he'd been surprised at his reaction; he was never one to be caught by the swing of a skirt—*Englisch* or *Amisch.* But following in the trail of her lithe form as they approached the place of his dreams had been enchanting.

But if someone had told him that his last walk down the mountain today would be filled with the stark but confusingly pleasant reality of having Mary as his *Amisch* wife, he would have told the person that he was crazy and put the thought far from his mind.

Yet there was no denying the reality and the fact that he felt as if taking her from the mountain was like removing some exotic wild creature from its natural habitat without a clue how to maintain its life in another world. He sighed beneath his breath as daylight broke over the trail and played on the gray firmness of the paved road. *There's no going back for now . . .*

It was a brief walk from the trail's end to the entrance of the Ice Mine, and Jude couldn't subdue the feeling of excitement that flooded him as they approached the protruding base of the mountain. A five-foot-wide boarded gap marked the entrance to the mine, the base of the wood covered by ferns and long grass.

"Would you like to try and transplant some ferns, Professor?" Mary teased.

Jude knew the joke now. He'd discovered in his research that the type of fern that grew outside the mine was peculiar and native only to the mountain, and the many attempts made by science in the past to transplant and grow the ferns elsewhere had failed. It was only one of the small, intricate mysteries related to the mountain.

"*Nee*, thank you." He smiled at her. "You forget

that I'm transplanting my own mountain flower and I must put every effort into that venture."

He admired the blush that stained her white cheeks at his obvious compliment. Then he indicated the grass with the toe of his boot. "I doubt anyone's been in here since us."

"Probably not," she agreed.

Jude knew, of course, that the *Amisch* didn't own the mine itself. It was maintained by the community but belonged to an *Englisch* farmer who had long ago left the area.

Mary turned to look up at him with consideration while she laid small, capable hands on the second gray board. "I've never asked you directly—why did you want to come here so badly?"

Jude blinked. It wasn't a question that he was prepared for, even though he had answered it a hundred times when he had sought funding from the university for the project. He pushed aside the thought that his father had offered him twice as much money not to come; that was beside the point.

"My grandfather always told me about this place when I was a boy. He and my grandmother visited the mine while they were on their honeymoon. Of course, that was when it was open for business and tours. One of my grandmother's most prized possessions was a snow globe of the mine she'd often show me, and I guess I was hooked." He trailed off, thinking hard. There was so much resonance in her question, so many layers. He knew he was giving the best answer he could, but it was simplistic. How could he truly explain the deep internal call he felt to the place—it had something to do with his spirit, and he was not yet ready to explore that ground.

But Mary nodded, a half smile on her pink lips as she pulled on the gray board. The wood gave when she slid a hammer from a crevice of rock—proof that this had been done before. He stood back, knowing that she needed no help. He allowed his gaze to travel to the bottom of her skirts and realized that she was barefoot, despite his reminder earlier that day to bring her shoes. The barefoot thing was something he'd read about her people but had found a bit hard to believe at the time. Now he knew. *Carol was right about one thing in her derogatory remarks, but I bet every woman in Atlanta would prize ankles so delicate and exposed . . .* But Ice Mountain, in *Amisch* terms of community, was Mountain Amish and probably about a hundred years behind the times. In fact, when he'd asked around Lancaster on a previous trip, the Paradise Amish community had referred vaguely to those of Ice Mountain as being a bit "odd." He could testify now to that oddness, but even after his shotgun marriage, he had to call the values system more old-fashioned and honor-driven than odd.

"Where are your shoes?" he asked, sliding off his gear and putting down her satchel.

She shrugged. "You're carrying them. They rather hurt my toes." She piled the boards neatly and Jude moved to stand on the precipice of the entrance to the cave, feeling the refreshing icy blast of cold air. Mary drew a lantern from inside the darkness, where he knew it hung on a convenient peg. She lit it while Bear whined a bit, then went into the cave. The animal returned a few seconds later, as if satisfied that it was safe to enter.

"*Sei se gut*—please, Professor. After you."

He took the lantern from her and stepped inside, feeling the ground both slick and rough at the same time. He looked up as the lantern light cast eerie shadows about the icy, jewel-like walls of the cave and down into the deep mine shaft, an ice-lined hole in the floor, more than eighty feet deep. He absorbed it all in a flash—the Native Americans using it as a cache to keep meat cool; the miners abandoning the site when they could not find the silver they sought; the hundred or so years of tours of people standing out on the remains of the wooden platform over the shaft, marveling at the natural wonder. And now him . . .

But it was a far different cave than when they'd visited at the beginning of the summer. Then ice had still clung thick to the walls in a dazzling display, with some icicles thicker than a man's thigh. Now the ice was nearly gone, except for what coated the shaft and a thin sheeting on the walls.

"It's still hard to believe," he said, swinging the light in Mary's direction. "I mean, the whole ice in the summer, no ice in the winter thing."

"As you gaze upon this mysterious ice, your life appears to unfold before you. Dreams seem more enduring and so does your faith. You feel the surge within you and the unknown becomes palpable, even unto the mystery of self . . ." Mary's soft voice echoed with times past.

"Isn't that a reflection from one of the earliest

visitors to the mine?" He turned to gaze down at her with wonder.

She nodded. "I—I read everything you loaned me."

This last bit seemed like a confession and he knew it was because advanced reading was not especially approved by the elders of her community. But he smiled in pleasure at her recitation and he thought of something as he gazed back at the wet walls of the cave in the mellow light.

"You feel that kind of faith when you're here, don't you, Mary?"

"*Jah.*" She paused. "But you don't?"

"No," he murmured. "I don't know how."

Mary remembered the consternation she'd felt when he'd admitted earlier in the summer to essentially not having a sense of faith. She'd never heard anyone be so negatively definitive about the subject before. To her, faith was as natural as breathing. She'd always been taught that worshipping God as Creator was as precious as life itself.

She knew by instinct that she must tread softly when he was willing to talk about it, like now.

She found herself praying in her spirit that she might have wisdom and discernment as to what to ask this man so different from she, yet still her husband. "Why don't you know how?"

She watched him bow his handsome head in the shifting light. "I—I don't have what you have, maybe the gift of what you have. When you're in this place, there is nothing here but the touch of *Gott*'s hand—

I know that's true for you. But I—have to have logical answers. I have to understand why things are the way they are. I guess my father taught me that."

"You sound sad at the teaching," she ventured.

"Yeah, he taught me well—by always crushing everything I was interested in. He didn't care how I felt; he needed proof that it was a worthwhile interest. I've never told you, but he didn't want me to come here."

"Why not?"

"He wants me to give up the *Amisch.*" He half laughed, a hollow sound. "He's a businessman, a huge contractor in Atlanta. Building things, you know? He wants me to put away the book and the professorship and work for him. And I can't do it."

Mary bit her lip, wondering what this new father-in-law would say about her, but she thrust the insecurity away. She needed to focus on Jude for the moment.

"So, you cannot be what your *fater* wants, and you do not know how to have faith? These two seem related somehow," she mused aloud.

He swung the lantern. "I suppose they are, but it makes my head hurt to think of it, and your feet are probably cold. Come on. Let's go. And thank you, Mary, for listening to me."

She knew the moment was broken but the talk had given her hope.

Jude was about to douse the lantern when something that seemed to shine caught his eye far down in the ice mine pit. He took a step nearer the edge and somehow lost his footing, dropped the lantern, and felt engulfing horror as he slipped into the pit. He caught the icy edge, dug his fingers in, and felt his legs dangle into nothingness. Everything seemed to move in slow motion as he watched the lantern roll, still lit, then looked up into Mary's terrified face. She'd caught his wrists but he knew she didn't have the strength to pull him up. The dog was barking, a faraway sound, and Mary's sobbing breaths mingled with the heartbeats he heard pound in his ears. *I'm going to die, right here, with her hands on mine* . . . And then, in the mixed light of the cave and the lantern, the shadow of a man appeared behind Mary. Somehow, someone had happened by . . .

He felt himself lifted by tensile strength, inexorably pulled from the pit until he lay on his belly on the wet ground, his cheek against the ice and gravel, his breath coming back to him in retching gasps. Mary's tears wet his face, and the dog licked at his raw fingers.

"Sugar," he managed to whisper. And then he felt her rifle through his pockets to find two hard candies and slip them between his lips. He sucked hard, eyes open, wondering who the man was and knowing he owed him his life.

It took a full three minutes before he felt up to standing, and even then, he leaned against Mary and the dog for support. As she led him out of the cave and into the warmth of the morning sunlight, he glanced over her head, looking for his rescuer.

"Where did he go?" he asked, regaining his bearings.

"Who?"

"The man."

He felt her eyes upon him, as if assessing whether he was truly all right.

"Do you need more sugar?" she asked, reaching toward his shirt pocket.

He caught her small wrist in his hand. "No, really, where did he go? Who was it?"

She stared at him, her beautiful eyes wide and uncertain. "What man?"

"The one who helped you pull me out." He was beginning to feel angry and confused. "Mary, you didn't pull me out alone. You don't have the strength. I saw the shadow of a man and felt myself lifted up."

She shook her head. "There was no one. Only me and Bear."

He let her go, staring down at his backpack on the ground. Perhaps, in his panic, he'd imagined the shadow, and nothing but adrenaline had helped Mary pull him up. But the explanation didn't feel right and he wanted to put the experience behind him.

He'd felt rattled as it was by how close he had let Mary come to his deepest feelings. He made it a rule never to talk about his father to anyone, let alone dwell on the man himself. But something about Mary's gentle concern moved him.

He helped her replace the boards after a few

moments and noticed that she rubbed her toes with apparent delight on the thick moss of the ground.

"Your feet are freezing," he scolded, dropping to one knee in front of her. He bent and cradled one of her feet against his thigh while she giggled and caught at his shoulders for support. Bear hovered near, his smell more than obvious.

"Jude, I'm fine."

He rubbed her foot and ankle hard, thrusting aside his desire to glance up the length of her leg beneath her skirt. "We're going to have to go shopping and get you some new shoes."

"Do—do you like women in shoes?"

He smiled up at her, opting not to tell her the *Englisch* adage about a wife being "barefoot and pregnant." Then he thought of Carol's obsession with shoes—the higher the heel, the better. Mary would probably kill herself in anything but sneakers. "No, I don't think I do. Shoes are too high, too cramped, and leave no room for a delicate arch such as yours, but they are a necessity on the hot pavement of Atlanta."

"*Ach,*" she mumbled.

He finished with his brisk movements, then stood to reach in his backpack. "If—uh, Bear will stand it, you'd better put him on a lead near the road here. And I don't know how he'll react to riding in a car." He handed her a length of rope and she slipped it with surprising ease around the dog's neck.

"All right, let's go see about my vehicle."

He'd housed his Expedition with an *Englischer*, Mr. Ellis, who lived down the road a short distance from the base of the mountain. He'd paid the man's hefty price for the solid insurance that the vehicle would be kept in fine running condition until the end of his three-month stay.

He held Mr. Ellis's gate for Mary and the monstrous dog, wondering how soon he could get the animal into a crate. Then he saw the blue Expedition, shining and sitting ready in the drive alongside the house, and forgot all about Bear. There was something to be said for the modernity of a fast vehicle and the prospect of driving again.

The front door of the old white home was opened, and Mr. Ellis, a short, older man with a bald head and a congenial attitude, appeared on the porch.

"So, you've come for your Beauty, have you? She's doing fine." There was pride in the man's voice. "I've kept her well."

"Yes, sir. Thank you." Jude nodded, anxious to load up and get moving.

"And what have you kept from your visit with the *Amisch*, Mr. Lyons?" Mr. Ellis gestured to Mary with a slight smile.

Jude spoke without thinking. "Someone worth keeping, Mr. Ellis."

The older man laughed and tossed him the keys as Jude wished he'd kept his mouth shut. Mary's gaze was distant and averted.

Chapter Nine

They had been driving for several hours when Mary clapped a hand over her mouth. "I'm going to be ill," she gasped.

In the fading light of the afternoon, Jude took in his wife's situation at a glance. Her skin was an odd mixture of white and green, and it was obvious that she was beyond carsick.

He pulled off the grass-lined highway and came around to her side. Then he eased her with gentle hands out of the seat and knelt beside her until her stomach was purged. He offered her a clean handkerchief and brushed the loosened tendrils of her hair back from her face.

"I'm so sorry," she whispered, sounding like a faint version of herself.

"Whatever for? You've never been in a vehicle before, right? We've been driving over four hours, and you know how sick I get when my blood sugar drops. Would you like to stop at a hotel or someplace and rest?"

"A hotel?" Mary's pale lips quivered and Bear whined softly by her side.

Jude pulled her close for a quick hug. "No worries, sweetheart. I promise."

Mary wished that she might have a shield of tree branches behind which she could hide—anything to keep out the stares of the men, women, and children in the hotel lobby. Instead, she clung with damp hands to Bear's makeshift lead.

"Are you all right?" Jude asked low when she nearly stumbled against him.

"I feel like they might see through my clothes," she admitted, glancing at the floor.

"Don't put ideas in my head."

"What?"

"Never mind." He caught her close to him and marched them up to the large ornate desk with its marble counter.

Mary forced herself to keep her chin up as the man at the desk swept them with an appraising glance.

Do I appear so different? Or is it simply that I am with the professor—an Englischer*? Surely the clerk has seen* Amisch *before, but then again, perhaps not, in such a place.*

She sighed to herself and wriggled her toes in the uncomfortable shoes she'd donned, clutching her satchel closer to her, when another man from the hotel hovered, seeming to want to take it from her. Bear made a low sound and the man inched off.

"We'd like a nice room." Her husband's voice was level and confident as he addressed the clerk.

"We don't take—um, dogs of that size normally, sir."

Mary watched Jude casually slip a hundred-dollar bill from his wallet and pass it to the clerk. She was amazed at seeing such a large denomination of money and didn't fully understand until she watched the man behind the desk pocket the bill with a swift, sidelong glance.

"Of course, sir, there are always exceptions. A suite or king-sized?"

"A suite, please."

Mary's head again whirled at the expense, but Jude seemed almost uninterested as he pulled a blue card from his wallet. She soon forgot everything, though, as her bag and Jude's backpack were loaded on a gilded trolley of sorts, and they crossed the parquet floor together.

She couldn't help but hear a little girl's voice as they reached a set of sleek metal doors that made a strange binging sound periodically.

"Mama, what's wrong with that lady? Why does she wear funny stuff? And look at that wolf!"

"Shhh," her mother hissed. "She's some sort of Amish or Mennonite. That's the way they dress. And no, don't ask to pet that thing."

Mary wanted to speak to the child, but the metal doors slid open, leaving her to stare inside at a small, gaping box of a hole.

"Don't be scared," Jude whispered, pressing his mouth against her temple. "It's an elevator."

"*Ach* . . ."

"Come on. I'll hold your hand."

She let herself be led inside, concentrating on his long fingers enveloping hers. Bear gave a gentle whine and Mary looked down at him in commiseration. But to her surprise, and despite her still-weak stomach, the ride wasn't too bad as she felt them rise a few floors before the doors slid open once more.

Jude showed her the intricacies of sliding the key card in the lock, and then they were standing in the most ornate room she'd ever seen. She felt Jude watching her and turned to look at him with an arched brow.

"It's amazing."

"It's a hotel room." He laughed. "But I forget that all of this is new to you. What are you thinking?"

She shrugged, then spread her hands. "May I take my shoes off?"

Jude stared at the expensive array of vegetables on his plate. He and Mary were seated in the hotel's elegant restaurant, and he knew he should be delighted with his wife's interest in everything concerning their surroundings. But he couldn't get past the heated flood of images that played through his mind from that afternoon when Mary had attempted to take a shower . . .

The strangled scream had been high-pitched and quick, and he'd flung open the bathroom door without knocking or thinking.

"Mary! What is it?"

The luxurious room was filled with steam and he bumped into his wife without being able to see her clearly.

"I got the water too hot for the shower and didn't realize."

He grabbed for her damp arm and hauled her back into the bedroom. He had been so frantic looking for scald marks that he didn't even notice that she was naked until his heartbeat slowed and he jerked his hand from her thigh as if he'd been the one burned.

He'd bit out a curse and grabbed the end of the comforter from the bed behind him. Then, wordlessly, he'd bundled her in it, swaddling her from head to toe.

"Mary, I . . ." He hadn't been able to think of what to say, and when she'd raised innocent eyes to him, he'd set her from him with a groan.

"Jude?"

"Next time, take a bath."

"Jude?"

He shook his head and realized Mary had been speaking to him from across the dinner table.

"Is everything all right?" she asked in soft tones.

No . . . no, everything is not all right. In fact, it's bad, far worse than I could have imagined . . .

He shifted in his chair. "It's fine. I'm thinking. How do you like the food?"

She smiled. "Well, it's not like home, but I love it. I never thought of slicing yellow squash so that it looks like a pretty fan."

"That's because the *Amisch* know the value of good food served simply. This place treats vegetables like they're paints on a palette."

"But I like that—not that I've ever painted, of course."

He considered her wistful expression. "Would you like to sometime? I think I can arrange that. My grandfather once loved to paint."

She blinked her beautiful eyes. "Your *grossdaedi*? You've not spoken much of him before."

"No, I guess I haven't. He's wonderful, really—the only one in the family who supported my going to Ice Mountain, in fact. He'll think you're great, I know."

"And—the rest of your family? What will they think?"

He stared at her, wondering where to begin, then opted for silence instead.

Chapter Ten

After dinner, Mary followed him into the hotel lobby, which housed more shops than she'd ever seen in her life. She felt like she was walking in a dream of color and shine and staring faces. Jude's obvious reluctance to talk about his family had left her drained and anxious, but she did her best to smile as he pulled her into a store with bright windows and women's short dresses displayed on figures without heads.

"Let's find you some comfortable shoes, sweetheart."

She gave a rueful glance at the old-fashioned black shoes she wore and knew her toes were as pinched as they appeared. "*Jah,*" she sighed. "I would like that, but—but I don't think I want to change my *Amisch* way of dressing."

He came to a dead stop and stared down at her. "I'd never ask you to do that, Mary. I know how important your plain dress is to your culture and who you are. Besides, I like the *kapp* strings." He gave the white string closest to her heart a gentle tug, and she felt comforted by his understanding.

"You respect people—me—I mean." She spoke the thought aloud and watched a look of tenderness cross his face.

"Thank you, Mary. I try, and I wish I could tell you more about my family, but—"

Mary glanced over his shoulder and he broke off as a tall woman in impossibly high heels and a very short dress approached them.

"Is there something I could help you with?"

Her words were polite sounding but Mary couldn't help but notice the veiled look of speculation in her eyes as she watched them. Yet Jude was entirely at ease with the situation. Mary longed for the private and quiet shopping of Kauffman's back on the mountain. Then she reminded herself that these very new experiences were why she was here and she decided to make the best of it.

"Shoes," Jude said. "She needs a comfortable pair of black shoes, and nothing with a heel."

The woman nodded. "She's—I'm sorry, I mean you're Amish, right?"

Mary decided the woman's eyes weren't cold but rather genuinely interested. "I am."

The woman nodded as she half turned from them to lead the way toward a beautiful circular display of various shoes. "I've watched some TV shows about the Amish. It doesn't seem like a fun life for a girl."

Mary shook her head. "*Ach,* but I had great fun growing up *Amisch.*"

"How could you, though? I guess I could never see myself dressing like that and being happy." There was a hollowness in her laugh, and something tugged at Mary's spirit. She looked into the woman's green eyes and found them sad in a way.

"But life is not about clothes and such . . . Of course, all of the things here are beautiful. And you are beautiful, but we have to find reasons to live beyond what we wear or how we look." She trailed off, realizing she was attracting the attentions of other customers. She sought Jude's eyes with an apology forming on her lips. But he simply watched her with a smile, one that entered her heart and made her feel glad.

The saleswoman sniffed. "I suppose you could be right, but fashion is my business. Now, what kind of a shoe are you allowed to wear? Only black?"

Mary realized the moment had passed for trying to speak of earnest things and concentrated on slipping her feet into the soft black "flats," as the saleswoman called them. She lifted her skirt an inch to show Jude and wriggled her toes in the surprising comfort.

"I like them. We'll take two pairs." He lifted a finger when she would have protested at the excess. "This is my shopping trip too, Mrs. Lyons, and one pair of those dainty things will wear out a lot faster than Ben Kauffman's shoe leather. So please accept them."

Mary giggled and felt young and carefree as he paid, then took the bag, leading her from the store. They were back in the elevator when she remembered the saleswoman.

"I don't think she was really happy."

Jude looked at her. "Hmm? Who? Oh, the saleswoman. No, sweetheart, probably not, for one reason or another. But you'd better get used to it—in my world, feelings rule."

"But what about the will and the spirit?" Mary asked.

He shook his head as the elevator doors slid open and they both heard what sounded like the loud howls of a wolf at bay.

"Let's worry about your dog for now, Mary. I think he may be scaring away guests."

She accepted the change in conversation somewhat gratefully, knowing his opinions on the matter of spirit were not much more favorable than his opinion of Bear.

She followed him down the hall to their room as the dog's cries echoed with ghostly intensity and she felt she could understand the sound.

Jude fingered his cell phone, really looking at it for the first time in months, and thought what an odd piece of connection it was. He'd retrieved it from the Expedition glove box after Mary had gone to bed with a satisfied Bear in attendance. He'd recharged the phone, deleting month-old messages without listening, and wondered if he should call his family to tell them of their impending arrival the next day.

He could imagine how that call would go. His mother would need a therapy session, his father would make sure not to be home when they got there, and his grandfather would congratulate him. And Carol . . . well, Carol would kill him, plain and simple.

He put the phone down, deciding against any forewarning. For the hundredth time, he wished he hadn't given up his apartment when he'd left, but the lease had been up. He'd rationalized at the time that he could stay briefly with his parents upon his return from Ice Mountain, then get a place to live near the university. Now he had a wife and a wolf and absolutely no idea what he was doing . . .

He glanced up as the adjoining door of the suite slid open and Mary appeared in one of her neck-to-toe nightdresses. Even completely covered, with her hair braided atop her head, she still managed to send his pulse racing.

"Can't you *shlofa*?" she asked in a whisper, coming toward him. Jude recognized the golden shine of Bear's eyes following her and sighed.

"No, I guess I can't. To tell you the truth, I—I mean—we—are going to have to see my parents and—everyone at some point. I have books and things at their house. I'll get us an apartment as soon as I can, but I was thinking that maybe we should stay at another hotel until we . . ."

"*Nee.*" She laid a small hand on his arm and he breathed in the comforting scent of her closeness—lavender and the mountain all drifting together. "No, Jude. I want us to stay wherever you see fit, of course, but I'd love to get to know your family."

"No, you really won't love it once you know them."

She laughed. "You got to know my *dat.*"

He had to smile and pulled her idly closer. "Your father is a good man—a loud man, but a good one."

"And—your *dat*?"

What am I supposed to say to you? How can I explain that my father has never believed in me, supported me, nothing . . .

He swallowed, staring into the shadows behind her head. "My dad is—who he is."

"I'm sorry. I won't press." She moved to step out of his arms but he pulled her back.

"You're very astute, little girl. I like that about you. I like what you said tonight to that saleswoman. You were right." He bent his head to brush his mouth across her forehead. "Oh, Mary King, what have I done? Bringing you here?"

"We are wed." Her voice was solemn and he realized how aroused he was becoming by her nearness.

"That's right." He spoke with abrupt haste, putting her from him and ignoring the quizzical growl from Bear. "You'd better go back to bed now. We're in for quite a day tomorrow."

He looked down, not wanting to see the confusion and concern in her pale face, and waited until the sound of the door closing let him know she had gone.

Mary burrowed her hand in Bear's neck and tried to stifle the tears that swelled at the back of her throat. A wedding into a marriage? But how? How could she reach a man who seemed so distant at times? Then she began to do what came naturally and started to pray.

Dearest Gott, *I need Your wisdom and guidance now. I'm going places and doing things I've never done and I get scared. But You know this . . . Ach,* Derr Herr, *let me become a wife to Jude, let me help him with his family, give him comfort . . . and* kinner *one day . . .*

She opened her eyes wide in the dark. Where had the thought of children come from? And how could that girlhood dream ever become a reality when he had yet to even share his heart and life with her? *I must go carefully* . . . She allowed herself to be lulled by the thought and finally found the peace of dreamless sleep.

Chapter Eleven

The following day, as they pulled into the wide circular sweep of the drive, Jude hoped in desperation that it would be Bas, the butler, who opened the door to them. He needed a little time before the confrontation he'd only begun to consider in detail since they took the exit for Marietta.

He glanced at Mary, her head bent in her white *kapp*, as they mounted the great stone steps to the front door of his family's home. He noticed her white-tipped fingers against Bear's lead.

"Hey," he whispered, squeezing her other hand tighter. "It's going to be all right." *All right. All right. It's going to be all right if only* . . . He wet his lips when she nodded. Then he rang the bell.

It was dinnertime, and probably everyone was in the dining room—or maybe they were out. Out would be good.

The door opened and his mother stood there, looking poised and beautiful—not a blond hair out of place.

"Mother . . . I—we're home."

He had to give it to Mrs. Lydia Lyons—her Southern graciousness was equal to the moment, and he and Mary were ushered in with a beautiful welcome, Bear and all. *But wait . . .*

"Jude, dear . . . you should have called. And you've brought a girl? Amish, am I right? Your skin is flawless . . ."

"Thank you," Mary whispered.

His mother stretched elegant fingers to Mary to touch the blue sleeve of her dress as if touching an exhibit at a museum.

Jude cleared his throat. "Mother, this is Mary Ki—Mary Lyons, my wife." *For a time. Only for a time.* He felt depressed. *I'm tired, that's all . . .*

Lydia Lyons rose to the occasion, though he knew that his mother and Carol were close friends.

"Your—wife? Jude, you must be joking." She laughed with faint nervousness.

Jude frowned and muttered under his breath as his father came into the large, elegant foyer. Ted Lyons looked younger than his sixty-three years, except when he was irritated and his strong-boned face flushed red, as it did now.

"Lydia, the second course is waiting. What are you . . . Jude, you're home. Get that smelly dog out of here."

Jude accepted the older man's embrace even as he barked orders, because he knew it was the right thing to do. But inside, he simmered as the familiar smells of expensive aftershave and woodsy cigar smoke enveloped him in negative memories.

"Ted, dear . . . Jude's just been playing a joke, and

at this lovely Amish girl's expense too." Lydia's voice fluttered like a butterfly drifting toward the glass ceiling.

"Hmm? A joke? Ha! You've brought your so-called work home with you, son? And a fine piece of work she is . . ." His father made to capture Mary's hands in his own and Jude pulled her back, instinctively protective. His father was a consumer—of companies, goods, people—and Mary was not up for swallowing. Jude slid his hands to her shoulders and felt the reverberation of Bear's growl against his leg.

His father frowned at him. "Jude, what is going on?"

"My wife, sir. Mary Lyons."

It was not the first time that he'd thought his father might strike him, but it was the most recent. Mary must have sensed his father's anger too, and the fine bones of her shoulders straightened beneath his hands as she tensed in reaction and Bear whined.

"You have a fiancée who happens to be dining in the next room, and this . . . joke . . . is in poor taste," his father hissed.

Carol's here . . . great. Just great.

Jude clenched his teeth. "Again—my wife, and I'd better introduce her to Carol."

"Have you been drinking, Jude?" his mother whispered in a discreet aside. "Or is your sugar low?"

He suppressed a groan, then looked up as the ominous click of high heels sounded on the marble floor. Carol appeared in the foyer, looking sleek and coldly beautiful. He felt a sudden headache begin to pound at his temples as he prepared to make one of the most interesting introductions of his life.

Mary studied the tall, blond-haired young woman with a sinking sensation in her chest. Here was the one the professor was to have married; she was sure of it. And for the first time in her life, she felt the sting of covetousness as she took in the fern green dress made of sleek fabric that seemed to cling in every flattering way it might to the other girl's body.

What must he really think of my way of dress? Mary tried to dismiss the absurd thought and then forced herself to concentrate on the Scripture passage that reminded a woman to "Not let it be the outward adornment" that mattered but "that of the heart."

"Jude, darling!"

The green blur had brushed Mary aside, and her long arms draped around the professor's neck. Mary felt her face flame and dropped her eyes, clutching her hand in her apron as she listened to her husband's voice. She felt Bear's increasing agitation.

"Caro, please. I know it's going to hurt, but I must introduce my wife to you."

"What?"

Mary looked up to find narrowed blue eyes riveted on her with deadly compulsion. "What have you done, you little Amish troll?" The woman drew a step nearer and Mary resisted the urge to move back, pressing against Bear's side.

"Carol," Jude interrupted, moving to place a firm arm around Mary's shoulders. "I have wronged you—it's true. So do what you want to me, say what you need, but don't ever, ever lay so much as a finger on Mary's head. She is innocent in all of this."

Carol flicked a narrow fingernail at Mary's loose *kapp* string and exhaled with slow, visible effort. "Innocent? Somehow I doubt that. Is she pregnant?"

Mary felt herself flush against her will as the other woman regarded her with disdain and then dismissal.

"I can overlook it," Carol bit out. "Send her and her brat away to some godforsaken Amish place and no one need ever know of your—indiscretion."

"Carol, I'm warning you—" Jude broke off as a sudden low purr of a sound entered the room. Mary saw an old man with Jude's bright blue eyes enter in some sort of mechanized wheelchair.

The grossdaedi. *Ach, the shame of being seen and met like this . . . Perhaps I should have stayed on the mountain, insisted against any wedding or role as a bride . . .*

But everyone stood silent and still as the old man moved closer to her, finally coming to a stop in front of her and Jude.

"You come bearing gifts, Jude?" The wise eyes stared up into hers, though he spoke to his grandson.

Am I a gift, old and dear one, or a curse upon this family?

"Yes, Grandfather—my wife, Mary Lyons."

She couldn't help but hear the relief that laced his tone and hoped that his world respected the old as much as hers, that his presence might bring about some peace for the moment.

"She wears no wedding ring," Carol observed

with bitterness, flashing a ring with a heavy stone in the light.

"The Amish do not wear jewelry," Mary whispered, trying to find some balance in the shift and tension of the talk. The sight of the ring that the other woman wore was enough to make her feel dizzy when she realized that it was her husband who had surely placed it on the hand of her would-be enemy. He must love Carol or he would never have asked her to marry him—and Mary understood that she herself was the interloper, and there was no escaping that knowledge now.

Jude closed the door of one of the guest suites behind him with a sigh. *I should have kept my lousy apartment or we should have gone to another hotel . . .*

But to his great surprise, Mary had accepted his mother's offer to stay at the mansion, as she'd told him she wanted to do, even in the face of obvious discomfort.

"Are you sure about this?" he'd demanded in an undertone while his family and Carol stood nearby, visibly listening.

"*Ach, jah.* I would so like the chance to stay here—your family is important."

He'd conceded with a frown. Of course Mary would think that family mattered above all. She was *Amisch* and had left her own home. But if she thought to find a loving *mamm* in his mother, he knew she was sadly mistaken. His mother was many things and he loved her dearly, but she oftentimes appeared to him as frivolous as a warbling bird.

So here he was, trapped in a bedroom suite with an untouchable wife, a smelly wolf dog, and an ex-fiancée down the hall who'd love to kill him. *Women!*

Of course, Carol would decide that she had nowhere else to go. Her parents were in Europe and she'd been staying at his family home having linens embroidered for the wedding. He should have known better than to ever think Carol might fly off offended to some spa to lick her wounds. No, she'd fight until the bitter end.

But he also knew his marriage had come as a shock, and Carol deserved some time to recoup so long as it didn't involve hurting Mary.

"I'm sorry, Jude."

His wife's gentle voice broke into his thoughts, and he realized she was staring at him, looking dismayed.

"What for?"

Mary gestured with a vague hand. "I didn't know about all of this . . . and Carol, well, she's beautiful—a girl to come home to maybe."

He chuckled and eased off the door to edge close to her. He trailed a gentle finger down her pink cheek. "I told you once, you saved me from a life of desperation. You have yet to see Carol at her worst."

"Then why did you ask her to marry you?"

The innocent question provoked him somehow. *Not because I made out with her, if that's what you're thinking . . .*

He shrugged and turned away. "I was drunk."

She said nothing in reply and he couldn't resist sneaking a peek at her over his shoulder. He knew how much she disliked alcohol as a Mountain

Amischer where moonshine was a disreputable and dangerous route to fast money.

She was petting Bear with careful strokes, her small hand disappearing and reappearing in the dense black fur. Jude met the dog's eyes with a sour look; even the beast looked appalled at his admitted behavior.

"Well," he asked after a moment. "What have you got to say about that? I know you're thinking something." His words came out rougher than he'd intended, and he regretted his irritation.

"You were drinking," she whispered. "Like Isaac Mast was?"

Jude never would have thought that she would link his casual words to the horror of being attacked, but he understood. "Mary, I'm sorry. I never thought how the truth might hurt you or resurrect those thoughts about Mast. But, yes, I was drinking, and I did make a poor decision."

"Have you told Carol that?"

"No," he admitted, dropping his gaze. "No, she'd take me any way she could. She's wanted to marry for years—I did not."

There was a long pause, and then her voice came sweet and serious. "I'm not sure then which is the more . . . difficult . . . situation, being drunk or unconscious. It seems we women will take advantage in either case."

"Mary," he groaned. "I didn't say that."

"*Nee*, I said it, and I suppose I don't sound very wifely at that."

"The *Amisch* are forthright and gentle, 'speaking the truth in love' as instructed." He mimicked a professor's tone and had to smile when she caught his eye. He turned and came nearer to where she stood, conscious of Bear forming an effective barrier in front of her.

"Are you joking about me?" she asked.

"The joke's on me, sweetheart. It's tough to be a petty man when such honesty comes from a mouth as beautiful as yours."

He was pleased to see her blush but also knew he was letting himself dance a thin line between his plans of annulment and intimacy. For once, he was glad of the dog.

"All right then, Mary Lyons." He clapped his hands in a brisk motion. "This is Lydia Lyons's second-best guest suite—Carol's got number one, but here we are and here we'll stay even if it'll probably drive me out of my mind. I understand, though, that family matters to you, and I will stick it out." He put up a hand at her wide smile. "But only for a little while, please, Mary. Then we'll get an apartment and I can wrap up the book."

"*Jah*, Jude." She gave him a demure look and he found himself wondering exactly how long they would be staying if she had her way.

Chapter Twelve

"Will there be anything else, ma'am?"

Mary turned from the bedroom window in the Saturday-morning light and stared blankly at Mrs. Bas, who'd been introduced as the housekeeper. The older woman was tall and spare, but her blue eyes twinkled with a warmth that Mary appreciated.

"*Ach*, please don't call me ma'am . . . Mary will be fine."

Mrs. Bas gave her a brief smile. "I had the joy of bouncing Mr. Jude on my knee when he was little. It's my pleasure to take care of his new wife. And if you Amish don't mind a bit of gossip, I think you're a fair sight more right for him than that other down the hall. She wanted to have me and the mister retire, don't you know?"

"But wouldn't that be up to Mr. and Mrs. Lyons?" Mary asked, too flustered to acknowledge the compliment mixed with the bit about Carol.

"Ha! That young miss has got her hands dipped in every pot around her, and I'll warn you, she'll not be fair going either."

"What—what do you mean?"

Mrs. Bas took a step nearer and leaned forward in a conspiratorial manner. "I mean that she's like to try every trick in the book to steal away Mr. Jude—and that means showing a bit of leg too."

Mary puzzled over this for a moment and the older woman laughed. "Never mind, honey. Your innocence shines as bright as day and is alluring enough in itself, I'm sure. Now, I've put your things in the wardrobe here and I must say that you've as fine a stitching as I've ever known."

Mary flushed with pleasure. "*Ach, danki* . . . I mean thank you. We're not to take pride in such things, but I do love to sew whenever I have the chance to find a bit of fabric."

Mrs. Bas reached out to pat her hand. "You wait, Mr. Jude's always generous to those he loves. He'll take you shopping."

"He bought me two pairs of shoes. I don't need anything else."

Mrs. Bas chuckled to herself as if at some private joke. "It's a wise woman who asks for little—she's bound to get more in the long run. You keep being yourself, honey, and everything will be fine. Now, please excuse me."

When the housekeeper had gone, Mary used the small set of stairs and climbed with a ginger tread into the high four-poster bed that had been hers since the previous night. Jude's room was adjacent, but his door was shut and she knew that he was probably working on his lessons. He'd told her that he was to start back to teaching classes in a few days and she didn't want to be a bother, but she felt lonely and tired.

She bounced a little on the thick luxury of the duvet cover, and a desire to pray rose within her. *Dearest Lord, you made marriage. You know what it's supposed to look and feel like to the heart, mind, and body. Please create intimacy between Jude and me, not only of the flesh but of the spirit also, and help me to have wisdom in this,* O Gott, *Amen.*

Then she lay back against the pillows and allowed herself to rest for a few moments even though she'd slept the night through.

"Jude . . . um, do you have any clean cloths about?"

He turned in his desk chair to look at his wife. She stood in the doorway of the guest room and appeared a bit pale and troubled.

"Cloths? I don't know. What about towels? What do you need them for?"

She bit her lip and her beautiful face was suffused with color. She rubbed absently at her abdomen. "I—it's that time."

He tilted his head, puzzled. "That time?" And then it hit him hard.

What is my problem? Am I so dense that I can't even discern when my wife is painfully trying to tell me that she has her period? He exhaled and rose from the desk chair.

"Mary, come in, will you? And close the door, please."

She obeyed slowly and he wondered now if she had pain with her periods. He knew it was common—before he'd decided on Amish studies, he'd taken a few premed courses and was infinitely glad for it at the moment.

She came to stand before him, her thick lashes downcast. "Jude—I'm sorry. I should have asked someone else but I didn't know . . . back home I just washed my cloths out in the creek each month, but here . . . Well, I need more for later today."

She trailed off and he remembered studying hygiene on the mountain and knew this was a common practice among the women.

"Sweetheart, you don't ever have to be embarrassed around me—about anything." He swallowed, then went on, reaching to catch her hand. "Come here. Sit on my lap." He sat in the desk chair and the old wood creaked with a comfortable sound as he pulled her down to rest against his chest.

"Does it hurt?" he asked, resting his chin on top of her *kapp* and trailing a hand down around her belly, rubbing softly.

"Only a bit." But he heard the discomfort in her voice and increased the pressure of his hand, feeling her relax a bit more against his chest.

"Mary, I am such a lout. Look, I'll take you to the store, all right?"

"Again?" Her voice dropped in dismay. "Besides the shoes?"

He had to chuckle. "Yes, again. And we'll get you fixed up for everything for your—uh—that time of the month, okay? Trust me?"

She turned her face into his shirt and nodded and he closed his eyes against the wash of emotion he felt at her vulnerability. He'd never been so needed or felt so helpless. He wished, for a vague moment, that there was such a thing as God and that His power would care for him personally as he cared for his wife. *My temporary wife . . .* His hand stilled against her at the thought. He needed to keep a rein on his thoughts . . . a few months . . . that was all. *That's all.*

Mary squirmed in her chair at the Lyons's elaborate luncheon table as she thought of their shopping expedition to the drugstore. She glanced at her husband across the table while he spoke with his grandfather, but then had to look away when he returned her gaze with a raised brow. At the store, he'd been calm and knowing, slanting her his oh-so-handsome, you-need-my-help grin, and she'd felt a curious tightening in her chest as he'd explained the various feminine products available in what she'd come to think of as his "professor voice." She wondered, as she played with a heavy silver fork, how he managed to know so much about women.

But she soon pushed thoughts of Jude aside as she tried to focus on having a genuine conversation with her new mother-in-law, who was seated to her left.

"Of course, he's always had a fascination with the Amish, even though Ted's tried to dissuade him." Mrs. Lyons spoke in an undertone with a glance down the long table at her husband, who was talking with Carol. "But you certainly are beautiful . . . and Jude was always affectionate when he was young. Will you be staying for the holidays? They're coming up fast and I must see about a new decorating firm for December. Do the Amish have trees at

Christmas? Wherever did you find that wolf? Will you have more salad? Bas, serve her more salad."

Mary blinked into the carefully made-up blue eyes of her hostess and struggled for a foothold to answer. The process made her head ache and she realized she'd never heard a person speak so much in one breath, not even Old John Beider—who was known on the mountain to be able to talk a man to sleep.

Bas was filling her plate with the mixture of greens, pecans, and orange slices, and only when she shook her head did the older man murmur and step back. She stared in dismay at the pile of salad, worried how she could possibly eat it all. At home, everyone served themselves when she brought food to the table.

Jude's mother was still eyeing her with a quizzical expression, and Mary put her fork down with a shaky hand. "I—we—yes, we have Christmas trees but we make the decorations."

"Lovely, I'm sure." Mrs. Lyons smiled. "Did you put that in your book, Jude? Handmade decorations . . . I don't know that I could manage. What do you think, Ted?"

Mary watched Jude's father cast his eyes over the table, clearly used to his wife's manner of speaking. "Oh, I don't know, Lydia. I am surprised that Jude has enough information for a book. Aren't your people private by nature?"

He didn't address her by name but tipped his crystal glass in Mary's direction with a faint smile that didn't reach his eyes.

There was a sudden silence around the table as Mary lifted her chin to reply. *I must speak well—this is Jude's* dat. *Please,* Gott, *give me words to say to this man who doesn't want* Amisch *for his son . . .* "Yes, usually private. Jude was the first one who Bishop Umble allowed to stay on the mountain. I think he got a lot of facts for his book and that it will be good."

She looked across the table at her husband to find him watching her with something sad and steady in his eyes.

But Mr. Lyons shook his head. "I'm afraid I'll have to disagree with you, honey. If your people are so private, won't a book about them destroy that privacy? Won't it bring the whole world to your—mountain? How wise a decision was it to allow Jude in—I mean by your bishop, of course."

"Dad."

There was a warning note in Jude's voice as he spoke and Mary understood that there was more to the conversation than she knew, not plain speaking but an undercurrent of dangerous anger. And she felt herself infected by the anger at the suggestion that Bishop Umble was less than wise, but she knew that she must not respond to the feeling. *What had Jude said—that here, people live by their feelings? I have been raised to control my emotions and my tongue, as* Derr Herr *instructs . . .*

"Come on, Jude," his father continued in a mild voice. "If you married her, she's got to be bright. No offense meant, Carol darling. But, son, let the girl answer a few questions. She must know that what you're doing is exploiting her culture, and for what, a better position and more—"

"That's enough," Jude said with quiet determination. He rose from his chair and Mary watched him squeeze his grandfather's shoulder before he came around the table and held out his hand to her. "Mother, please excuse us."

Mary put her hand in his and followed him from the room, but she couldn't resist a glance back at the table. She saw the looks of satisfaction on the faces of Carol and Jude's father. It was an image she would not forget.

Chapter Thirteen

"Are you driving fast?" Mary asked, her voice faint.

Jude nodded and slowed. "Yeah."

He looked over at her beautiful, concerned face in the play of sunlight and shadows as he took back roads to Roswell, wanting to go somewhere and walk. He had expected his father to be what he always was, but not so soon or so openly. And he hadn't expected it to hurt so much when his dad found the right buttons to push—always enough truth to make him uncertain whether they were really lies. He realized that, in the past, he probably would have sought out a drink about now, but he had no desire to hurt Mary by doing so.

"Look, Mary, I'm sorry about lunch. My father is . . ."

"I understand, I think. Back home once, one of Ben Kauffman's older *bruders* wanted to leave the *Amisch* and the mountain—Ben's *fater* was alive then. He fought with his *sohn*, in private and in public. I only remember bits and pieces because I was young, but the *fater* fought because he was angry and worried for his son. That is what your *dat* must be for you."

Jude gripped the steering wheel hard. "I wish it were that easy, sweetheart. I really do, but my father is a hard man—one who's used to getting everything he wants. It's not only that I'm a disappointment to him, it's that I'm different than he is—and he cannot accept that."

He swung the Expedition into the turn for Bulloch Hall, an old plantation that was open for historical tours, and turned the engine off. He stared out the front window at the old magnolia trees and the wide sweep of grass in front of the big old house. "And what he said about exploiting you and the Mountain Amish . . . I would never hurt your people or you. The university's press will not . . ."

She leaned over and pressed warm fingers against his lips, stilling his words. "Jude, do you think that I do not trust you? Because I do, we all do back home. I believe in what you write. I know your *fater* doesn't understand your work, but I've tried—all summer. And now I'm here with you."

She moved to draw her hand away and he caught her wrist, thumbing over the steady pulse point, then closing his eyes against the wash of emotion her simple words evoked. *She believes in what I write . . .* He opened his eyes to find a soft smile on the pink wash of her lips and had to mentally shake himself for a moment. Then he let go of her hand and reached over to undo her seat belt.

"Do you want to walk with me?" he asked. "There are paths behind some of the outbuildings, and there's a flower garden."

She nodded, reaching for the door handle, but he knew she wanted to say more. However, unlike many women he'd been around, she didn't pressure him. He caught her hand as they walked over the roots of the trees, passing a few tourists on their way to the large front porch of the hall.

"What is this place?" Mary asked after a few moments of silence.

"An old plantation. It still has one of its slave quarters intact. People come and see how it was to live here before the Civil War."

"Ach . . ." She didn't go on and he wondered how much history she knew. After an eighth-grade education, all that was required for the *Amisch*, there wasn't a lot of room for facts and rhetorical discussion. But he knew she liked to read.

"Do you want a tour?" he asked, even though he longed to skip the business. He wanted the coolness of the shadowed paths, a place he'd often gone to think.

"Nee, though I must say that many *Amisch* aided in the Underground Railroad in Pennsylvania."

He stopped and looked down at her in surprise and she laughed.

"Jah, I know some history, Jude, and besides, the *Amisch* have mostly always opposed slavery because of the persecution they themselves suffered before coming to Penn's Woods."

"I didn't know." He resumed walking and she shrugged.

"Maybe there's a lot more to know about everyone."

Her words echoed in his mind as they turned

down a bank to the head of one of the interwoven trails. There was something secret and sensual about the filtered sunlight and densely tangled undergrowth of the path that had appealed to him for years. He remembered being in high school and bringing a girl to the place for a walk, fantasizing the whole time that she'd kiss him so that he wouldn't have to risk trying it first with her. *What was her name anyway?*

"What are you thinking about?" His wife's quiet voice broke into his thoughts and he felt himself flush.

"Nothing."

She raised a delicate brow at him in question and he had to laugh. "All right, but no getting angry with me if I tell you."

"I will not get angry," she promised with a knowing nod.

"All right—a girl. I was thinking about a girl I brought here once in high school."

"*Ach* . . . I'm angry." She sounded so surprised that they both laughed together.

"Don't be, sweetheart. I can't even remember her name, and even if I did . . . well, it wasn't that successful a walk back then."

He watched her reach to brush her delicate fingertips across the soft petals of a stray flower and had the sudden desire for her to touch him with the same intimacy. He pushed the thought away, but she caught his short blue shirtsleeve.

"What do you mean by 'not that successful'?"

Her tone rang with genuine curiosity and he shook his head.

"Look, I wanted her to kiss me because—I was afraid to try kissing her first." He admitted the last bit in a rush, wanting to get it over with, and not especially proud of admitting to a lack of prowess. *Arrogant idiot . . .*

"Are you still afraid?" she asked, lifting then dropping her thick, dark lashes.

You know I'm not . . . you know . . . she wants me to kiss her. His last thought was somewhat of a revelation; Mary was trying, in all her innocence, to flirt with him, and it felt so good it almost hurt. Then he realized how dangerous a situation it would become if she decided to practice tempting him, but he was here now, and he wanted to put away the lingering memories of a past when he'd been so unsure.

"Nee," he whispered in *Amisch,* stepping nearer to her. "I'm not afraid now."

"Gut," she breathed.

He drove her home as if demons pursued them, and she had to hold on instead of repairing her hair in its *kapp*. Her mouth stung and her lips felt swollen from the intensity of his kiss and the faint roughness of his skin. She hadn't expected how she'd react to him or what it seemed to do to him. When she'd twined her arms about his broad shoulders, he'd wrenched himself from her to stagger a step away. He'd bent over and clasped his knees, muttering a curse. His breathing had echoed her own, coming in harsh, ragged gasps.

She watched now as road signs flashed by and snuck a glance at him. His own mouth looked red, but his fine lips were set in a grim line. She wondered if she sinned somehow in desiring him, yet she was his wife. *But he wants an annulment . . . and I want a marriage.*

Her head began to ache as he turned into the drive of his family's home. She felt the intensity of his gaze and wet her lips before looking at him.

"I'm sorry," he bit out. "I was out of control. It won't happen again."

She longed to protest that she liked him when he lacked control, but he was already out of the Expedition. He slammed the door and she watched him walk around the side of the house toward the backyard.

She opened her own door and made haste to go up the front steps and slip inside the great door. She longed to get to her room and repair her hair before she met any of the family. She had reached the spiral staircase when Carol's voice hissed from behind her.

"So, the little Amish troll is really an Amish tramp. What were you doing, rolling in the hay? You have no real idea how he likes to be touched anyway. You're nothing but an ignorant, temporary diversion."

Mary turned to face her adversary, hearing the pain laced with anger in the other woman's voice, and prayed for the right words to respond. But, to her great surprise, she felt the simmer of indignation come to her and she spoke with level clarity.

"You have lost what you never had, yet still you mourn. I too would be angry if another had him, and you wear that ring with hope. I tell you not to hope and that a woman is worth more than any jewel—if she is true to herself."

She watched Carol's face flush crimson as confusion showed in her narrowed eyes. Then Mary turned back to the stairs, knowing her words had found their mark.

Chapter Fourteen

Jude stalked around the house, seeking the privacy of the garden. He stopped short at the sight of his grandfather and Bear enjoying an apparent time of connection, with the big dog pressed hard against the side of the wheelchair.

"Ah, Jude, a fine animal you've got here. Smart too—fetched me my paper."

Jude crossed the grass with reluctance, not wanting to see anyone at the moment. Bear growled faintly at his approach and Jude rolled his eyes. *Yes, I was having an insane kiss with your mistress, you weird, knowing beast.*

"She reminds me of your grandmother."

Jude dropped into a chair near the old man he loved, knowing his grandfather spoke of Mary. "Does she, Grandfather? Why is that?" *Tell me something so that I can refute it in my crazed head . . .*

"My Amelia was beautiful, of course, but there's more to beauty than a pretty face. Your grandmother's soul was beautiful and so, I think, is your wife's."

Jude passed a hand over his eyes in mute frustration. "Well, I can't see her soul or anyone else's, for that matter." He kept his tone light, meaning no disrespect.

"Yes, the soul is not easily seen, more felt, I believe. I must confess that when your mother first brought your father home as a potential suitor, Amelia was not happy. She said she feared your father's soul."

"She should have feared *for* it," Jude muttered in a dry tone. "Not that I believe that rot."

His grandfather waved his paper at a bug and went on as if Jude hadn't spoken. "She feared the darkness in him, and I must tell you that I have tried to shield you from that darkness as much as I've been able without dishonoring your father . . . Of course, he really only wanted the other one of you."

Jude leaned forward, confused. "The other one of me? Grandfather, is the sun too hot for you?"

The old man squinted as if looking at the past and shook his head in a vague manner. "No, it feels good."

Jude reached out to clasp the old man's knee with concern, deciding to dismiss the confusing statement. "I love you, you know that?"

"And I you. But now you have this young wife to love you and to stand between you and the world, Jude."

"Isn't it supposed to be the other way around? I'm supposed to protect her."

"No." His grandfather spoke with serious intent.

"No, a woman can bear much more than a man can—bear children and grief and death and life. You remember that, Jude. She may let you think you are stronger, but sometimes you won't be. And there's nothing wrong with that."

Jude nodded, wondering where he could go for solace, as his grandfather's talk only made him feel more confused and churned up inside.

"Do you want me to take the dog in, Grandfather?" he asked as he rose.

"Hmm? No, leave it. Good company for an old man who prattles on."

"Never that," Jude said, bending for a quick hug. "I'll see you at dinner."

He left the backyard and entered the house through a side door, deciding he might as well face Mary after running off like a teenager.

Mary sat in front of the large mirror in her room. Her hands shook a bit as she pulled off her *kapp* and started on the many hairpins that held the intricate mass in place. *I cannot believe I spoke that way to Carol—no matter that her words hurt me. But what I said was the truth. And yet what reason do I have to hope myself?* She bit her lip as she blinked back tears and shook out her hair.

"Beautiful." Jude's voice was hoarse as he loomed in the mirror behind her.

She almost jumped but then sat still, meeting his eyes in the mirror. *"Danki,"* she whispered. It felt strange to have him staring at her with such intent. For her people, only a husband could view a wife's hair unbound, and Jude seemed to be claiming that right as he lifted a wooden-handled paddle brush from the dresser.

He started to brush her hair and she shivered in delight, forgetting for the moment why she had been discouraged. He stroked the brush from the crown of her head down the length of her back to where her hair fell past her bottom. Then he straightened and appeared to shake himself, though he continued to brush at the top of her head.

"I came to apologize, Mary."

"But I liked your kiss," she said before she could think.

"And I liked yours, but I shouldn't have run off like that when we got home. It wasn't very mature or gentlemanlike. I apologize."

"You said—you said you'd 'never let it happen again.'" She couldn't keep the anxiety out of her tone. She didn't want to lose his physical touch even as she remembered *Grossmuder* May's warning that there was much more to a marriage.

He gave a rueful laugh as he let his hand run over the smoothness of the hair at her shoulders. "I can't promise to not kiss you again, especially when I remember you looking like this. But I meant that I'd try not ever to lose control of myself. I owe you that."

"Is control always such a good thing?"

He shook his head at her in the mirror, put the brush down, then leaned very close to stroke the dark strands back from her ear. He put his mouth against the small lobe and she closed her eyes. "Yes, sweet *Amisch* Mary. You above all people should know that control is a good thing." His voice was a husky sigh, his breath warm and sweet against her.

And then he was gone, and she opened her eyes to see him close the door between their rooms. She picked up the brush and began to bundle her hair back up with determination forming in her heart.

Jude looked up from some notes as he heard the door to the hall creak open. He glanced over, expecting to see Mary, and a smile hovered about his mouth. Instead Carol stepped in and he sighed. She was dressed in a brief pink dress that bared her thin shoulders and emphasized her lean waist. He knew she was dressed to look her best, from her hair to her heels, and he had the sudden wish that she'd simply find someone else to think she was in love with. She reached a hand to smooth an imaginary wrinkle from her dress and the sun caught on the jeweled shine of his grandmother's engagement ring. *I forgot the ring.* He put the papers down on his desk and weighed the options in his mind.

Certainly, Mary did not want or need such finery; as she had said, her people did not wear jewelry. But it would be nice to let her hold the ring, to feel close to his beloved grandmother.

"What do you want, Caro?"

She smiled like a cat licking cream. "Now that, my dear Jude, begs for an inappropriate answer."

"Well then, I'm afraid you'll be disappointed."

"Will I?" She moved close and tangled her arms about his shoulders. "I've heard you don't sleep in the same bed with her. So what does that make for you, Jude? A little less than four months since you've—"

He shook his head. "Don't, Caro. Don't lower yourself to this."

He watched her eyes take on a sullen look and then, to his amazement, well up with angry tears.

"Caro? Are you actually crying? Because it's not going to work—I'm only surprised to see it. I mean, in all the years . . ."

"Shut up, Jude! The little troll is right. She's right!" He watched in fascination as Caro yanked the engagement ring from her finger and threw it at him. It bounced off his chest and he caught it with one hand.

Then Carol stalked up to him, slapped him hard in thc face, and turned with a sniff. "There," she announced. "I did it."

He rubbed with absent fingers at his cheek as he listened to her heels click out into the hall. His head rang in the sudden silence after the door slammed.

He was looking at the ring in his hand, turning Caro's words over in his mind, when a soft knock from the adjoining bedroom door made him lift his head.

"*Kumme* in," he called in *Amisch,* knowing it was Mary.

His wife peeped into the room and he motioned her forward, wondering with curiosity what it was that his seemingly meek wife had said to Caro.

"I couldn't help overhearing the last bits," Mary murmured.

"I'm sorry for Carol's name-calling, Mary."

"Don't be."

He was surprised to see a half smile tug at her beautiful mouth. He took a step closer to her, cupping the ring in his hand. "And why not?"

"Well, she said I was right, didn't she?"

He nodded. "Yes, and that's got me curious. When did you speak to Carol?"

She put her hands behind her back and shrugged in a way that he found charming. "*Ach,* I don't know . . . here and there. I told her the truth, that was all, but I probably could have been more loving when I spoke."

"The truth, hmmm?" he mused aloud. "And what would that be?"

She shook her head. "It's not for you to know."

"Ever?" he pried gently.

"Maybe sometime."

He smiled and opened his hand, holding it out to her. "It's the worst of form, I imagine, to present your ex-fiancée's ring to your wife, and I know you don't want it. But I thought maybe—I don't know, that you might feel closer to my grandmother if you looked at it."

She moved toward his outstretched hand, then reached to take the ring from him. He watched her cradle it in one palm, and the sunlight from the casement window caught on the stone's brilliance. "Would I know you better, if I could have known your grandmother?"

"Yes," he whispered, her words washing over him like rivulets of warm water.

"I'd like that—to understand you, to know you, to know your heart . . ."

He felt overcome by some sensory hypnosis. *Who has ever really wanted to know my heart, except my grandparents?* "Mary, I . . ."

"Jude!"

The moment was splintered by a frantic pounding on his hall door. Mary plopped the ring back in his hand and he would have spoken, but his mother's wailing increased. He was used to drama from his mom, but Mary appeared visibly shaken. He bit the inside of his mouth and crossed the room in quick strides to open the door.

His mother fell against him sobbing. "Oh, Jude. It's terrible!"

He felt his heart begin to pound. "Is it Grandfather?"

"No, it's Betty the cook. She's cut her arm and there's blood all over the kitchen. And I'm to have five women here for dinner in two hours. It's the Bases' night off, Carol's left, and your father is working late. What am I going to do?"

Jude pivoted with his mother in his arms, automatically patting her back. He met Mary's confused gaze and arched an eyebrow at her. *See, Mary, this is my life . . .*

"Well, Mother, I expect you'll have to cancel or cook yourself."

"Jude Lyons!" she sobbed louder. "How ever can you be so cruel?"

"I can cook," Mary announced above the din.

Jude's head began to ache.

Chapter Fifteen

Mary leaned over the now-pristine granite countertop and pored over her mother's cookbook, which she had brought from the mountain. She and Jude had helped Betty, the cook, into the hastily phoned ambulance and Jude had gone along with her at Mary's insistence.

She had cleaned the blood from the countertop, washed the offending knife, and run upstairs for the recipes she loved. She was glad for the moments of quiet in the vast kitchen—Jude's mother was dressing and his grandfather was napping with a now-faithful Bear in attendance.

Mary ran her finger down the handwritten words on the browned page in the middle of her *mamm*'s book. She loved how her mother's handwriting looped and blended and blurred with easy-to-follow ingredients and instructions. The simplicity was a comfort when she glanced behind her to consider the large cookstove.

"I'll have to figure it out," she mused aloud, then

turned back to the age-old recipes. "All right, meat loaf, mashed potatoes, fresh corn, and pineapple upside-down cake—it's going to have to do."

"Oh, it sounds divine, darling." Jude's mother entered the kitchen in a flurry of yellow chiffon. "Anything you make is sure to be good. I mean, you and all of those lovely produce stands, right? Will you be a dear and zip me up? Thank heavens you cleaned up the blood. I simply could never have been a nurse. I hate hospitals. I've heard the Amish women have their babies at home. Will you and Jude use the hospital? I do hope so—they have a lovely florist. Do you like flowers? I do."

Mrs. Lyons whirled around and Mary sought the zipper with unfamiliar fingers, her head ringing. Her own people held clothes together with clever pins and hooks and eyes, but she managed the yellow zipper with ease, unprepared for the quick hug and wash of perfumed scent as Jude's mother expressed her gratitude. Then the older woman was gone from the kitchen as quickly as she'd come, and Mary shook her head. *I suppose it takes many kinds of different people to make a world . . . and I will not think about the idea of having Jude's baby . . .*

She grasped a large metal bowl with determination and began to poke into the cupboards and then inside the mammoth icebox, *nee*, refrigerator, looking for ingredients. At home, she would have used a mixture of ground beef and ground pork for the basis of the meat loaf, but she knew she had to settle for the white-wrapped package marked "Ground Round" in the refrigerator because she had no idea how to quickly thaw any of the meats in the deep freeze. Eggs were easy to find on a convenient shelf, but it made her homesick for a moment for the summer when she'd taught Jude how to hunt for stray nests. *But I'm here with him now . . . isn't he my home?* The question resonated too deeply for her to dwell on the issue as she began to assemble labeled spice jars with grateful hands.

She bit her lip when she realized she'd have to master the stove top in order to brown the bacon for the top of the meat loaf. But to her surprise, she followed the simple, circular drawings with a few quick turns of the black knobs and produced more constant heat than she could have found with her woodstove at any time.

She'd progressed to peeling the last of the potatoes when she was startled by the sound of the doorbell chiming an intricate ring. Soon the echoes of women's laughter and chatter came closer and closer. Mary paused in mid-peel to look up as the kitchen door swung open and Mrs. Lyons entered, followed by five other women.

Mary felt enveloped by varying colors of dress and scents of perfume. It seemed there were more people like Jude's mother in the world than she had realized.

"Ladies, meet my new daughter-in-law, Mary. Don't ask about Carol—I love her, of course, but Jude . . . Don't mind Mary's dress—she's Amish. You know Jude's fascination with all things Amish. Her skin is positively flawless and the dear thing is making us meat loaf. Barbara, remember that meat loaf we had at the church dinner when Mitty died?

I wish I had the recipe. I hope we're not bothering you, dear, while you cook. I thought it would be fun for the ladies to meet you and see you work. Do you think you could make lasagna sometime? It's the only thing I know how to bake." Mrs. Lyons stared at her as Mary was surrounded by the interested guests.

"I . . ." Mary began.

Jude's mother waved her hand in dismissal. "This is Barbara, and Eve, and Michelle, and Letty, and Jane. I'll go check on the dining room seating."

Mary nodded a cautious greeting as her mother-in-law fluttered out of the room, unsure whether to speak or to go on peeling.

"Is that your only dress?" Barbara asked, blinking heavily made-up green eyes.

"Did you make it yourself?" Michelle enquired, reaching to pick a slice of raw potato from the bowl on the counter.

"What did your family think about your marrying?" Eve questioned with a flick of her bejeweled wrist.

"Are there Amish in Georgia?" Letty murmured in a soft accent.

"And do tell us before Lydia gets back," Jane, the youngest looking, demanded. "What's it like to be with Jude? He's simply gorgeous . . ."

All the ladies giggled as Mary tried to fathom the prying intimacy of the last question. She drew a deep breath. "I have more than one dress. I made them all myself. My father thinks Jude is *schmart* . . . smart, and he wanted the wedding. I don't know about *Amisch* in Georgia; I'm from Pennsylvania. And . . . and what I do with my husband is always good." *Though I bet it could get even better . . .* She rebuked herself silently for the naughty thought.

There was a distinct silence and Mary waited, wondering if she'd offended them somehow, but then they all broke into gales of laughter as Mrs. Lyons reentered the room.

"Having fun, darlings? Good. Let's go have a drink, girls. I think Betty left a pitcher of something made up, and I can try my hand at serving you all. It's almost like a slumber party, don't you think? I used to have a pink sleepover bag with white elephants on it . . . so sweet."

Mary spoke up with quick inspiration. "Mrs. Lyons?"

"Lydia, dear."

"*Jah*, Lydia. I would be happy to serve you if you will all go and be seated."

"That's really nice," Barbara said, reaching to pat Mary's hand where she still held a potato.

"Wonderful!" Lydia cried. "Let's go, darlings. I bought the most beautiful vase the other day at the antique store on Old Canton. I've got to show it to you all and . . ." Lydia moved on ahead as Jane leaned over to Mary.

"We'll talk later," the other younger woman whispered with a conspiratorial wink. "I want all the details."

Jane left with the rest of the group and Mary half laughed aloud, breathing a sigh of relief as she went back to peeling with hurried hands.

* * *

Jude saw Betty safely tucked up in her bedroom on the third floor, gave her the pain medicine the ER had provided, then went in search of his wife. He heard the high-pitched laughter of his mother and her friends in the smaller dining room and was going to slip past when Mary exited the room carrying a large tray.

"What are you doing?" he demanded, surprised by the anger he felt in seeing her acting like a servant. He took the tray from her.

"Shh," she warned and turned from him to head down one of the hallways toward the kitchen.

He stalked behind her trim form, his irritation growing. They entered the kitchen and he slid the tray onto a granite countertop while Mary began cutting slices of delicious-smelling pineapple upside-down cake.

"I know you can cook, but I did not expect my mother to make you serve," he bit out.

She shook her head, not glancing up from the cake. "Jude, Betty was with you. Your mother had no one, and I don't mind serving supper one bit. It's kind of fun."

"You're my wife, not the cook or the maid." If his voice held a ring of proprietorship, he didn't want to think about it.

She did pause then in her deft cutting to blink wide hazel eyes at him. "I think you sound . . . what's the word? *Ach*, snotty. *Jah*. We are commanded to serve one another."

He wanted to grind his teeth at her accuracy but settled for snatching a red cherry from a circle of pineapple. She slapped his hand as if he were an errant child and he found his humor restored.

He sucked on the cherry, savoring its sweetness, then rounded the counter to gently remove the knife from her hand and lay it down. He put aside his resolutions of a few hours before and decided that a little light play might not hurt either of them.

"Jude, they'll be wanting dessert soon."

And so do I . . . "I know." He lowered his lashes. "But I think I need more sugar, maybe another cherry." He sighed as if he were tired and had to suppress a feeling of chagrin at her sudden, intense concern.

"*Ach*, Jude, are you feeling faint? I'm sorry. Here." She thrust her small hand into the glass jar of cherries sitting nearby and withdrew several, heedless of the sticky redness that ran in thin rivulets down her wrist.

He caught her hand and drew her wrist to his mouth, letting his teeth edge against the sweetness of her skin. She stood still, watching him, and he felt his cheeks heat with color but continued. He lapped at the juice and closed his eyes against the small sound of mingled shock and pleasure she made when his tongue crossed the pulse point in her wrist. Time had slowed to a lazy sprawl of moments as he worked his mouth to diligently remove every trace of sugary stickiness from her fingers and hand. Then he opened his eyes.

She was staring up at him, her fingers still clasping the three cherries she'd pulled from the jar.

"Are you—feeling better?" Her voice was high and breathless, her breasts rising and falling.

"I need the cherries, I think," he murmured with a trace of an apology. He twined the fingers of his right hand with hers, so that the sweet fruit was clasped between them. Then he bent his head. He felt the pulsing burn of his own skin as he licked across his fingers to get to hers and taste the first cherry.

She watched him in delicious fascination, her heart beating hard in her throat. She gripped the counter behind her with her free hand as his lips closed over the bright red fruit between her fingers.

"Mmm," he murmured, his blue eyes narrowing. The sound reverberated down her backbone and forward to her belly, washing her in delicious sensation. Her lips parted and she longed to lean forward, to meet his mouth with her own, but she didn't move.

She knew he angled his head to deepen the intensity of what he was so thoroughly doing with his clever mouth. He sucked hard at the juncture between her thumb and then licked his own skin again. "Oh, Mary," he moaned. "We taste so good together. I—can't . . ." Then he captured the second cherry with the tip of his tongue. He closed his damp mouth on the fresh redness and some instinct made her let go of the counter.

She trailed her fingers up to touch his lips, feeling the heat from his mouth. He half shook his head, in some distant protest, she knew, of her questing hand. But she also understood that he was too caught up in the moment with her to stop. Pleasure spiraled almost painfully through her as she nestled in to hear his ragged breathing and to see how dark his blue eyes had become. She stroked the remaining cherry caught between their fingers, and he made a tight, half-choked sound from the back of his throat.

"Well, well, son," Ted Lyons barked out. "Dallying with the help? Unless, of course, this is your idea of research."

Chapter Sixteen

Jude felt her jump at the mocking voice of his father, and the last cherry fell to the parquet floor like a drop of blood. Mary bent to pick it up but Jude caught her first, pulled her up straight beside him, and slid his arm around her shoulders in a comforting manner.

"Would—would you like some cake?" Mary asked his *daed.* The quaver in her voice brought anger surging through Jude's already heated blood.

"He's fine," Jude snapped, then frowned as she looked at him askance.

His father laughed low. "Ah, Jude, I must congratulate you, a wife charming in both form and manner. What more could any man want?"

Jude loosed his arm from around Mary's shoulders. "I'll take the cake in to Mother, Mary. You've had a long day. Why not go up to bed?"

He saw her struggle with a protest, her feelings playing with rapidity over her expressive face. But her *Amisch* demeanor of wifely duty won out and she gave a quick bow of her head. "*Jah*, Jude. *Gut nacht* . . . Good night, Mr. Lyons."

"Ted, honey. Call me, Ted."

She nodded and slipped away from Jude, stepping with care over the cherry.

Jude turned to his father when she'd gone. "Go on, Dad. Say it." He kept his voice quiet, not wanting to rouse his mother's guests or his father's further ire.

"What would you like me to say, Jude?"

Jude mentally tried to hang on to something, anything, that would give him a feeling of peace. *The other man at the Ice Mine . . . now, why would I think of that?* He drew a deep breath. "Say what you've said a hundred times over. That you want me to work at the company for you and give up Amish studies."

His father snared a pineapple ring from the cake and swallowed it in one gulp. "Well, that might be a bit difficult now, son—since you saw fit to marry yourself to a pretty piece of it."

"Leave her out of this," Jude growled.

"Come on, son. I don't blame you for it—I mean, look at her. But did you really think that I'd accept her—on any level? Ever? Because if you did, you're a bigger fool than I've thought." His father snatched a cherry up and tossed it in the air, but Jude caught it in an abrupt move before it could hit his dad's mouth.

"Sorry, Dad. No bites this time. For you or your argument. I've got cake to serve." He smashed the cherry on the counter and ignored his father's sardonic grin. He caught up the cake and the knife and turned in one swift move.

"All right, Jude. Have your cake, but from what I've heard from the servants, you're not getting to eat it too. Separate bedrooms, really? I thought your Amish were a bit more—earthy. You know, muck and mud and all that?"

Jude bit the inside of his mouth until he tasted blood. *I will not respond.* He hit the kitchen door with his hip, then turned to his father.

"Have a good night, Dad."

He was pleased to see the brief shadow of confusion cross the older man's face.

Jude left the kitchen, feeling his heart pound. *But for once, I held it together. Didn't give up—didn't give in.* His father's words still burned in his mind, but something about remembering his fall at the Ice Mine made his heart slow to steadiness. And he went to serve the cake with a smile.

Mary broke off her listening at the kitchen door when she heard Jude's father call his son a fool. She slipped with silent feet up the back stairs while her eyes welled with tears. The Amish took seriously the Bible's command to "call no man a fool," and to hear it hurled from a father to a son was almost more than she could bear. It didn't matter what Mr. Lyons had said about accepting her; all she could think of was Jude growing up as a child under such meanness.

She gained her bedroom and paced, feeling restless and lonesome, her heart aching for Jude. She sat down at the delicate white desk and chair provided for her and drew out some paper and a pencil, deciding to write a letter home to her own family. Mr. Ellis, who'd housed Jude's vehicle, got the mail for the mountaintop, and one of Ben Kauffman's oldest *buwes* made a trip down to pick up and send every few days.

August 25

Dear Dat, Joseph, and Edward,

I wanted to write and tell you how much I miss you all. Jude is a gut husband, though, and treats me real well. His family are—she paused, biting with anxiety on the pencil tip, then began writing again—*all here; his mother, father, and grossdaudi. They live in a big haus and we are staying with them for a time, so you can write to me here in care of this address. Dat, how is your sore hip? Joseph, your syrup should start to run in a few weeks, I bet. And Edward, how are the animals doing from Jude's cabin?*

I do miss church meeting and have been thinking of starting a quilt pattern that looks like one of the trees they have here—a Magnolia. I will send it to you if I finish it. Please give my love to all.

Your Loving Dochder and Schwechder,
Mary

She licked the envelope, then looked up to see her door ease open and Bear's gleaming eyes as Jude followed the dog into the room.

Mary swallowed hard as she put the letter down and buried her hands in Bear's fur, wondering what in the world a wife might say to her husband at this kind of time to give him comfort. But then, like a fiery dart to her soul, she remembered that she was only a bride and found no true acceptance with the father Jude struggled against.

Jude watched her sitting at the desk, very upright, very Amish, and realized that he had no photograph of her to carry with him. He slid his cell phone from his pocket and approached her in the twilight of the fading day.

"What arc you up to?" he asked.

"Writing a letter back home."

He frowned. "Are you homesick, Mary? I've never asked you yet."

"*Ach, nee* . . . I . . . you're here."

He felt a surge of unexpected pleasure and something warm flooded his heart. "That's right. I'm here. Here for you, sweetheart."

She nodded, looking a bit confused, and he knelt down on the other side of Bear. "Mary, I want to ask you something that I know you won't want to do."

"*Jah*," she said slowly.

He held out his phone. "May I take a photograph of you? I know the rules, and the thing about graven images, but I want—I need . . ." He couldn't seem to explain to himself why he needed her picture, and he stumbled over his words.

"Yes," she said with determination. "Yes, you may."

"What?" He blinked at her, at her unexpected agreeableness when he'd been forbidden to so much as take a picture of a squirrel all summer on the mountain.

"I said *jah,* Jude. Please."

"Okaaay, that's great. Thank you. But may I ask why you . . ."

"I want to give to you, to make up for your father calling you . . ."

Jude laughed at this unexpected admission. "Mary Lyons, were you eavesdropping?"

She flushed gracefully and he caught her hand in Bear's fur.

"So your husband sends you to bed, but you do not obey as a good Amish woman should?"

She bit her lip and shook her head and he wanted to kiss her hard, right then. But he was also genuinely grateful that she wanted to be a balm to his spirits after his father's mockery. And he didn't want to lose the opportunity to have a photo of her.

She blinked after the brief flash of light and then Bear barked once, breaking the moment. Jude smiled and leaned forward to press a warm kiss on her forehead.

"Thank you, Mary. Have sweet dreams."

He walked away, then gently closed the door between them, staring down at his phone.

Chapter Seventeen

Mary slid into the wooden desk chair and closed her fingers on themselves with care. An uneasy week in his parents' home had passed since they'd come to Atlanta, and Jude's university was to start classes. She told herself that she should be proud that he'd asked her to accompany him on the first day and should not be quaking like a lone leaf inside. But she felt rather disconnected from him; he'd been kind but had not really touched her since the night he took her photograph.

"Nervous?" Jude asked. He adjusted his glasses and smiled at her. "Don't be. They're only a bunch of college kids."

"That doesn't help, really," she confessed. "Aren't they my age?"

He frowned a bit. "Yes, but I find every day that you are wise beyond your years. So don't be intimidated."

He turned and walked back to his desk at the front of the room. "It's about time. Oh, and they might ask you questions—answer what you like. Don't worry. I'll help you."

Mary tightened her fingertips and tried to concentrate on the smell of old wood, stuffy, filtered sunlight, and the fact that here, she recognized her husband in his element. His tall body was relaxed yet poised as he leaned against the front of the teacher's desk and smiled and nodded as students began to enter.

Mary became aware of a multitude of sensory details as the various people glanced her way, then dropped into seats. There were boys with large numbers on their shirts who bobbed their heads with reckless abandon while thin wires dangled from their ears. And girls, perfumed with cloying scents, who wore long boots with short skirts and tight tops who took extra time to sidle past Jude, who appeared not to notice. Even the more serious and plain-looking students seemed alien to her with their mountainous book bags and careful preparations with pencils and papers and small computers. They all waited for her husband to speak and she realized that she was waiting too.

He flashed a smile in her direction and she felt herself flush; then he began to talk.

"If you're here, you're in Amish Studies 100, and I'm Professor Lyons. Here is the syllabus, nothing too bad, I promise."

One of the booted girls raised a hand and smiled in what Mary considered a coy fashion. "Professor Lyons? May I ask who the Amish girl is at the back of the room?"

Jude smiled easily. "Of course. May I introduce Mary Lyons, a special guest for today."

"Lyons?" The apparently bold *Englisch* girl persisted. "Is she related to you, Professor?"

Again, Mary couldn't keep the heat from her cheeks when he grinned. "Indeed. I forgot to add that she's my wife."

There was a subtle murmuring of disappointment from the girls as a whole while Mary watched the boys in the room apparently share some private joke at the situation from the smiles they wore.

A serious-looking girl raised her hand and Jude nodded. "May we ask Mrs. Lyons questions?"

"Of course, but remember, she's no different than you are, really, so be respectful."

Mary squared her shoulders in her seat in response.

"How did you and the professor meet?" It was a booted girl again, and Mary fidgeted a little, trying to think of what to say, when Jude interrupted.

"I'll take that one, if you don't mind. I had the privilege of spending a few months this past summer at a place called Ice Mountain, Pennsylvania. I met my wife there."

"But wasn't it hard to get the bishop to allow you to marry, with you being *Englisch*?" The serious-looking girl knew her stuff, Mary thought with grim acknowledgment, wondering what he'd say.

But Jude only smiled. "You're right. For those of you who are new to the *Amisch* culture, anyone who is not *Amisch* is called *Englisch* or is an *Englischer*. Each *Amisch* community is governed by the spiritual and literal leadership of the bishop. In Ice Mountain, it was Bishop Umble who heard my case, and I became a very lucky man."

Lies or half-truths. He does it so easily, but ach, *he did not shame me about my family forcing him . . . about me forcing him . . .* Mary shifted in the wooden seat.

Another boy closer to her seat spoke. "So are you going to stop being *Amisch* eventually—I mean, wear regular clothes and stuff?"

"I—" Mary opened her mouth then closed it again as the question tore through her. *Stop being* Amisch*? Could I? Could I give up everything I know and value if it would allow me to stay in Jude's life? But what about the annulment he wants?*

She realized the boy had repeated the question and shook her head. "I am *Amisch.* It's not really about my clothing."

"Then what does make you *Amisch*?" one of the girls asked with disbelief and a faint challenge.

Mary bit her lip, then began to answer one of the most difficult questions of her life.

Jude clutched the ridge of the desk behind him. *This was a bad idea, bringing Mary here to expose her to prying eyes and questions . . .* But this question, this answer—the one she wet her lips and stumbled over, made his heart beat faster. He felt he was able to gain a very intimate view of her within the confines of a small crowd, and he felt his eyes burn as she struggled over the words.

"I-I do dress differently, *jah.* But I'm still *Amisch* without my clothing." She blushed when she realized what she'd said, and the appreciative males in the audience laughed. "I mean to say that being Amish—for me—means loving *Derr Herr*, the Lord, and the community and nature He's given us. I—we *Amisch* read often from *The Book of Martyrs*, stories about the first *Amisch* in Europe, who were tortured for their faith. I think of those people and how they came to Pennsylvania to find a new life, and I guess my faith helps me to find that new life too—every day."

She looked at Jude when she'd finished, her beautiful eyes wide and seeking his approval. He nodded and smiled at her. She summed it up so well. Of course there was more to being *Amisch*, but that was what it meant first to her. His conscience pricked him though at her easy speaking of God in a nonsectarian university. *How can I ever be with her and not believe as she does? I can't, that's all. I can't . . .*

He cleared his throat and took back the class's attention, laying out the plans for the semester and studiously avoiding Mary's gaze.

After the last student had gone, she watched his lean hands scoop papers up from the wood of the large desk and a sudden impulse took over, sending a tightening to her belly as she bit the inside of her cheek.

"You're a wonderful teacher." Mary couldn't keep the excitement out of her voice. She'd loved sitting in on Jude's class, loved hearing him talk about her people with a knowledge and respect that made her proud to be his wife—even if only in name. But she also knew that something she had said had put him off a bit because he didn't seem to want to connect with her for the rest of the class.

Her enthusiasm dissipated at her last thought and she wondered how far she'd come in building a marriage from a simple wedding.

"I'm glad you like the class. What's wrong?" he asked, looking up.

She shrugged in what she hoped was a casual way and put out a finger to run circles around a knot-hole in the desk. "Well, since you're such a *gut* teacher, I-I thought, well, that you might teach me how you—like to be touched. I mean, your mom said you always were affectionate, and Carol seemed to know . . ."

"Ah, Carol." He laughed shortly, his blue eyes bright. Then he dropped back into the wooden desk chair, slid slightly on its coasters, and gazed up at her. "So, Carol said something that got your *Amisch* dander up?"

She sniffed in a prim fashion. "I don't know what you mean."

He laughed again, then sighed. "How I like to be touched? Well, let's see—Carol certainly never asked." He rose to his feet and brushed past her briefly.

Mary felt her heart jump. "Really?"

"Yes, really. Carol is a taker, not a giver, but you, sweet Mary, are something else entirely." His voice lowered as he locked the classroom door and sauntered back to the desk.

"Am I?"

"Yep." He dropped into his desk chair and sprawled his legs apart. "Come here, will you? And I'll try to give you a—lesson."

Nervous now at having achieved her goal, she

glanced at the closed classroom door behind her, then moved hesitantly to stand before him.

Then he removed his dark-rimmed spectacles and closed his eyes, leaning his head far back against the chair. "Touch my throat," he murmured. "Please."

She set her teeth at his sudden and intimate request, then stopped and took a small step back.

"Oh, no, Mrs. Lyons." He reached out and caught her hand. "No running away. I'm afraid you asked for some teaching. Am I right?" His blue eyes gleamed at her from beneath thick lashes.

She waved her other hand before her in a vague gesture while her fingertips burned against his palm. She had the intriguing idea that she had somehow happened upon a large wild cat lazing in the sun, and she wasn't so sure that she wanted to have a pet . . .

He knew he shouldn't be playing such a hazardous game with her. But she tempted him with her innocent provocation, and he rationalized that a touch couldn't hurt. He felt torn between panic and the pressing desire to forget everything but the probability of kissing his wife. *My wife* . . . He swallowed hard. "Closer . . . *sei se gut.*" He bumped her with his knee as he rumbled the Amish words, dropping her hand. Then he arched his neck against the low chair back. "My throat. I like to be touched there." He closed his eyes, heart pounding, waiting for what seemed a forever moment, and then felt her dress press against the insides of his legs. He felt her fingers stroke down his throat quickly; a butterfly's touch, and he tightened his grip on the chair arms.

"Slower."

"Like this?"

He felt her lean into him, using both of her hands, touching him in languorous motions that sent him wondering if she could feel the thrumming of the blood in his veins.

"Yeah . . . like that."

"Where else?" Her voice sounded husky, warm, and confident. "Like that day in the blueberry patch?"

He was hot, burning up between the slanted sunlight of the old office window and the fall of the Amish dress against his thighs.

"Mmm . . . yes," he whispered. "I can't forget."

Her small hands dropped to skim his shoulders, then down his arms, and images of that day on the mountain slammed into his consciousness. She'd touched him then too, and he'd kissed her and worked his shirt off at the same time. She'd laughed, a small breezy sound, as he pulled her hands against his chest, staining his skin with the purple juice that clung to her fingertips. He'd wanted her then; he couldn't deny it. Fast. Hard. Right there . . . against the green of the grass and the shelter of the bushes.

He came to himself in the pressing wood of his desk chair and stared up at her in confusion, the past still looping pleasantly with the present in his brain. Then he shook his head and slid back from her in a rough motion. He stood up and turned away from her, knowing he was probably confusing her beyond measure. But he didn't fully understand himself—didn't want to, in truth.

"I'm sorry, Mary," he managed to say, thrusting his hands into the front pockets of his jeans.

"Did I—do something wrong?"

Wrong? Wrong? His mind screamed. *No, that was about as right a touch as I've ever had and now I hurt and want and . . .*

He swung around to face her, then stopped still at the bleak look in her eyes.

"I'm sorry, Mary," he repeated. "I—I'm not focusing very well on our deal, am I? Things like this won't help an annulment much. But for the record, no, you did nothing wrong."

She still looked dejected and he was about to gather her in his arms when a quick knock at the door surprised both of them.

He crossed the room quickly and unlocked the door, twisting the knob. His best friend, an associate professor of history, Sam Riley, poked his blond head into the classroom.

"Cheerio. Not interrupting anything, am I?" Sam asked in a fake British accent.

"No." Jude shook his head "Nothing. Come in and meet my wife."

Chapter Eighteen

"Who is she?" Sam hissed the words when Mary walked out of earshot in the restaurant where they'd gone for lunch.

Jude sighed. "I told you—she's my wife."

Sam rubbed his hand over his blue eyes as if to clear them and leaned closer across the table. "But what about Carol? You know—the fiancée near and dear to my heart?"

"You and Carol never did get along," Jude acknowledged, accepting a glass of sweet tea from the smiling waitress.

"Yeah, so? I'm not denying that, but coming back here with a girl who could be a model—an Amish model, mind you—and who looks about as innocent as a baby is not exactly what I expected as completed book research. She's not pregnant, is she?"

"Carol asked the same thing. And no, she's not."

"Then why are you married?"

"Maybe I fell in love."

"Jude—come on. How long have I known you? Junior high? You haven't been a monk, but you also haven't been in love with anyone or anything but your books and your research and the Amish since— Wait, that's it, isn't it? She's a research project—your own personal Amish research project."

"Sam . . ." Jude swallowed, startled at how close to the bone his friend's surmising struck. Sam's words echoed what his father had suggested. "Of course she's not a project." *But maybe she is* . . . He pushed away the dangerous thought that she also might be something else entirely and chose to take refuge in the colder part of his being. Maybe his father was right . . . *A project—research, up close and personal.* He shifted in his chair when he thought about exactly how personal things could become.

"So how long are you planning on keeping her?" Sam asked, his nonchalance striking a chord of anger in Jude.

"I told you, I'm not keeping her like she's something in a cage. We're married. End of story."

"Remind me to get you drunk one night, my friend. You tend to be more forthcoming when you're intoxicated."

"I've decided to give up drinking," he announced, realizing it was true.

Sam stared at him in puzzled consternation. "Is your sugar low?"

"No," Jude growled. "Now here she comes. Drop it."

Mary slid back into her seat and Jude focused on the beauty of his wife's face and found himself relaxing in spite of his tension a few moments before.

"What would you like to eat, sweetheart?"

He watched her give a self-conscious glance at

Sam, then look down at the menu. "It doesn't matter. Pie, I guess."

Sam gave an appreciative sigh. "A girl after my own heart. Pie for lunch. Do you have a specialty Amish pie that you make?"

"Raisin . . . Jude likes it."

"I bet he does. I've never had it."

Jude wanted to roll his eyes at the open wistfulness in his friend's voice. "Well, you might as well come over some afternoon and have a slice—if my wife will be so kind as to bake for you."

"*Ach*, I'd love to," Mary murmured.

"Thank you. How is it staying at your mom and dad's? Not much fun, I bet?" Sam asked.

Jude met Mary's eyes and smiled. "It's as interesting as ever."

"I'm sorry, old man. I'd have you with me but you know my place is only an efficiency."

"Don't worry about it, Sam. I—" Jude broke off as a jovial older man in a suit approached their table.

"Don't get up, boys." The short, balding man waved them back down into their seats.

"Dean Walters." Jude spoke with pleasure. "Please join us. You must meet my wife, Mary."

"Aha! I heard it gossiped round the department this morning that you had a bride and a most fitting one for you, Jude. My dear, I'm James Walters. A pleasure to meet you."

Jude watched with pride as Mary's delicate hand was engulfed by his mentor's. The dean of the department had secured the funds for him to travel to Ice Mountain and was also in charge of the funding for his book to be published. And the older man was someone Jude respected and trusted. *Like introducing Mary to a real father . . .*

He pushed the thought aside and joined in the pleasant talk of completing his book.

Mary knelt on the floor in the vast Lyons family library. Jude had brought her home after lunch and she had found good company. Jude's grandfather was in his chair, drawn near the fall of afternoon sunlight through the tall windows that looked out onto the garden with Bear at his feet.

"You have a gentle and quiet spirit, my dear." The old man smiled down at her with Jude's blue eyes. "Not unlike, I might add, my own dear wife, Amelia."

Mary heard the sadness lacing his words and smiled with gentle sympathy. "How long has she been gone from you?"

"Ah, ten years now."

"My mother died giving birth to me. I miss her though I never knew her. So you must truly miss someone you were able to hold and love."

"But life goes on," he said after a quiet moment. "Now you fill my grandson's arms, and I am grateful for that."

Mary bowed her head and nodded, not wanting this man who loved Jude so to know that she was a wife in name only.

He cleared his throat. "Are you homesick, child?"

She looked up with a bright smile. "*Ach, nee* . . . there's so much to see and do."

The old man grunted. "Especially in this house."

"*Nee*, really. Every family is . . . different. But the Bible teaches that *Gott* places us in families, and I am so glad to be part of yours."

"Again, you are gracious and good, child. But should you ever grow homesick . . . Will you go to the desk in the far corner over there?"

Mary rose and went to where he asked. The large mahogany desk had a beautiful grain, but she felt it was probably more a decoration of sorts than actually for everyday use.

"In the top drawer, my dear. On the right. You'll find a small item wrapped in brown paper. Will you bring it here?"

She found what he wanted and felt its odd heaviness as she carried it to him. Then she resumed her place on the floor near him.

His elderly hands carefully undid the paper as he spoke. "This was from our honeymoon—mine and Amelia's. We stopped on our way to New York at a little place in the mountains of Pennsylvania called Coudersport, at a miraculous spot called the Ice Mine." He held up the glass globe of water, then gave it to her.

She took it with careful hands, amazed to see that the ball was a miniature of the Ice Mine, complete with thick icicles and faint colors, as if the sun shone on the ice.

"*Ach*, it's—beautiful." To her surprise, her eyes filled with tears and she realized that she did miss the mountain, its peacefulness and steadiness. "I'm sorry for crying," she whispered, swiping at her cheeks with one hand.

But Jude's *grossdaudi* smiled. "Take it, child. Keep it for when you miss the mountain, as I have remembered it in all of its mystery and glory."

"I can't do that," she said, nonplussed, leaning forward as if to hand it back. "*Ach*, I can't . . ."

"What can't you do?" Jude asked from where he stood in the open doorway of the vast room.

Mary looked up in surprise and Bear gave a welcoming snort as Jude's grandfather laughed. "Come in, my boy! Come in."

Jude crossed the intricately woven carpet, pleased to see his wife sitting with his grandfather. The afternoon's class had gone well and he had enjoyed their lunch with the dean, who had assured him that the university's press was more than ready for his book.

He bent to hug his grandfather in greeting and glanced down at Mary. "Oh, you've shown her the snow globe . . . Mary, what can't you do?"

"He wants me to have it . . . I said I could not."

Jude dropped to the floor beside her, sitting cross-legged, and reached out to give the globe a little shake in her hands. A mixture of snow and sparkle added to the background of the ice and she gasped again at its loveliness.

"Oh, I can't think of a better person to have it, sweetheart. It's perfect." He smiled at her. "Thank you, Grandfather."

"You may enjoy it together." The old man laughed, and the sound was pure joy to Jude's heart. He put his arm around Mary and pulled her close for a warm, snuggling hug.

"You make Grandfather happy, Mary. I won't ever forget that."

He'd meant it lightly, not to speak of the future, wanting only to dwell in the moment, but he caught the shadow of doubt in her lovely eyes as she gazed back at the globe. And he wondered how it would be when she was back in her world, and he alone in his.

Chapter Nineteen

A few days later, Mary discovered that Mrs. Bas and Betty had gone out shopping. She sought out Bas and asked his permission to use the kitchen since Sam was coming over that evening for raisin pie.

"My missus and Betty are a bit over-the-top with the kitchen," Bas had confided. "Feel real bad about you having to cook the other evening. But if you want to bake something, by all means, go and do it now, Miss Mary."

So Mary had hurriedly assembled the piecrust ingredients and was poised with the soured milk to add to the flour when Carol strolled into the room.

Mary decided to concentrate on the crust, though she nodded a greeting. Carol had been absent from the house for hours at a time for a few days before finally declaring that she would remain if Jude would allow it. And, of course, Mary thought, with the slightest trace of bitterness, he had. *Because he's kind and gentle . . . would I want him any other way?*

She paused in forking the damp flour, breaking from her thoughts, and realized that Carol had spoken to her. "I'm sorry, what was that?"

Carol shrugged a slim shoulder. "Nothing. I—I wondered what you were making, that's all."

"Raisin pie. Professor Sam is coming over tonight."

"Sam? Sam Riley? That snot!" Carol popped a plumped raisin into her lips. "That man drives me up the wall."

Mary frowned, puzzling out the turn of phrase, and Carol sighed.

"He bothers me."

"*Ach* . . . I thought he was nice."

"Ha! If you like brainy, blond egomaniacs who'd rather discuss the War of the Roses than have normal human conversation."

Mary arched a brow at her in surprise. "You like him."

"What?" Carol snapped. "I do not. Listen, honey, you might be able to tell me the truth about one or two things . . . and I might listen, but I do *not* like Sam Riley."

Mary smiled in confusion. "But you were going to marry Jude?" It was a question, sincerely meant.

Carol gave her a dry look. "'Were' is the operative word there, honey . . . Anyway, I—I wanted to say thanks for what you said the other day—about a woman's worth and jewels and all that."

Mary stared at her. "It's sort of from the Bible."

"Oh," Carol laughed. "Then that's why I didn't know it—not that I don't go to church. But anyway . . . I'll go."

She turned on her high heel to start to walk away and Mary bit her lip for a moment.

"Carol, would you like to join us for pie tonight?"

Mary watched the other woman pause, then glance back at her over her shoulder. "How do you know I'm not trying to be nice to you to get Jude back?" Carol asked.

Mary shrugged. "Because you like . . ."

"Don't say it. I'll think about pie tonight. I do love raisins. Bye, honey."

Mary once again pondered the strangeness of those around her and wished for the straightforward talk of home. But then she smiled to herself as she mixed the raisins and sugar; Carol liked Sam Riley!

They were assembled in the den, watching a movie on the big flat screen and eating pie, though Jude found his wife's wide-eyed fascination with the large television to be sweeter diversion than the confection that melted in his mouth. And to his great surprise, Carol had joined them, apparently at Mary's invitation.

He glanced at his ex-fiancée now as she sat, delicately forking up pie and ignoring Sam. Jude couldn't quite understand the animosity between the two, but Mary seemed more than happy to make up for breaks in the conversation. *Women . . . they are beyond any study . . .*

He looked up to see his father stroll into the room, pie plate in hand. Jude reached for the remote and paused the movie. He sensed the discomfiture in the room. Sam had never been well received by his father, and Mary was used to leaving whenever he was around. *But not tonight* . . .

"Excellent pie, honey."

Jude felt Mary's glance and waited.

"Thank you," she murmured.

"Yes, and I need it after a day like today. My vice president up and quit on me. Man couldn't stand a little input now and then."

I can imagine what kind of input . . . Jude tilted his head. "I'm sorry, Dad. You should be able to get someone soon, though, right?"

His father snorted, clattering his empty plate and fork on a side table. "Like you care, Jude. No, the man I really want in that position is you. I think it's a great opportunity." His gaze raked Mary. "What with you choosing to start a family and all."

Sam got to his feet with haste. "I, um, I'll take my plate into the kitchen. Find something to drink and all that."

"I'll join you," Carol announced with an audible sigh.

Jude stared after them as they left, finding their behavior nearly as provoking as his father's.

Mary rustled a bit beside him. "Jude, do you want me to go?"

"No, please no. Dad, I've gone over this with you a million times. I've got a job that I love at the university and I'm finishing my book. I can't work for you."

His father stared at him, silent for a rare first time. "Right . . . right, you can't." He got to his feet suddenly. "Well, I'll leave you two newlyweds alone. I have some business to attend to."

Jude had an uneasy feeling but decided he was overreacting as he watched his dad leave without a fight.

"That was odd," he said, smiling at Mary.

She shook her head, a touch of sadness on her face. "I wish it could be easier."

He touched her hand. "Let's forget it—we've got a moment to ourselves and we're on a couch. Do you want to make out?"

"Make—out?" She turned puzzled, beautiful eyes on him and his smile widened.

"Yes, let me teach you the meaning of that particular *Englisch* expression . . ." He leaner closer to her and dipped his head with pleasure.

A full twenty minutes later, Mary raised her eyes and spoke in a hushed voice. "Where are Sam and Carol?"

Jude nuzzled the length of her neck. "Who cares," he muttered.

"I bet they're—making out too."

"What?" Jude lifted his head and stared down at her. She smiled up into his handsome face and gazed at his reddened mouth.

"Carol likes Sam."

Jude peered at her closely, having laid aside his glasses long before. "Sweetheart, have I kissed you delirious? They can't stand each other."

Mary giggled. "Let's go find them and see."

"You want me to give up kissing you to go

sneaking around my own house? They probably left or something."

"Please—*sei se gut*, Jude, for fun."

He sighed and repositioned his glasses, then straightened her *kapp*. "All right, since you never usually mention fun as a diversion, I'll agree. But we're coming back to this couch once I prove you wrong."

"All right." She smiled.

He got up and pulled her to her feet, then bent to kiss her nose. "Onward, wife. Where should we look for them?"

"The kitchen. Sam said he was taking his plate back."

"The kitchen it is." He swept a hand before her. "Shall we?"

Mary caught his hand. "All right, but we have to be quiet."

"As quiet as thieves," he quipped and she squeezed his hand in response.

"What the . . ." Jude stared at the tangled couple leaning against the kitchen counter. Carol's perfect hair was a mess and Sam looked flushed and giddy.

"I told you," Mary said with a knowing smile. "They're making out."

Jude shook his head. "You know, in some cultures, getting caught like this is a reason to get married." He gave his wife a deliberately wolfish smile and she blushed, much to his pleasure.

"Yes, well." Sam cleared his throat. "I'd better be heading home . . . I've got some things to read and all that . . ."

"Oh, and I think I'll run out to the stores for a bit," Carol declared. "Honey, thank you for the pie."

Jude watched them slink out of the kitchen like two high-schoolers and could only stare after them in confusion.

"I was right," Mary declared.

"You were, but I have no idea how . . ."

"Even Amish women have intuition, but I do wonder why Carol would go shopping this late in the evening?"

Jude laughed out loud. "Mary, they're going to . . . well, never mind. Some women shop late."

He felt her thoughtful gaze. "You're not telling me something," she said.

"No," he agreed. "I'm not, but it's nothing worth knowing. Now, how about that couch?"

"I've got to wash the pie plates."

He caught her close, loving the feel of her soft body curving against him. "I'll wash the pie plates, sweetheart. You go wait on the couch."

"Will we make out again?"

"Do you want to?" He knew there was an anxious note in his voice.

"*Jah*, very much."

"*Gut*," he whispered, kissing her once and hard. "That's good."

He watched her leave the kitchen, his eyes on the slightly off-kilter apron band at her waist, then he went whistling to wash up the pie plates, contentment in his heart.

Chapter Twenty

Jude smiled at Dean Walters's secretary, Joan, as he entered the office where he'd been requested. The gray-haired woman, a terror of undergraduates, usually smiled on him but today simply held out a candy jar filled with chocolates.

"Miss Joan? Your secret stash? What's wrong?" he asked as he helped himself to a piece.

She eyed him and shook her head, her faded brown eyes sad. "Bad news, kid," she whispered.

"What?" he asked, jokingly. "Am I fired?"

She extended the jar once more and he stared at her, then brushed past her to knock at the blurred glass of the inner office door.

"Come in." Dean Walters's voice sounded faint and Jude entered, sucking hard on the disappearing chocolate in his mouth. Another tall man whom he didn't recognize stood behind the dean, looking impressive and serious.

"Jude, please sit down, but, uh, first . . . I'd like you to meet Mr. John Eliason . . . he's the university's vice president and chief financial officer.

There are—some problems we need to discuss with you."

Jude shook hands with the cold-eyed CFO, then sank into a leather chair, feeling as if his future was about to change forever.

"But really, Mrs. Bas, I want to do it." Mary tried to keep the note of desperation out of her voice as she spoke with the older woman.

Mary had asked Mrs. Bas if she might have the privilege of cleaning both her and Jude's rooms. The older woman had disagreed, but Mary explained that she needed to do something productive.

"You're pretty, honey. That's productive enough."

Mary nodded her thanks. "I appreciate your words, Mrs. Bas, but, well, back home on Ice Mountain, I'd be cooking and cleaning for him. He'd be . . . mine . . . to take care of and look after."

"Oh, I see." Mrs. Bas gave over the dust rag and bottle of furniture polish with reluctance. "Well, if that's it, and it'll make you happy, go and dust your heart out, luv."

Mary gave the housekeeper a brief hug, and Mrs. Bas sniffed.

"Go on with you, now."

Mary darted away up the stairs with Bear at her heels, feeling that she'd been given a secret family recipe and was about to try it out. It would be so nice to be able to do something for Jude while he was out teaching.

She decided to clean his room first and entered

to find the window open and sheets of his yellow notepad blown about the hardwood floor. The September air smelled sweet and a breeze had picked up, making the draperies dance.

She knelt to gather the notes happily, glad that she might help him organize a bit. She'd collected three yellow-lined sheets when her eyes fell on the neat handwriting of the fourth. She lifted the paper slowly, as if seeing herself in a dream, then began to read . . .

"Mary as Research Project"

> I should admit the truth to myself, I suppose. Being married to Mary is better research than I've been able to find in any type of intensive study. Her dialect, demeanor, dress, religion, and even the way she holds her body, all scream Mountain *Amisch* domesticity, in loud and clear tones. There is no doubt that this marriage, even temporary, has helped the development of the book, and I suppose I should be grateful that my hand was literally forced in being bound to her. Yet . . .

Mary dropped the sheet of paper and then the others. She could not read one more word. She pressed her hands to her mouth and rocked slowly back and forth as tears filled her eyes and fell down her cheeks. It was as though she had gotten a true look at herself from Jude's heart and she realized that she would never be a true wife to him.

Then, resonant and clear, she calmed herself as an inner voice seemed to take over. *I must leave. Now.*

Before Jude comes home. She got to her feet, resolute, and went to her room. She slipped off the flat shoes he had bought her and clambered into her old ones, and then she finished packing her satchel with the few things she had originally brought with her. She glanced around the room and her eyes fell on the Ice Mine snow globe. She picked it up with care. Then she went in search of the one person she knew would help her.

Jude watched Dean Walters shuffle the papers before him in an awkward way before he began to speak.

"Jude, uh, there's been some difficulty with funding, and, um—" The older man broke off and shot an imploring glance at Jude, as if willing him to understand.

"For the book?" Jude asked. *If that's the problem, I'll put together everything I have of my own and . . .*

"For the book, yes, and for your position." The dean took out a handkerchief and swiped at his round forehead.

"My position? Why? What's wrong? What have I done?" He directed his questions to the CFO.

Mr. Eliason stared at him as if he was a bug. "Funding, Professor Lyons. You do understand. The university has made a decision to cancel its Amish studies classes for next semester, so your position is null and void. And the university's press is no longer interested in your book. We're moving on to—bigger things." The man gave Jude a brief smile. "So no antics, if you please. You'll finish out the term teaching, of course, but then—well, it's a big world."

Jude looked at the face of Dean Walters, who appeared to have tears in his eyes, and slowly nodded. "All right . . . all right."

He got to his feet and stared down at his mentor, then turned to go.

Mr. Eliason's voice stopped him. "Oh, and Professor Lyons? Give my regards to your father."

Jude pivoted, staring hard into the impassive face of the CFO; then he opened and closed the door.

He automatically took the chocolate Joan put in his hand. *Give my regards to your father* . . . He sucked hard on the candy, then swallowed. "Joan, was my father here sometime recently? Ted Lyons? Tall man, but stocky, always wears a suit and . . ."

The older woman shook her head and whispered, "Jude, I'm sorry. I can't—I need this job."

Dean Walters slipped from his office and leaned hard on the closed door. "Jude, you have to understand. I'm being forced to retire early—I wanted nothing to do with this. But a new undergraduate library . . . paid for down to the last book . . ." He shook his head. "I'm sorry. I'm so sorry."

Everything clicked in slow motion in Jude's brain. He made himself go and shake hands with the dean, who looked instantly relieved. Then he took another chocolate and walked out. Walked away from the destruction his father had bought. Jude suddenly wanted nothing more than to see Mary and to rest a few moments in the true comfort of her arms . . .

Chapter Twenty-One

Jude opened the door to the mansion to the unearthly sound of Bear howling. It was a mournful wolf's cry, eerie and low, and it made Jude's heart pound for some reason.

He met the butler in the hallway. "Bas, what's wrong with Bear? Where's Mary?"

The older man looked like he had to resist an urge to wring his hands. "She's gone, sir."

"What?" Jude had to raise his voice above the din.

Bas mouthed the words. "She's gone."

Jude took the stairs two at a time to their guest suite. He flung open the door to Mary's room and took in the sight of Bear sitting in the middle of her bed, on his haunches, his nose pointed to the sky.

"Mary! Mary?" Jude went to his room, striding over the strewn yellow pages on the floor, then back to hers and opened her wardrobe. He saw with a sick feeling that her simple satchel was missing. He sat down on the bed and methodically began to try to quiet the dog, then gave up and went to the hall door. It opened in on him and he stepped back as Carol entered, carrying an envelope.

"Here, Jude. I had to help her. She begged . . ."

He snatched the envelope from her and ripped it open, reading as he paced.

Dear Jude,

I owe you my apology and the truth. I felt guilty when Dat trapped you into the marriage, but I wanted it at the same time. I've been dishonorable to you, knowing I have never been a match for who you are. And I have sinned against you, by trapping and trying to hold you as well. I cannot go on living like this, knowing what I've done to you, am doing to you. I wanted desperately to turn our hasty wedding into a marriage and I was working toward that all the time—working against what I said in words. That I would go back to Ice Mtn. In truth, I should have gone long ago. I hope your work goes well and that your book about Ice Mtn. is well received. Please do not come after me or try to reach me; I must do what's right by my faith. I'm sorry that I have to leave Bear—I didn't know how to take him. I will ask Joseph or Edward, perhaps, to come off the mountain and drive to get him soon.

Mary

Jude spun on his heel to face Carol. "Why? Why did she leave?"

"I didn't say anything, if that's what you're implying. I'm happy enough with that big lug, Sam." A faint coloring of her cheeks testified to the truth of her words. "And I thought she explained it in the letter—she said she did. She wouldn't tell me much, only begged me to help her go and used some of her Bible talk again about women and jewels and their worth . . . I didn't know what else to do."

"How did she go? And she has no money! I've got to find her . . ." He started to leave the room when Carol caught his arm.

"Jude, I watched her plane take off for State College, Pennsylvania. She's to take a taxi the rest of the way to her mountain. I made sure she had plenty of money. I'm—I'm sorry."

He stared out the open door, into the darkness of the hall, and Bear's cries expressed his own feelings perfectly . . . mournful and lost.

"Ma'am, are you all right?"

The stewardess's voice penetrated the door of the plane's bathroom and Mary paused in her retching to gasp a feeble *"jah."*

She wished the woman would go away and let her simply die, but Carol had told her something about "first class" and "getting more attention," so Mary knew the lady was simply doing her job.

Carefully, she pushed the folding bathroom door open, then wandered down the aisle, sliding into her seat, praying the lady next to her wouldn't start a conversation. Nothing would come out of her strangled throat now, much less friendly talk. Even her tears had frozen behind her eyelids. Thankfully, she had the window seat, so she leaned against the plane's cold inside wall to stare at the twinkling

Atlanta lights slowly fading out of sight—like her soul—fading—emotionless. The one she loved and hoped to become a good wife to was forever lost. She tried to cling to the belief that *Gott* had a perfect will for her life, and eventually His plan would be revealed. But for now, she would take her bruised heart home to Ice Mountain, knowing that she was nothing more than one man's research and not his dream.

I can't think about her . . . not now, maybe not ever. What did I expect? What did I really expect—that she was going to stop being Amisch *or keep on with no community but me? Maybe it's better this way. She'll marry someone on the mountain . . .* He ignored the sick feeling the thought produced and turned as the door was opened.

Jude was surprised at the dead calm he felt when his father strode into their library. He'd been drinking; Jude could smell the alcohol from where he stood near the window. He faced his father—this strange, hurtful, alien man who was his own flesh and blood.

"Somebody should shoot that dog if it's going to carry on because your little Amish skirt finally wised up . . . I suppose you're howling too, though, aren't you, son? Your mother said your wife's left you."

"I find that we all howl, now and then . . . when we don't get what we want, what we expect . . . no matter how much we give." Jude shrugged. "Like you, Dad, not getting me."

His father stalked closer to him and missed a

step, catching himself on the back of an ornate chair. "Not getting you, huh? I paid a king's ransom for you, and if I can't get what I want, then neither can you. At least I'll have the satisfaction of that."

"Why do you need satisfaction?" Jude asked, feeling disturbed to realize he was genuinely interested in the answer. *Why do I even care?*

"Why do I need satisfaction?" His father laughed aloud, a hollow, eerie sound, as he spread his arms wide and staggered toward the desk. "I need satisfaction, you miserable wretch, because you took the only hope I had . . . took it all . . . and choked the life out of him."

Jude tilted his head at the slurred words. "What? Choked who?"

His father continued to laugh, then drew a harsh breath. He grabbed something from the desktop and whirled, throwing it with sudden violence at Jude, who moved out of the way.

Jude saw the Ice Mine snow globe shatter against the wall and its water run down the ornate wallpaper. *Mary must have left it here . . .*

He felt a sob rise in his own throat as he bent to stare down at the cracked glass, and then his father's breath was close against his ear, the older man's hands tight around his neck.

"Who? You dare to ask who?" His father shook him and Jude twisted from his grip to back away. "Your brother, you fool. Your twin. Born first. My firstborn son . . . Ted Lyons Junior . . . but your cord was wrapped around his neck and he was dead before he ever breathed air."

Jude froze in horror, his grandfather's strange

conversation in the garden about the "other one"—his dad only wanting the other one of him—making sudden terrible sense.

His father sneered at him. "You should see your face, Professor Lyons. Quite a study . . . Your mother didn't want you to know, to bear the burden, but I named you—Jude. Close enough to Judas for my taste, and I was right. You've betrayed me since your first breath." He ground the broken glass beneath his foot.

"But why couldn't you have been grateful for one son?" Jude's voice was raised.

"One son? Don't you, with all of your Amish superstition, know the truth about twins . . . my own mother told me. It's only the first who's gifted, who really matters . . . He was the 'what could have been' and you—are the what never was . . . All I wanted was a son, mine to follow me, and you come along with your Amish and your studies, and you're too good for what I want . . . Well, now you know. So live with it . . . you murderer."

Jude watched as the violence drained from the other man and his shoulders sagged as if in defeat, and he saw his father as a broken man—one never strong enough to face the pain of his loss. Instead, Ted Lyons had built layers of hardness to surround his heart, and in the end, he'd lost not only one son but both.

A thousand emotions roared through Jude's mind, like the pounding of an oncoming train, and he thought of Mary's smile. Then his sugar plummeted while the embroidered rug rose up fast to meet him as he fell.

Chapter Twenty-Two

"Your head's bleeding, sir." Bas's urgent voice brought Jude to his senses and he remembered what he'd been thinking of when he collapsed . . .

"They'll shun her, Bas."

"Shun? Who, sir?"

Jude staggered to his feet and in three gulps swallowed the orange juice Bas provided. He swiped his hand across his mouth. "The *Amisch* on Ice Mountain . . . Mary. She can't leave her husband." He handed the glass back with a nod of thanks.

"I'm not sure, sir . . . but we should attend to your head."

"I'm all right." He remembered the conversation with his father. *Murderer* . . . "Where's my . . . father?"

Bas shook his head. "He went out, sir. I'm not sure where, but . . ."

"Jude! Jude, Bas, are you in there?" Jude's mother raced into the room, half screaming, and Jude felt his head begin to pound.

"Mother, what is it?" He was tired and didn't want to play drama games.

"It's my father . . . I think he's dead or not breathing. Oh, Bas, call for an ambulance!"

Jude straightened fully. "Grandfather? Where is he? His room?"

"Yes, oh yes . . ."

He brushed past her and raced down the hall to his grandfather's suite on the first floor. The ominous discoloration of the old man's face as he lay on his bed stopped Jude cold for a moment, but then he ran forward and put his head on the frail chest. He heard a faint heartbeat.

"Grandfather, oh, Grandfather. Don't do this, please, not now. Don't leave me now." Jude swiped at the tears that filled his eyes as his grandfather drew a shuddering breath and suddenly opened his eyes.

"Jude . . . I feel strange."

"Yes, I know . . . an ambulance is coming."

"I heard Ted's voice screaming . . . was he screaming at you again?"

"No, no, everything's fine."

Another staggered breath. "Jude, you must know, you had a twin when you were born."

"I know. I understand. Don't try to talk. Save your strength." Jude held the thick-veined hand nearest him tightly.

"You know? Ah, then Ted told you . . . Lydia wouldn't . . ." A choking cough emanated from the shrunken chest and Jude bit back a sob.

"It's all right . . . it's all right." *All right . . . all right.*

"Don't believe . . . don't . . . believe."

Jude felt the sudden slackening of the hand in his. "Don't believe what, grandfather?"

"Don't believe . . . her . . . Mary . . . Oh, the globe's broken, Amelia! It's broken . . ."

His grandfather's body surged upward for a brief second as he cried out the words, and then he slumped back against the pillows and Jude knew that he was gone. *How did he know about the snow globe?* He laid his head on the old man and cried, for everything that he once thought was real and true and good . . .

He drew away only when the ambulance attendants entered the room. He moved aside to make room for the useless stretcher, putting an arm around his mother as she sobbed, but his own tears were dry now.

"You sure you wanna get out here? It's pitch black . . ." The taxicab driver peered out the window in doubt.

It *was* dark, but Mary knew it must be sometime close to morning, and she knew the mountain blindfolded. "I will be fine."

She carefully counted out money for him plus a tip as Carol had instructed, then put the rest of the bills in her satchel. She would have to mail Carol back the money when she'd earned it, even though the other woman had told her to "forget it."

She got out of the car, aware that the driver still wasn't moving, and she hurried past the beams of the headlights, finding the edge of the path up the mountain and stepping without hesitation into the inky darkness.

A few moments later, she heard the car drive away and breathed a sigh of relief. Then she stumbled over a root and fell facedown into the chill earth of the path.

She lay for a brief time, stunned, then turned her face into the familiar comforting smell of the dirt and began to sob—hoarse, choking sobs that wrung her heart and then her stomach. *Why,* Gott*? Why did you let me go with him? Because I was willful, because I wanted it? And it seems all for nothing . . . But You have a plan; You must have a plan. I will not believe anything less.*

Then she crawled to her feet and continued on, walking in darkness.

Chapter Twenty-Three

"Are you ever going to get off that couch, old man?"

Jude caught the pillow Sam lobbed at him as he lay down. Following his grandfather's funeral, he'd taken up residence in Sam's efficiency with a depressed Bear, quit the university, and knew he was wallowing. He'd also decided that if Mary was shunned, she could always technically repent of marrying an *Englischer* or tell them they'd never consummated . . . His eyes burned at the thought.

"Do you want me to move out?" he asked Sam, his voice indicating he couldn't care less.

"I want you to get up. It's been weeks now, and I'm worried about you. You've got to—" He broke off at a knock on the door and returned to the couch with a brown paper-wrapped box. "Here, it's for you."

Jude grunted at the dropped weight and peered at the postmark. "It's from my mother, no doubt. I'll open it later."

"Open it now."

Jude glared at his friend and tore the wrappers off, tossing them on the floor. But then he sat up straighter as he read the brief note from his mother.

Jude Darling,

Mrs. Bas found these in the desk in Mary's room. I thought I'd send them to you to return to her. I miss you . . .

Love,
Mother

He opened the box and stared inside at the three books as Mary's delicate scent wafted to him. He closed his eyes briefly against the swamping rush of pain.

"Well, what is it?"

"Nothing."

"Nothing, but you've got better color than I've seen on your face in a while."

"They're some books Mary left behind . . . her Bible, her mother's cookbook, and *Wuthering Heights.*"

"Well, you've got the brooding Heathcliff down to a science, why not read the Bible and let me borrow the cookbook? I'm going to Carol's parents' tonight to cook her dinner."

"Great," Jude said in an absent voice; then he set the books carefully on the floor and pulled a cover up to his chin, closing his eyes. "I'm taking a nap."

"Nap?" Sam cried. "It's nine-thirty in the morning."

"All the better," Jude mumbled, already losing himself in the veiled comfort of sleep as the weight of Bear's body on his legs soothed him for the moment.

Mary sat on the backless bench in Ben Kauffman's barn, waiting for church services to begin. She sat beside Rachel Miller, near the other widows. There was no direct place for a woman who'd left her husband, but she'd thankfully found acceptance and community among her people.

Her thoughts drifted back to the morning she'd first climbed the mountain after leaving Jude and had gone to knock on her father's door.

Joseph had opened the heavy wood and stared at her in disbelief as she'd collapsed with weariness into his arms. She knew she must have appeared quite a sight—a million miles from where she was supposed to be, her head bleeding from where she'd scraped it in the darkness, and her clothes torn and dirty.

"Mary?" Joseph had picked her up in his strong arms and carried her to her bed.

She'd lain, feverish and weak, for three days while her *fater* and *bruders* did everything they knew to comfort her.

And then Bishop Umble had arrived at her bedside.

"Can you tell me what happened, child?"

"I-I grew homesick, Bishop. Beyond what I could bear. I had to return."

The old man had studied her with warm and wise eyes. "I see . . . homesick. It can be a terrible thing, this homesickness. Even in the Bible, Paul sent Epaphroditus back to his home because of longing. We do not begrudge your homesickness for your community. But should you ever want to tell me . . . more, I am here to listen and advise. We look forward to seeing you back at worship services when you are ready, child."

Her *fater* had cried and blown his nose in his hankie. "So you'll not shun her, Bishop? I am grateful. I think now that maybe I acted in haste in the hurrying of the marriage."

Mary had blinked back tears as Bishop Umble patted her *dat*'s shoulder. "Now, Abner, we cannot undo the past but must learn from it, and look forward to *Gott*'s future plans."

He'd nodded to Mary as he'd left the room and she'd felt great gratitude for the bishop's mercy, even if his eyes said that he knew more than she was willing to speak.

Mary blinked, brought back to the present, as Rachel handed her a Bible. "Here, child. Take this. I noticed you were without and I have several at home."

Mary stared down at the Book, remembering suddenly that she'd left hers at Jude's house. She whispered her thanks to Rachel, then closed her eyes and began to pray that he might find her Bible and read it someday.

Jude rolled over on the couch, ignoring a groan from Bear at his movement. He stretched his hand down to the floor and caught up Mary's heavy Bible. He scrabbled for his glasses on the end table, then propped himself up on one elbow to glance through the words. Written in High German, which he'd had to learn for his now-defunct *Amisch* studies career, the Bible seemed alien and strange to him even though he knew it was at the heart of what Mary believed. He sighed and was about to close it when he noticed the penciled writing in the front cover.

He peered closer at the double-sided flap and saw that Mary had handwritten notes and dates all over the white space—half in *Englisch*, half in Pennsylvania Dutch. He set his mind to translating and reviewing the quotes and thoughts she must have written during her private study or service. One in particular drew his eye and gave him pause.

Gott *is the only One Who can put a man back together again, and only if the man (or woman) will really embrace the pain of his life and be willing to become an authentic person.*

He read the lines again, then felt his scruffy face and stared around the tiny room. *My father would never embrace the pain of his life . . . and I'm being exactly like him by lying here!*

He sat up straight and pushed away the cover, ignoring Bear's grunt of annoyance. He laid the Bible on the table, got up, and went to shower for the first time in days.

Chapter Twenty-Four

Mary awoke to the distinct feeling of snow in the air and pushed back the quilt on her narrow bed to look out the frosted cabin window. Sure enough, the first snow of the season had come, and early too, as it was only the first week in October. She shivered as she dressed with quick fingers, unable to keep flashes of Jude out of her mind as she secured straight pins in her dress. But she was growing used to the pain of missing him and trying to pick up the threads of life here on the mountain. She refocused on the snow and hurried out to the kitchen to find the stove already going and Joseph making hot chocolate and coffee.

She gazed in appreciation at her tall older *bruder*. She and Joseph had become especially close since her return, and she accepted the mug of chocolate from him with shivering gratitude as she pulled a chair nearer to the stove.

"I think I'll put baked beans in the oven for lunch and set the bread to rise and then go visit

Rachel Miller. She said her stomach was upset at the quilting yesterday."

Joseph sat down adjacent to her and stretched his long legs toward the stove. "You're not happy, are you, Mary?"

"What?" she stuttered, burning her tongue on her drink.

"I know; I think I do anyway. Sometimes I get restless, feel like there's got to be something more—maybe someone more," he confided in a whisper.

"Joseph, is there someone, a girl here?"

"*Nee* . . . I seem to feel like I've known everyone and everything for too long at times. At least, well, at least you had the chance to see a difference, even though you cannot hide that it cost you."

Mary reached out her hand to her *bruder*, who took it easily. "*Gott* has a plan," she said.

He sighed. "I know. I guess you're better waiting on it, though, than I am."

She squeezed his hand in gratitude, then bustled about with the beans and brown sugar and bacon, intent on visiting with Rachel for a bit before the rest of the daily chores.

She pulled on her cloak and mittens, then set out, trudging through a good few inches of snow until she came to the path that led to Rachel's house. She was surprised to see the snow marked by what seemed like dozens of cat paw prints, and she climbed the steps outside to be greeted by the frantic mewling of a variety of cats and kittens.

She scooped up two of the nearest felines, realizing they were hungry, and tapped on the door. No one answered. She tried the latch and it gave easily.

"Rachel?" she called as the cats streamed around her skirt.

A faint cough alerted her to Rachel's presence and she made her way to the back bedroom. The cabin was freezing and the bedroom was even colder as she eased open the wooden door.

"Rachel!" she cried out when she realized that the window was wide open while the old woman lay in a voluminous nightdress beneath a light sheet on the bed.

"Rachel, what are you doing?" Mary grasped the other woman's hand and Rachel opened her eyes to stare at Mary with fever-bright eyes.

"Early influenza, missy. Tryin' to drive it off with the chill." Rachel's thick, wet cough alarmed Mary, who went to shut the window.

"I'll go fetch *Grossmuder* May," Mary announced as she piled spare quilts from a chest atop Rachel.

"Not yet, *sei se gut*, missy. I need—the chamber pot—bad."

"*Ach*, surely." Mary hauled the covers back off and helped raise Rachel to a sitting position before bending to find the chamber pot beneath the end of the bed. She helped the woman with her needs, alarmed at the rabid heat of her body through her nightdress, then tucked her back up beneath the quilts.

Then she went to the small kitchen area and washed her hands and hurriedly set out what dry cat food she could find for the grateful cats. The sound of Rachel's cough rang in Mary's ears as she closed the door and noticed in a brief glance that one of the larger cats had killed a beaver and was sharing it with several of its mates. Then she took off running through the snow.

It had taken Jude a bit of time to roll things over in his mind, but the determination not to be like his father kept him moving. One day, he found himself actually at his parents' home and decided that the afternoon was as good a time to enter as any, given that his father would probably be at work.

He got out of the Expedition in the warm sunshine of autumn, glad to see Bas when the older man greeted him at the door.

"Mr. Jude, sir." The butler held out a hand and Jude brushed it away to hug him instead.

"Bas, is Mother in? How are Mrs. Bas and Betty?"

"Oh, all well, sir, thank you. But your mother's gone to play Bunco and your . . . father . . . he's at work."

Jude clapped him on the shoulder. "That's all right then. If you don't mind, I'll go and say hello to your wife and be on my way."

"Certainly, sir. But—uh—Mr. Jude, there's something I saved for you, if you'd like. I know it was presumptuous, but I thought . . ."

"What is it, Bas?"

"Your notes, sir. The research for your book on the Amish—you left so suddenly and I thought perhaps you forgot."

Jude drew a deep breath. He wasn't sure that he was ready to face the book or the lack of it, but then he remembered Mary's note on the necessity of "embracing pain" and nodded to his old friend.

"All right, Bas. Let me have it. And—thanks."

He left a half hour later with one of Mrs. Bas's fruitcakes and an armful of yellow notebooks and single pages. He got into the Expedition and piled the lot on the passenger seat, glancing down once at the top sheet. "Mary as Research Project."

"Well, Lyons," he murmured aloud, throwing the vehicle into reverse. "That's one project that didn't turn out the way you'd hoped." He met his own eyes in the rearview mirror and saw the raw emotion reflected there. *That's one person who was never truly a project at all . . .*

Word had a way of spreading throughout the Mountain *Amisch* community as if by invisible lips and sharp ears, but soon, everyone knew how very sick Rachel Miller was and who else in the community was ill.

Mary was surprised to learn that there were as many as ten other cases, all early influenza, or so *Grossmuder* May said as she was driven about in a sled from home to home. All had high fevers and all badly needed the chamber pot at regular intervals. This last bit seemed to puzzle the old healer, who spoke in an aside to Mary when she elected to stay and nurse Rachel for a time.

"I understand the fevers, headaches, and coughs, but the bowels . . . hmmm? I haven't seen influenza quite this hard on the stomach region before."

"But, Rachel—they'll all be all right?" Mary felt anxious for some reason, especially when Rachel refused the fluids she needed so badly.

"As *Derr Herr* wills, child. But *jah*, they should recover in a few days."

Mary saw the old healer to the door, then went back to Rachel's bedside. She did some small chores for the woman and was adjusting the quilts when Rachel caught her hand.

"Where's that man of yours, the professor? He would know what to do."

Mary sighed. She knew Rachel had been told of Mary's return along with the rest of the community, but her fever was making her talk out of her head.

"*Jah*, he would know," Mary agreed, alarmed at the faintness of the patient's pulse as she checked it automatically. "Rachel, are you all right? Will you take a drink?"

Mary was panicked by the rattling sound that came from the old chest with abrupt suddenness.

Rachel smiled. "I'm swimmin'. In the crystal sea. It's so . . ."

Mary felt for a pulse and couldn't find it. "Rachel? Rachel!" she cried. Then she knew that she was in the Presence of something greater than her, beyond her, and she wanted to reach through the somethingness and nothingness and pull her old friend back to her. But her mind acknowledged what her heart would not; Rachel was dead. And Mary bent her head to pray . . .

Chapter Twenty-Five

It was late October in Atlanta as Jude looked up from the small table in the restaurant where he was to meet Sam and Carol for lunch. He watched them enter together, laughing about something, and then they stood, openly giddy, at the table.

"Are you two going to sit? Or do I have to call the waitress to make you behave?"

Carol laughed out loud, careless of the looks she received. Jude wanted to groan at their infatuation.

"Jude, old man, I've—that is, we've got a favor to ask you." Sam clapped a hand on his shoulder.

"Okaaay."

"We're getting married!" Carol squealed. "Right now, during Sam's lunch hour."

"What?" Jude looked at them as if they'd lost their minds. "You've only been dating for what . . . Married? Sam?"

His friend had the grace to look sheepish but then turned an adoring glance back to Carol. "I want you to be my best man, Jude. Right now, will you? We've got a judge waiting and . . ."

Jude peered at them over his glasses, feeling old and stodgy. "Have you two thought about this? What about the wedding, the invitations, the reception?"

Carol waved a dismissive hand that sported a tiny diamond on a simple gold band. "Oh, Jude, I know things didn't work out for you, but do we really need all those things when we have love?" She cuddled against Sam's shoulder.

"I guess not," Jude returned dryly. "All right." He put down his napkin. "Who am I to judge? I'll do it."

Sam hugged him close. "Thanks, old man. And you can keep the studio while we go on our honeymoon. I've got a little nest egg saved and we're jetting off across the pond."

"To England." Carol giggled.

"Uh-huh."

"If we could hurry." Sam laughed. "I've got to get back to teach a class, but we're leaving right after. Carol's going to find a receptionist at the courthouse to be her maid of honor or whatever."

"Fine." Jude couldn't resist their beaming smiles. "It's fine, really. Congratulations." He hugged them both, then followed their hurried steps out of the restaurant.

Half an hour later, he waved them off—Mr. and Mrs. Riley—then stood undecided on the courthouse steps, alone and still hungry.

"Jude? Oh, Jude!"

He turned to see his mother rushing toward him and gave her a genuine smile.

"Mother, what are you doing here at the courthouse?"

She looked irritated for a moment. "A speeding ticket—I don't want your father to know."

Jude didn't respond and she flushed. "I mean, well—never mind."

He tucked her hand in his arm. "Let's go get some lunch, shall we?"

"I'd love to, darling."

He found an elegant bistro tucked away in one of the side streets and enjoyed some time with his parent, though she was careful not to mention his father again. *I suppose this is as good a time as any to talk about it . . .*

His mother fished in her purse a moment, distracting him. "Oh, Jude. I almost forgot . . . a letter for you, dear. It's—from Pennsylvania."

"Thank you." He took the envelope from her, noting the Coudersport postmark. It was dated six days earlier. He felt his heart begin to throb as he opened the letter and scanned the contents with growing franticness.

October 20th

To Professor Jude Lyons,

Fater doesn't know I'm writing, but I thought it best. Mary's real sick. We had an early bout of the influenza up here and something else is going around too, some stomach illness, making the 'flu worse. Mary nursed many through, but now she's got it herself. Rachel Miller passed on from it. Mary calls for you when her fever's high. I fear for her. I thought you should know.

Joseph King

Jude reread the short missive once more.

"Jude, you're pale, darling. Not bad news, I hope?"

"Mary's sick." *I fear for her, and this letter is six days old.*

"Oh, dear, the poor child."

Jude didn't respond. He'd pulled out his cell phone and found, to his amazement, that he was praying inside. Over and over . . . *Dear God, dear Father in Heaven, let her be well, please let her be well . . .*

"Sam?" he said into the phone quickly. "Yes, I know you're leaving for your honeymoon. Look, do you still have that friend at the CDC in Atlanta? Mary's very ill and I think there's an epidemic in Pennsylvania on Ice Mountain . . ."

Chapter Twenty-Six

Mary was dreaming; she knew, on some level, that it was a fever dream, but she still felt entranced by its realness.

Jude was sitting in a desk chair, his shirt off, and his hair ruffled. He had on a pair of jeans and boots and was trying to coax her to come nearer.

But she was hot, clad only in her shift, and felt shy in front of him.

"Please," he whispered, wanting something from her that caused confusion and delight to mingle together in the back of her mind.

She took a few steps closer to him, wondering what he'd do if she sat on his lap and caught her hands about his neck to stroke his throat.

Her fingertips tingled and she drew closer but then something blocked her feet. She gazed down to see a swirling mass of yellow note paper, churning and growing higher at the same time until it encircled her.

She was caught in a yellow cyclone of words and phrases and their movement seemed to steal her breath. She coughed, struggling, and cried out for Jude. But he was gone from the chair with only his words left behind to consume her.

Less than twenty-four hours after reading Joseph's note, Jude led Dr. Julie Matthews and her intern, Kyle, both from the Centers for Disease Control, up Ice Mountain, with Bear barking joyously in the lead. Sam had friends in high places, apparently, as the disease specialist carried a bulk of supplies and medicines.

"I had a chance to skim some notes about the *Amisch* and polio vaccinations, Dr. Lyons," Dr. Matthews said behind him, not winded by the climb.

"Call me Jude. Yes, but that wasn't Mountain *Amisch* and I think, with people dying, we won't have to go through a community approval to help. If the bishop agrees, then we're good."

"Excellent . . . Jude."

There was enough lingering over his name for Jude to glance back at her once. She was pretty, in a professional sort of way, with dark hair and green eyes, but he did not need or want the attraction of his best potential help when Mary was sick. *I fear for her . . .* He increased the speed of his steps, ignoring the panting of Kyle, who lagged a few steps behind, carrying equipment.

They broke through the clearing at the top of the mountain and Jude let Bear off his lead. The dog took off in quivering, howling joy, and Jude followed with the team.

"We'll stop at the bishop's first." *Because I have no*

idea how or if I'll be received . . . Maybe they won't even let me see her. Maybe it's too late. The thought made him sick, but he trudged on and they soon made the turn to Bishop Umble's house.

Jude climbed the stairs and knocked on the wooden door, hope and fear mingling painfully in his chest.

"Her fever burns too high," Joseph said wearily, lifting his hand from Mary's head.

Mary heard the words from far away, heard her *fater*'s sobs . . . *Don't cry,* Dat. *Don't cry* . . . Snatches of a child's rhyme she used to sing as a little girl ran through her mind like rivulets of heat and she thought she could see her *Mamm.* How strange, for she had no idea what her mother even looked like . . .

"And this woman doctor, she can help, do you think?" Bishop Umble stroked his long, gray beard and Jude nodded, concealing impatience. He wanted to see Mary.

But he knew he had to get past the bishop first, who strangely had mentioned nothing yet about the broken marriage but had urged Jude alone into the kitchen while his wife provided tea to the others.

"Yes, sir. Dr. Matthews studies different illnesses and helps decide what medicine might best treat them. I know Rachel Miller died . . . maybe that could have been prevented."

"You would prevent *Gott*'s will?" the old man asked mildly.

Jude knew there was something going on here, something more than debate over medicine and doctors . . . He bent his head. "Perhaps it is God's will that Rachel died, as my grandfather died recently. But please, sir . . . *sei se gut* . . . don't let Mary die. Let me have a chance."

The kind, wise old eyes studied him carefully. "Do you know why Mary said she left you?"

"I—uh . . ." Jude didn't know what to say. *Because I'm an idiot. Because I expected too much.*

"Because she was homesick." Bishop Umble spoke with gentleness. "And you forgive her this?"

"Forgive—her?" Jude was confounded. *Was that what she told them?*

"*Jah*, forgive her."

Jude straightened his back. "Sir, there is nothing she's done that requires my forgiveness. In fact, it is I who . . ."

The bishop held up a hand. "That's fine then, *sohn*. I am sorry to hear of your grandfather's passing. Both you and your help can move freely about the community with my blessing."

"Yes, sir. *Danki*." Jude shook the bishop's hand with deep gratitude, then went to round up his team.

Jude once more knocked on the thick wooden door of Mary's home with trepidation, but when Joseph opened it, he broke into a wan smile.

"*Ach*, Professor Lyons. *Kumme* in. I have prayed you might be here soon."

Jude noted with alarm Joseph's red-rimmed eyes and looked frantically toward Mary's door. "Is she . . . how's Mary?"

Joseph shook his head. "There's nothing else to do, I think."

"That's where we come in," Dr. Matthews asserted with quiet authority. "Show me where she is."

Joseph looked at the woman and back to Jude, who gave a slight nod.

"This way."

Jude was overwhelmed by the heavy smell of sickness as he entered Mary's room. Abner King sat on her hope chest, blowing his nose, while Edward crouched in a corner, his head in his hands. Bear had secured a watchful spot at the base of the window.

Jude stepped to the bed and stared with horror at his wife's shrunken features. *She's so thin, and her eyes . . . Don't die. Dear God, don't let her die . . .*

He felt for her hand beneath the pile of quilts.

"Jude? Jude?"

"Yes, Mary. I'm here," he choked out.

Joseph spoke softly. "She doesn't know. She's called for you often, and said something else . . . over and over . . . that she's a 'research project,' that she doesn't want to be a research project. I expect it's the fever talking."

But Jude understood and his eyes filled with tears. He flashed back to the strewn yellow-paper notes that he'd walked on the night she'd left and then remembered the note on top of the pile from the

Expedition. *She read my notes, my stupid meandering notes to myself. No wonder she left. Oh, Mary . . .*

"Professor Lyons? Jude? If you could move out of the way, we need to start an IV."

There was faint impatience in Dr. Matthews's tone and Jude stumbled back away from the bed.

"Kyle, load me up some antivirals, and then you and Jude go have a look round the first victim's house, if you can. Find anything that looks like it matters. This is more than regular influenza; I can feel it."

Jude didn't want to leave the room, but he wanted to help. If it wasn't simple influenza, then what else could it be?

Abner and the boys followed him into the kitchen like lost puppies. "You came. *Danki* for that." Abner blew his nose and stared up at Jude.

"Of course I came, sir. Mary is—she's . . ."

"Do you forgive her then, *sohn*? For deserting you? I would not want her to—to die—knowing she was unforgiven."

Sohn . . . son. Jude wanted to drop to his knees and beg for forgiveness himself from his strange, short father-in-law. How could he explain what it felt like to be called *sohn* by this man, by Mary's father?

"There is nothing to forgive," he managed to say.

Abner patted his arm with a ham-like hand. "*Gut*, that's *gut*."

Jude put his hands on his father-in-law's shoulders and shook him a bit. "And Mary is not dying . . . do you hear me? She's not."

Abner nodded. "All right . . . it's only . . . her *mamm* . . . my wife . . ."

Jude shook harder. "She's not!" *Not . . . not . . . not . . . Dear God . . .*

Mary was consumed by light, embraced by it, as it shot from her fingers and toes. She knew great peace and sensed vibrant colors to rival those of the mountain in full autumn. She felt safe, calm, and peered ahead. But blocking her view was Jude, illuminated and standing hand in hand with himself, almost as if there were two of him . . . *A twin. His twin.*

Mary smiled to herself; she didn't want to leave the warmth, the cocooning feeling of endless hope, but two of Jude was reason enough to *kumme* back to her bed. Even if it was cold.

Chapter Twenty-Seven

"I'm only an intern," Kyle said, his young voice strident. "But I am also an epidemiology geek."

Jude grunted as they walked through the snow. "A disease geek? That oughta get you some dates."

Kyle nodded beside him. "You'd be surprised."

Jude led the way to Rachel Miller's house and he remembered the mermaid *fraktur* the woman had given them as a wedding gift. He couldn't believe she was gone.

One of Ben Kauffman's sons was there outside, his arms full of cats. "Hiya, Professor Lyons. My *Dat* says to gather up *Frau* Miller's cats and bring them over to our barn."

"That's good," Jude murmured, bending toward a black kitten.

"Don't touch it," Kyle shrieked.

Jude straightened. "What?"

"Don't touch that cat and, young man, put those animals down and come here and disinfect your hands." Kyle produced a bottle of clear liquid from his backpack.

"What's wrong?" Jude asked.

"There are beaver skeletons here. Two of them." Kyle indicted the ground near him with a grimace.

"So?"

"Beavers can transmit *Giardia lamblia* to other animals and then on to humans. Of course, I'll have to run some tests, but . . ."

Jude racked his brain. "You mean *giardiasis*?"

Kyle nodded, squeezing out disinfectant. "That's right, Professor. Sometimes called 'Beaver Fever,' the parasite, along with influenza, would be enough to dehydrate and drain anyone—even to the death."

"Can you cure it?"

Kyle gave him a lopsided grin and shook the disinfectant bottle. "You betcha."

Mary opened her eyes slowly. The light from the window hurt her eyes . . . not like the light in her dream. She gazed to her right and saw Jude fast asleep in a bedside chair. He opened his eyes immediately, though, when she stirred.

"Jude?"

"Oh, Mary, thank God."

"Why . . . where . . ." She felt strange and wasn't sure how to begin with her questions.

"You've been very ill. Joseph wrote to me and I came."

"*Ach* . . . Rachel Miller died. I remember now."

"Yes, I'm sorry."

She gazed into his concern-filled blue eyes. "You had a twin."

He blinked once. "What? What did you say?"

"I saw it . . . in the light in my dream. You were holding hands, but with another you . . . I suppose it sounds strange."

"It sounds true," he whispered and bowed his head. "My father told me the night you left."

She blinked back sudden hot tears, remembering why she'd gone. She drew a deep breath. "You didn't have to come."

He lifted his head. "Mary—I know you saw my notes about you."

"I did."

"Well, I—"

A quick knock on the door interrupted him, and Mary watched a young *Englisch* woman in a dark blue sweater and white coat, come in.

"Jude, how is she?"

Jude . . . She's calling him Jude.

Mary saw Jude rise and go to engulf the woman in a hug. "She's better. Oh, thank you, she's better."

The *Englisch* woman slipped from Jude's arms and came to the bedside. She laid a cool hand on Mary's brow and gave her a bright smile.

"So you're back, hmm? Had me worried for a few minutes, but . . . I'm Dr. Matthews from the CDC in Atlanta."

"Atlanta? You . . . came with Jude, then?"

"Yes, I and my intern, Kyle. He's the one who actually discovered the root cause of your illness."

Mary nodded, feeling sudden exhaustion. She longed to close her eyes but felt it would be impolite. *Here's the right kind of match for him . . . an* Englisch *woman, a doctor. His equal . . .* She drew a strained breath and felt her eyes closing against her will.

"She's going back to sleep," she heard the *Englisch* doctor murmur.

"Good," Jude said and Mary could imagine the smile on his face as he spoke. Perhaps he wanted time alone with this woman doctor . . .

Jude accepted the hot mug from Joseph and took a grateful sip.

"Why not go and lie down in our room?" Joseph asked while Edward nodded in agreement.

"It sounds like a tempting offer," Jude said. It was the first time he'd been able to relax in days and he knew he was running on pure adrenaline.

"There's nothing to do right now, *sohn*," Abner pressed, turning from the stove where he was frying ham slices for lunch. "That Dr. Matthews said she was going around to finish the last of the flu shots, and the others who were sick are all improving. I heard this morning over at Ben Kauffman's store."

"What happened to Rachel's cats?" Jude asked tiredly.

"All of them got a *gut* dose of something too, I heard. The ones that were feral went back to the woods, but the rest are living cozy in Ben Kauffman's barn. I bet there'll be a cat from Rachel Miller in every house come this spring."

Jude heard the lighthearted note in Abner's voice and rejoiced in it on some level. *Mary is safe . . . thank God. Thank you, God . . .*

He decided that an hour or so of sleep wouldn't hurt and went to lie down in Joseph's bed.

Chapter Twenty-Eight

Jude awakened to find the window in the cabin room pitch dark but for the light of the moon. He rubbed a hand over his face and groaned. *I must have been asleep for hours.*

He got up, pulled on his boots, and walked out into the kitchen. Dr. Matthews was asleep on the couch in the living area and Kyle snored on the floor. The door to Abner's room was closed, but Mary's showed a crack of light shining beneath the portal. He went and knocked with a quiet hand.

Mary's soft voice bid him enter and he was surprised to discover her sitting up, propped against pillows. She looked infinitely better than she had a few hours before, and he couldn't believe how much she had improved in such a short time.

"Hello," he said, taking the chair next to her bed. "You look so much better than this afternoon."

She smiled at him. "This afternoon? They tell me you've been asleep for two days straight now."

"What?" He moved to pull his cell phone out of

his pocket, then remembered there was no service. He glanced at the wind-up clock on her small bedside table. A bit after twelve . . .

"Only past midnight. You must have been so tired." Her tone was sympathetic.

He ran a hand through his hair, then touched his scruffy chin. "Yeah, I've never slept so long."

She eyed him quietly and he noticed, up close, that she still appeared frail. He put out his hand to cover hers, glad when she didn't withdraw.

"Mary, I wanted to talk to you about those notes you read."

"*Nee*, it's of no matter."

"It's why you left, isn't it?"

She shook her head slightly and he frowned.

"Mary, please, talk to me."

"I cannot."

"But why?"

He was startled to see her beautiful eyes well with tears. "Because Dr. Matthews calls you Jude, because she's far more *schmart* than I'll ever be and is a better match for you, because . . ."

"Wait, whoa!" he whispered in a frantic tone. "Dr. Matthews? Julie?"

Mary swiped at her tears with the back of her hand like a small child.

"Sweetheart, you're exhausted, and I promise you that there is nothing, I repeat, nothing, between Julie Matthews and me—I don't even know her."

"Well, you could get to—maybe she wouldn't be a research project in your eyes."

He thought for a minute, then slid his chair back. "Will you give me a moment to get something out of my backpack? I think it might clear things up a bit . . ."

He hurried out of the room through the shadows and grabbed his pack from the kitchen, then lugged it back to her room.

Rooting inside, he came up with a single yellow sheet of paper and handed it to her with a faint smile.

Mary stared in bleary-eyed disbelief at the words on the page—"Mary as Research Project." *How dare he?* She slapped it into his hand with as much force as she could muster.

"Did you ever read the back?" he asked, and she heard the tenderness in his voice. It made her want to cry more.

"The—back?"

He took the page and straightened his glasses, then began to read. "I suppose I should be grateful that my hand was literally forced in being bound to her. Yet . . ." She felt his brief gaze as he flipped the page. "Yet there is so much more than gratitude in both my heart and mind where Mary is concerned. She is so special—wise, beautiful, and kind. I can only learn the best about myself when I am with her, and I am so simply happy when I am with her. To have been given this gift, Mary as my wife, even if it does turn out to be only for a short time, will be one of the greatest things that's ever happened to me in my life."

There was a distinct moment of silence.

Mary covered her flushed cheeks with her hands. "*Ach*, the back."

He smiled. "*Ach*, indeed."

He seemed about to say more when a pitiful howling sounded outside her window. Jude looked at her.

"Where's Bear?"

She shrugged, worriedly grasping at the quilts. "Joseph said he wanted to go out earlier."

"I'll go check."

She waited for what seemed like an eternity, then caught her breath when Jude reappeared in the doorway, his hands and shirt covered with blood.

"It's Bear," he spoke rapidly. "I think he tangled with a real bear and got the worst of it."

Mary put her hand on the covers and he raised a bloody finger. "Do not get out of that bed, Mary Lyons. I'll wake up Dr. Matthews—she probably can do some minor surgery or something . . . I've got to hurry, and I mean it—stay there. I'll keep you posted."

He was gone and she heard him raising the household and felt the chill of the front door opening and closing. She began to pray.

Jude grabbed the sheet off Abner's bed while the older man stood shivering and dressing fast.

"If we can get this sheet under him, we can all lift him and get him inside," Jude explained, but the amount of sticky blood on his hands made him wonder if there was time.

He returned to the kitchen to see Kyle setting up

all the kerosene lamps and candles that he could find near the table while Julie rummaged, mumbling aloud, through her supplies.

Joseph and Edward were already outside and Jude hurried after them. The ominous puddle of blood in the snow at the side of the dog reflected eerily in the light of the brothers' lanterns. There was a heavy, musky scent in the air as well.

"Bear, a real bear," Joseph said, helping Jude slide the sheet under the dog. "And I don't like the idea of a wounded bear roaming the community."

"It's not roaming," Edward said suddenly, standing a few feet away, his lantern held high. "It's here, dead, and there's an arrow in its side. The dog must have killed it, though, praise *Gott*. Any one of us could have run into it out doing chores in the morning."

Jude laid a hand on the shaggy black fur of the dog that had become his friend. "Good boy, Bear. Good boy."

He got a whimper in response and then they hefted the sheet up and began to walk back to the house.

Jude was glad he'd closed Mary's door when they laid the animal on the kitchen table. Even Dr. Matthews seemed nonplussed for a moment at the gruesome sight of the dog's multiple injuries, but then she snapped on some gloves.

"Right, let's get started. It would not be good for my patient to lose her dog, so we're not going to lose him, got it? I can't risk giving him anything to knock him out, though, because of the blood loss.

Could one of you hold his head? He may bite." Her gaze swept the group.

Abner blew his nose and Jude saw Julie frown.

"I'll do it," Jude offered. "He won't bite." *Please don't bite me, Bear.*

"Okay then, the biggest problem is blood loss, and I see the main reason. There's an artery here in the neck area . . . Kyle!"

Her intern hastily slapped a metal tool in her hand and she bent carefully over the open wound for a few minutes. "There," she said with satisfaction, lifting her head. "Now we'll disinfect and suture the major scratches. Let's hope the real bear didn't have rabies, but . . ." She paused for a second. "You all don't vaccinate dogs up here, do you?"

"I did!" Jude cried, and the debacle of his visit with Bear to the vet in Atlanta suddenly became worthwhile. "I had all his shots done about two weeks ago."

"Wonderful." Julie resumed her work.

A full hour later, the operation was over.

"Now, we wait and see," Julie said, stripping off her gloves and reaching to rub her lower back. "Infection could set in, though I've given him a heavy load of antibiotics. We'll have to watch."

"And pray," Abner added.

Jude saw Julie's slight smile. "It certainly couldn't hurt."

Mary looked up from the Bible Rachel had given her as her door was eased open and Jude and her brothers came carrying an inert Bear through the doorway on a sheet. "We'll keep him in here on the floor. He can probably sense your presence and it'll keep him calm."

"What happened exactly?" Mary asked in a low voice. "Bear wouldn't go after a bear without reason."

"Somebody poaching," Joseph said in anger. "Got an arrow in the bear but then didn't track it. The dog saved us from what could have been a deadly tangle with that animal."

"*Ach*, Bear . . ." Mary whispered.

Jude nodded. "He's a hero for sure, and he's going to get better." He met Mary's gaze. "Dr. Matthews says so."

Mary knew an inward pang at the sin of her jealousy of the woman who'd helped to save Bear. She would have to talk to her as soon as she could, but now, with Bear's heavy breathing sounding in the room, she felt like she couldn't keep her eyes open.

Jude smiled down at her and she was awash in the gentleness of the look.

"Go to sleep, sweetheart. I'll keep watch over both of you."

Mary knew he would and sank down beneath the quilts, her heart full.

Chapter Twenty-Nine

The following morning, Mary was still sleeping and Bear still breathed. Jude sat back down in the hard chair by the bed, then looked up as the door creaked open.

"Letter for you, sent overnight or something, Mr. Ellis said," Edward whispered and handed him the blue envelope.

"Danki." Jude smiled at the younger man, who nodded, then closed the door.

With an eye on Mary, Jude slit the envelope and pulled out the single page. He recognized the handwriting as his mother's and straightened his glasses to read the sprawling cursive.

Jude Darling,

I have to confess . . . I lied to you. I was not at the courthouse that day for a speeding ticket; I was there to file divorce papers against your father. I can't live with him anymore. We have led separate lives for years as it is, but with Father gone, I realized that your father is full of too much hate and bitterness, especially against you. He told me that you know of your brother, your twin. I want you to understand that it is Ted's own foolishness that would not allow him to accept you as the gift you are in place of the son we lost. Seeing you together with Mary while you were here reminded me of when I was young and had hopes and dreams of my own . . . these had gone missing for quite a while under the veil of your father's anger . . . I had a postcard from Sam and Carol—they've invited me to spend two days with them in England! Carol says she wants to celebrate with me and Sam agrees. Can you imagine? The three of us on honeymoon . . . but I've always wanted to go abroad.

Please do not worry about me or my future. My father left me more than enough funds and the small house on the Cape—I may even take up painting! Well, I've got to run, darling. If you need me, send a letter to Bas, who is staying on with Mrs. Bas at the house with your father. Bas will know how to reach me. Please know that I love you always and give Mary my love as well.

Yours,
Mother

"What is it, Jude?"

He looked up at Mary's face in the fall of the morning sunlight.

"My parents are getting divorced." Even as he said the words, he couldn't believe them.

"What?"

He handed her the letter and watched her read

as images of his mother and father drifted across his mind.

"Jude . . . I don't know what to say."

He leaned forward and put his head in his hands, thumbing beneath his glasses to massage at his eyes. She touched his hair and he stayed still. Everything felt like it was falling apart . . . *or maybe falling into place. Now, why did I think that?*

"Why not take a walk, Jude? Go over to the bishop's house—he's a wise man."

Jude lifted his gaze and saw the true sympathy in Mary's eyes. "He's also an *Amisch* man who doesn't believe in divorce. I—I'd probably seem like a mess to him."

"Nee," she said tenderly. "He understands people, I think."

Jude considered. "Will you be all right for a bit if I get someone to sit with you?"

"Of course." She smiled, though there were still bruise-like smudges beneath her eyes.

"All right. I'll take your advice."

He bent and brushed a kiss on her forehead, then walked to the edge of the bed to bend down and check on Bear. This time, the dog opened its mouth a bit and Jude quickly swabbed the swollen tongue with a damp cloth as Julie had instructed.

He got to his feet. "I think your wolf dog may yet be well."

"I have prayed for it."

He gave a brief nod, then left the room.

* * *

Mary dozed for a bit and awoke to see Dr. Matthews bent over Bear on the floor. Mary sat up anxiously. "*Ach*, is he all right?"

The other woman turned with a smile. "Yes, I think so. He took a bit of water." She got up, snapped off blue plastic gloves, then went to wash her hands, using the bowl and pitcher on Mary's dresser. She smiled at Mary once more and made as if to exit the door.

"*Ach*, wait, *sei se gut*," Mary called.

The doctor came back to the bed. "Is everything feeling all right?"

"*Jah*, it's—it's just I wanted to apologize to you."

Dr. Matthews sat down in the chair by the bed with a surprised thump. "Apologize? Whatever for?"

Mary wet her lips. "You see, I thought that you and Jude . . . well, I accused him of liking you and I thought of you with jealousy. I was wrong. Please forgive me."

The doctor shook her head and smiled, then to Mary's surprise, she wiped a tear from her eyes.

"I didn't mean to upset you," Mary cried softly.

"No, it's not you. It's your honesty—so typical of your people. I remember it from growing up and miss it now."

"You—you're familiar with the *Amisch*?"

"Mennonite, actually. My grandparents raised me; they were Mennonite. A bit more liberal, but still that same emphasis on honesty of the heart. Thank you, Mary."

"I have to thank you . . . I mean, what you've done for everyone and Bear especially." Mary had a sudden inspiration and gave the other woman a shy smile. "Would you accept a gift? Please—from the heart."

"Oh, I don't know . . ."

"Please go to that chest over by the window, if you can step around Bear, and open it."

Mary watched the doctor's reluctant movements and then heard the creak of the chest opening. "Way at the bottom, there's a quilt with red and green and yellow."

Dr. Matthews found the quilt and held it up for Mary's inspection. "*Jah.* It's a Christmas Roses pattern. You might know it. I worked it when I was sixteen. I want you to have it."

"I can't take this," the doctor said, tears thick in her voice.

"You can, please, and will. I want to remember—what did you call it? The honesty of the heart always."

Mary watched the doctor come forward and bend to offer her a hug. Mary returned the embrace with gladness, the quilt between them, and true joy in the giving.

Martha Umble, the bishop's wife, opened the door to Jude. He glanced with some hesitancy at the old *Amisch* woman, not sure what to expect, as she was usually a rather dour person. But to his surprise, she broke into a wide smile and waved him into the warm kitchen. He slipped off his boots on the rug to the side of the door and hung up his coat next to the bishop's black wool one and Martha's cloak.

The long, narrow kitchen was painted a bright, light blue and plants grew in coffee cans on the windowsills. The smell of cinnamon and fresh bread hung heavy and comforting in the air.

"You want a sticky bun?" Martha asked as he took the seat she offered at the narrow kitchen table bench.

"Danki, jah." He wasn't hungry but he didn't want to give offense, and soon a mug of coffee and two gooey spirals of cinnamon bread were set before him.

"I'll fetch the bishop," Martha said, leaving Jude alone with his thoughts for a moment. He moved the heavy-ended fork through the brown sugar topping and took a reluctant bite. It tasted heavenly, but he could only think of his mother's letter. *Things falling into place . . .*

"So, Jude Lyons, you come early for breakfast, and Martha has left us alone. She has sort of a sixth sense as a bishop's wife—always can tell when a man wants to talk."

Soon, the older man eased a leg over the bench on the opposite side of the table with his own mug and sticky bun. He peered at Jude over his wire-rim spectacles and stroked his long gray beard back out of the way of his napkin. "So, *sohn*, what is it?"

Jude hunched his shoulders. *Sohn . . .* "Maybe this was a bad idea."

"You think? Who sent you?"

"Mary."

"Mmm." The bishop savored a bite and waved his fork. "Not a bad idea, then—what can I do for you?"

"My mother is divorcing my father." *There. That gave the old man pause.*

"I see."

Well, I don't, not really . . . Jude sighed. "I know the *Amisch* don't practice divorce."

"Mmm-hmm. Annulments, neither. We don't practice those."

Jude threw him a sour look. "I should go."

"Stay right there and finish that sticky bun or you'll hurt Martha to the quick. How do you feel inside, about this divorce?"

"Like I have no family left . . . like I'm ten years old and want to cry . . . like there's no place for me." Jude spat the words out, feeling angry with himself for not simply being able to accept the news.

"That's not the truth?" The bishop pointed his fork at him.

"What? What's not true?"

"That there is no place for you. Tell me, young man, what are your intentions toward Mary?"

"I . . ." Jude stared into the wise and wizened face. He didn't know where to stop or how to begin. *Mary . . . Dear God . . .*

The bishop wiped his whiskers and smiled at Jude. "Eat your sticky bun, *buwe.* I expect we have some time for it while we talk."

Chapter Thirty

Mary appreciated the hand that Jude held at the small of her back as they navigated their way into Henry Miller's largest barn for the church services that were held every two weeks. She still felt weak at times but was infinitely better than three weeks earlier and had been truly sorry to bid farewell to Julie and Kyle when they returned to Atlanta.

"Are you all right?" Jude bent to whisper near the edge of her bonnet. "These backless benches are brutal. I think I'd better sit near you in case you feel weak or something."

"I'm fine," she whispered back. She slid down onto the bench she'd occupied with Rachel, wondering if Jude would notice that she didn't sit with the married women. *He must know but I'm not sure what he's thinking, what his plans are about us . . .*

She peeked up at him from beneath the rim of her bonnet and saw his slight frown, but then he patted her shoulder. "I'll go find my seat."

She smiled and watched him make his way through the crowd of black coats, his own navy blue standing out obviously. But the bishop had invited him . . .

The worship service began and she prayed she would not feel ill during the next three hours. But soon she discovered that the familiar order of the hymns soothed her and she eagerly drank in the prayers with a thirsty spirit.

Some time later, Bishop Umble stood up to give the main sermon and Mary waited eagerly in anticipation. The bishop's talks were anything but common; he always had a way of applying the Bible to everyday life that seemed relevant for that particular moment in the community.

But today, to Mary's surprise, he began to speak on forgiveness. Of course, there was always a need to be of a forgiving nature, but she'd expected something about illness and healing, in light of Julie and Kyle's recent help to the community. Still, she listened intently.

"Forgiveness is not forgetting," the old man said, his hands behind his back as he paced from one side of the benches to the other. "*Nee*, forgiving does not involve forgetting but does involve choosing not to remember a sin—a subtle difference but *ach*, so powerful."

He stopped and Mary watched him search the faces of his people. "Who has wronged you? Who has hurt you, wounded you, expected the worst of you, lied about you? Who has done these things? You all can bring someone to mind . . . all of you. But I challenge you in Christ's name to choose to forget those sins and move on in right relationship with that person . . . Now, I don't mean to say that you must become bosom friends, but that you can greet the other with a deliberate consciousness, a deliberate action to no longer recall what they did to you. That is how *Gott* sees us. He remembers our sins no more . . . And now, I would ask one to come before you, one who would speak about forgiveness and ask something of you all—Jude." The bishop lifted his hand in the direction of the blue coat and Mary caught her breath. Was Jude going to speak? And if so, *was en der weldt* was he going to say?

Jude knew it was coming, this call to come before the community. But he felt nervous nonetheless. What he was about to do involved no turning back, no looking back, only going forward to a possible new future.

Jude adjusted his glasses and clenched his hands behind his back as he looked out on the community of *Amisch*. Mary's eyes, in particular, were large and searching. *Well, here goes . . .*

"I thank you all for the chance to speak and thank you, Bishop Umble. You all know that I spent the summer here, married one of your own, and that she came back because of homesickness. I have discovered too that I have homesickness, but I will speak of that in a moment.

"First, I must beg for your forgiveness in the situation of my marriage to Mary. I have confessed to the bishop and now, I do the same here before you, that it was my first intention to seek an annulment from Mary, to put her aside, send her back here and go on with my life . . ."

Jude swallowed at the faint rustling among the worshippers and avoided looking in Abner's direction. He went on.

"But I have found that my life outside this mountain has become distant and I am homesick for this place. Here, I have found *faters, bruders,* sisters, my wife, and most importantly, the need to cry out to *Gott.* I would ask you to consider my staying on to become a permanent part of the community."

He saw the shock on Mary's face as her beautiful mouth formed a silent gasp.

"I would study with Bishop Umble, with all of you, if you will have me, and I will give up my other life to find community here among you. I ask you to please consider—*danki.*"

He dropped onto the bench beside the bishop, who handed him a peppermint candy, unwrapped. Jude took it with pleasure as the older man rose to speak again.

"So, you have heard both his confession and his petition. May I have an indication of what you would like to do regarding Jude Lyons?"

There was an infinitesimal pause and then a chorus of *"Jahs"* that slowly rose to echo in the great barn. Jude's eyes filled with tears. He glanced behind him to see Mary wiping her cheeks and smiling at him and he knew he'd done the right thing. Now she could be his wife in truth . . .

"I agree with your decision and thank you," Bishop Umble said from the front and Jude turned back around. "There is one thing, though . . . as I was the one who participated in Jude and Mary Lyons's rather hasty marriage, I feel it only right that Jude complete some of his studies for the next month while staying under my roof—Mary under her *fater*'s. And while this may seem odd to you, I find it *gut* judgment, to give Jude time to focus—ahem—on the desires of *Gott* and not the desires of the flesh. It will also give the couple a month's time to court in the *Amisch* way, for he should learn of this as well. Are we in agreement?"

The bishop's eyes twinkled as Jude stared at him. *The old goat . . . so now, I have to court my wife instead of . . .* But a new resounding affirmation from the community, as well as some laughter, drowned out his thoughts and he knew he had no choice but to agree. Although now the prospect of intense study didn't seem as pleasurable as it might have with his wife as his tutor.

Jude was engulfed by handshakes and well wishes and had nearly made it back to Mary when the barn door suddenly swung open, letting in the cold, bright light. The community turned as one to stare at the silhouetted figure in the door—a man, carrying another man.

"Please," Mahlon Mast called out, stepping farther into the barn. "Someone help my *sohn*—he's sick bad."

Whispers of "It's Isaac" blew in Jude's direction and then he had to keep himself from leaping over heads when he saw Mary slowly make her way back to the open door and Mahlon Mast.

Chapter Thirty-One

"Are you out of your mind? Is your fever back? That kid tried to rape you, do you remember?" Jude hissed the words, furious with her.

But she merely turned serene eyes on him and half smiled. "I'm choosing not to remember. You know, forgiveness?"

"That's all well and good in theory, but you cannot trust him. You cannot be alone with him."

"I didn't say that I would be. *Herr* Mast will be here."

"No, absolutely not, that guy is a loon."

He watched her think for a moment. "Well, you could always help me."

He was speechless for a moment, then took her arm and led her farther into the shadows of the barn, realizing they were attracting attention. "Mary, I don't want to take care of that freak . . . the world would be well rid of him, in fact."

"I'm not listening to this." She turned to go and he realized how serious she was.

"All right." His voice stopped her and she slowly

turned back to face him. "All right, I'll help you. But you are never to be alone with him, not even for a few seconds, out of his head with fever or not . . . agreed?"

"*Jah*, agreed. *Danki*, Jude."

Jude closed his eyes for a second on the wash of anger that still surged through him. *And she's just getting over being sick . . . It's a good thing Julie Matthews left antibiotics . . .*

He realized that Mary had gone on ahead and hurried to catch up with her. Henry Miller's wife opened the door to the family's home, then allowed Mahlon and the men now helping him to carry Isaac Mast into the main-floor master bedroom.

Jude saw that Mary's *bruder*, Joseph, walked beside him. "Why is she doing this?" the younger man asked.

Jude shrugged. "Do you think I understand a woman's mind?"

Joseph didn't respond and Jude's frown deepened as he saw Mary standing by the bed, bent over the unconscious Isaac Mast, with her hand on his brow.

Mary's heart raced and she had to keep her hand from shaking as she touched the man who had meant to do her so much harm. She didn't know what had compelled her to move from her place after service to go and offer help to Mahlon Mast. She only understood that somehow the bishop's talk had touched her deep inside and she wanted to live out what she had been taught. And also, if she was honest with herself, there had been a small voice inside, prompting her, moving her, and she knew that she had to obey.

"How long has he been this way?" she asked.

"Found him this morning, out in the snow, outside the cabin. He hasn't been back since yer man ran him off the mountain."

"He needs the medicine the *Englisch* doctor brought . . . Did the rest of your family get a shot or medicine to take?" Mary asked, deciding to ignore the negative comment.

"We don't need none of that. Ain't nobody sick at our place."

"Well, Isaac is and . . ."

"And you don't need to be tendin' him none. I told you once, you're a hex."

"Mr. Mast, if you'd be so kind as to not be rude to my wife, I'd deeply appreciate it. Because, you know, it's a merciful thing that she's willing to do." Mary heard Jude's low voice come level and clear as people left the bedroom.

Only the bishop and Henry and Esther Miller stood by. Mary looked at Jude with gratitude as he came to stand at the foot of the bed and stared down with a solemn expression at Isaac.

"Now, Joseph's gone for my knapsack and we'll try some medicine for your son, and with that, you'll have to be content."

"Don't tell me what to do, you—*Englischer*," Mahlon bit out.

"Enough." The bishop spoke with calm authority. "Mary, do you feel well enough and called to give care to this young man?"

"*Jah,* I do."

"And I'll help her," Jude added.

"Fair enough, and I'm sure Henry and Esther will join you?"

The Millers nodded in accord.

"All right then, Mahlon, go on home to the rest of your family. We'll send word when he's better." The bishop turned in dismissal and Mary watched Isaac's *fater* stomp out of the room.

"Jude, I'll expect you at my house tonight and, Mary, you'll go home to your *dat*'s. I don't want you tiring yourself."

Mary nodded, though she bit her lip as she felt Isaac's forehead once more.

"What is it?" Jude asked.

"He is so feverish . . . and lying in the snow . . . for who knows how long . . . *Ach,* Jude, I hope he lives. I pray that he lives."

"That is beyond us and up to *Derr Herr,*" the bishop admonished gently. "It is enough that we will care for him our best and with well-intentioned hearts."

Mary murmured in agreement but didn't look at Jude, because she knew where his heart lay in regard to Isaac.

Jude couldn't help thinking of the *Amisch* school shootings that had happened a few years earlier and the world's amazement at the *Amisch* response to the family of the shooter. They had expressed kindness and forgiveness, mercy and grace. And their outpouring of love had been an example to live by for the entire world. *So why should I expect any less of Mary?*

He glanced at the small wind-up clock by the bed as Mary held a damp cloth to Isaac Mast's forehead. Two o'clock in the afternoon. He was glad the bishop had expressed his wishes for Mary to return home in the evening to get a good night's rest . . . *Even if she'll be sleeping alone for a month.* He shifted in his chair, then spoke without thinking in the quiet room.

"I love you."

"What?" she asked, looking startled.

What . . . this is my first profession of love to my wife, in the bedroom of her smelly would-be attacker?

He leaned forward in his chair and locked eyes with her. "I said . . . I love you."

"*Ach,* Jude . . . I love you too."

She flushed prettily and he wanted to go and kiss her, but he leaned back instead, feeling his heart beat and knowing gratitude at simply being alive in her presence.

"*Gut,*" he murmured. "That's so good."

He wanted to say more but Esther Miller entered with a clean basin of water. "How is he?" she asked.

Jude watched Mary refocus and was pleased at the slightly dazed look in her eyes. *I probably look the same.*

"I think he grows no worse, but no better either. I suppose it will take time for the medicine to work," Mary said finally.

"I will sit with him for a while and keep the door ajar. I've prepared a meal for you. Please, wash up and go and eat." Esther straightened the covers and prepared to take up watch.

Jude thanked her and took Mary's hand as they went to wash up at the kitchen sink pump.

Then he noticed the loaded table and his stomach rumbled. But Henry was not yet seated. Instead, he stood over a pile of men's *Amisch* clothes on the couch in the living area.

"Used to be quite a bit thinner some years back," the older man said, patting his stomach with a smile. "I've had these things in the back of the closet and thought you might like to have them, Jude, seeing how you're becoming *Amisch* and all that."

Jude walked over to shake the farmer's work-worn hand. "Thank you, Henry. I'll put something on right now before lunch."

He selected some clothes from the ample pile and turned to smile at Mary. She dropped her gaze with a faint blush and fiddled with a napkin at the table while he strode to a smaller side room and got dressed.

There was no mirror, so he wasn't completely sure how he looked. The clothes fit quite well, though, even if they did feel odd. He straightened his suspenders and opened the door.

Mary turned to see him walk with visible self-consciousness into the room. But he needn't have worried. *My, but he looks wunderbaar!* She'd never seen any man appear so handsome in *Amisch* dress before, and even as she chastised herself for being so interested in outward appearances, she found that she couldn't drag her eyes away from him. He'd chosen a forest green shirt, and the black pants and suspenders seemed to fit him more than well, emphasizing his lean waist and the broad expanse of his shoulders.

Henry Miller too seemed to have no concern for guarding against vanity, because he laughed outright in pleasure when Jude appeared. "Well, now, that's fine. More than fine. You look like you were born *Amisch, buwe*!"

"Danki," Jude returned, then glanced at her. "Mary, what do you think?"

She looked into his blue eyes and smiled, strange feelings churning and tightening in her belly. "You look . . . great."

Henry laughed again. "Now there's an *Englisch* word for you—great! *Kumme*, let's eat so that Esther may take a turn. I think the food will be—great."

Mary had to smile at Henry's humor and went to the table to eat, secretly eyeing her husband all the while.

Chapter Thirty-Two

The hours of the afternoon lingered on, and Isaac Mast grew no better. Jude sat beside the young man on the bed and didn't like the increase in the patient's pulse. He turned to look at Mary, who'd finally agreed to sit in the chair and rest for a few minutes.

"What is it?" she asked as Mast coughed laboriously.

"I've given him everything that Julie Matthews left and then some. I'm afraid the influenza may have settled deep in his chest. I don't like the way he's breathing or how his pulse is galloping."

"What can we do? Perhaps *Grossmuder* May?"

"No," Jude replied. "She's still recovering herself, I heard. I suppose I could give him some syrup of ipecac and try to get him to throw up a little of the congestion in his chest, but then he also might aspirate . . . I don't know whether to risk it. What he needs is a hospital, but I think the trip itself might kill him."

"We have to do something," Mary insisted.

Jude drew a deep breath and put his arm beneath Mast's shoulders, raising him. He held the ipecac bottle poised at the bluish lips and wished he had thought first of an empty syringe, but suddenly Mast's eyes opened and he stared up at Jude with a strange fervor.

Jude slowly eased him back against the pillows, arranging him so that he was semi-propped up. "Isaac? It's Jude Lyons . . ."

The dilated pupils focused and Jude once more saw an odd distance that disturbed him.

"Ma—Mary," Isaac gasped.

Jude had to suppress a rush of anger at the mention of his wife's name, but he realized how sick Mast was and turned to Mary.

"He's asking for you."

Mary rose from the chair and Jude slid back out of the way so that she could sit near Mast, but Jude kept a firm hold on her shoulder, not willing to risk anything.

"*Jah,* Isaac, it's Mary."

Mast began to move in an agitated manner and Jude almost drew her back, but she caught one of the patient's flailing hands in her own and he seemed to settle a bit.

"Mary . . . I was wrong. Going to hell."

"*Ach, nee,* Isaac. *Gott* forgives. I forgive you. That's why I'm—we're—working to help you get well."

Jude saw a spasm of pain cross Mast's face as he coughed again and shook his shaggy head. "No—getting well. Dying . . . I deserve . . ."

"We all deserve to die," Jude said roughly. "You'll pull through." *Now, where did that come from?*

Mary reached up to touch the hand he held on her shoulder and he grasped her fingers. "Jude," she whispered. "Rachel was like this. Maybe Henry should go for Isaac's family."

"*Nee.*" Mast coughed, this time so long and hard that blood and spittle appeared on the edge of his mouth. Then his strange eyes became fixed and his body heaved once and went limp.

Jude pulled Mary out of the way and bent his head to listen to Mast's chest. Then he began to do chest compressions. "Come on! Come on, Mast! Breathe." He continued for several moments until he felt a heavy hand on his shoulder. Jude looked over his shoulder to see Henry, standing tall and sober beside him.

"It's *nee gut, sohn. Derr Herr* has taken him."

Jude slackened his touch and bowed his head. For some strange reason, he felt like bawling.

Mary withdrew into a corner of the Millers' couch as the bishop and Mahlon Mast arrived. Jude came and sat beside her.

"We did what we could," he said, but his tone was dull and she looked hard at him in the fading afternoon light.

"We did, but Jude, are you all right? I mean, I know you told me about being with your grandfather when he died . . . and now Isaac."

"It's not that. I-I said things earlier today that I shouldn't have—about Mast not being around. I was wrong, and even though I still didn't trust him, I felt . . . pity or something for him."

"Mercy?" she suggested, realizing she'd felt it too.

"Yeah . . . mercy." He seemed to taste the word on his tongue, then leaned forward to put his head in his hands. "The whole time that kid was dying, I was thinking about my father on some level. I want—I want to let go of the anger I feel toward my father. But I don't know how to do that."

"Isn't there an *Englisch* saying that, 'People need mercy the most when they deserve it the least'? That's true, I think."

She watched him lean back and stretch out his long legs in their black *Amisch* pants. "It is true, I suppose, and I . . ."

"*Hex!* You're a witch, I say, like your mother before you, and you killed my *sohn*!" Mahlon Mast stood less than three feet away from the couch and pointed down at Mary, his face red with rage.

Jude stood up and Mary resisted the urge to sink farther back into the couch.

"Look, Mast, I'm sorry about your son—I really am, but I will not let you call my wife a witch. Isaac apologized to Mary before he passed; he knew she was trying to help him," Jude snapped.

"Liar!" Mast snarled.

Mary watched the bishop edge with slow dignity between the two men. "That's enough. Mahlon, you will not do this; it is your pain and loss speaking. It should bring you comfort to know that Isaac asked for forgiveness for his actions before he died. Go home to your wife and other children and tell them the news. I will join you shortly."

Mary saw the struggle in Mahlon's face, but he

finally nodded and jerked away, leaving with a loud slam of the front door.

"Is that guy a threat to my wife?" Jude asked. "Because he acts like an idiot."

"If you're going to be *Amisch*," the bishop suggested mildly, "you might refrain from calling others idiots—you might think it, but cast out the thought. And *nee*, I don't believe that Mahlon Mast is a threat to anyone but himself. He has always been . . . odd in nature."

Mary spoke up with hesitancy. "Bishop Umble, he mentioned my *mamm*—like my mother before me—why is that?"

The bishop glanced at Henry Miller, then back to her. "Mahlon Mast once had a fancy for your mother when they were both young, but she chose your *fater*. I don't think Mahlon's ever forgotten."

"Well, he'd better forget. I don't want any trouble," Jude said, reaching up as if to ease an ache in the back of his neck. Mary had the urge to massage the tension from him and folded her fingers at the sudden heat in her hands.

"There will be no trouble," the bishop assured him. "Right now, I expect some of the women will have heard about Isaac and will be coming to help prepare the body for burial. Henry, would you mind taking Mary home on the sled? I'll see to you, *sohn*." He gestured to Jude, who blew out what sounded like a disgusted breath.

"You mean I can't even see my wife to her door?"

"*Nee*." The bishop shook his head. "But you may go and visit, er, um, court with her tonight when all the others have gone to sleep in her house. But you're not to be seen by anyone entering or leaving . . ."

Mary had to suppress a giggle at the look of pure joy that crossed Jude's face. And despite the sad and exhausting afternoon, she decided that she liked the idea of courting with her husband.

"So, I've read about *Amisch* courtship, of course, but what really goes on when young couples meet and no one's around?" Jude asked, eyeing the bishop over the rim of a mug and trying to gauge what his boundaries were in courting his wife.

"What do you mean, 'What goes on'? What do you think goes on?" The old man gave him a placid look and Jude wanted to grind his teeth. He'd waited hours for the bishop to return home from visiting with the Mast family, and now it was dark and the moon was full. He knew Abner and Mary's *bruders* would soon be asleep and he was anxious to be gone.

"Even when our young couples practiced bundling, there was nothing going on," the bishop finally conceded.

"Bundling? You mean bed courtship, where nothing but a bundling board separated the engaged couple in a bed?"

The bishop sniffed. "Fully clothed, mind you. And sometimes the man was sewn into a snug sack—as a matter of fact, I was . . . up to my neck."

"Don't get any ideas," Jude muttered.

"The purpose of courtship is to meet, get to know one another, steal a kiss or two, and make plans for the wedding."

"Uh-huh. Well, I seem to have gotten the last two down." Jude drained his mug and went to the sink to wash it up. Then he returned to stand by the table while the bishop peered up at him.

"Well, Jude Lyons, let's agree that you did things a bit out of order, so why not spend your courtship time getting to know Mary better?"

"I know her." *Not in the biblical sense, but . . .*

"What's her favorite season?"

"I—uh . . ."

"Her deepest fear? Her best memory? What secret does she hold closest to her heart?" The bishop thumped the table with each question.

"Hey . . . what's—what's your wife's favorite color?" Jude returned, feeling cornered.

"Blue," the old man answered unequivocally. "And don't bother telling me you know Mary's. So, like I said, get to know her a little."

Jude knew how to accept defeat gracefully. He smiled at his mentor and nodded. "All right. You win. I'll try."

"*Gut* man."

But I'm not promising to refrain from kissing her sweet mouth . . . And he knew an aching satisfaction at the thought.

Chapter Thirty-Three

Mary couldn't help but feel excited knowing that Jude would be coming that night. She realized that she had missed this *Amisch* aspect of dating, the secret alone time, and was grateful for the chance to experience it.

She'd gone to her room to wash up and redo her hair into its heavy mass beneath her prayer *kapp*. And then she chose a clean blouse of light blue to put on beneath her black dress and apron. She added a few drops of homemade rosewater to the places behind her ears, hoping that Jude would discover the scent, then went out to the main room to sit with Bear for a bit.

The dog was still tired often but had made an amazing recovery, though he'd lost his right eye and limped a bit when he walked. But even her *Dat* considered him the family hero for killing a wounded bear, and he'd gained a great deal of loving attention from everyone as he grew better.

Mary sat on the couch, keeping quiet and still, glad that her *fater* and *bruders* had gone to bed and no light shone from beneath their doors. Normally, the first time an *Amisch* man would come to court, he'd already have identified the girl's bedroom window and would throw pebbles at the glass to let the girl know he was outside. Then she would decide to let him in or not. Mary smiled at the thought of teasing Jude and not letting him in but knew that she didn't have the heart to do it to him. And as it was, she was having trouble controlling her own excitement at the prospect of maybe a few kisses or a caress from her handsome husband.

She closed her eyes, daydreaming as she rubbed Bear's fur, then was startled back to the moment by a light knock at the front door. She gave a quieting pat to Bear's head and skimmed across the floor to open the door. Her eyes drank their fill of Jude in the black *Amisch* coat and hat, and he already had a subtle shadow of beard growth on his fine face, making him look faintly piratical and all the more appealing.

"A *gut nacht* to you, Mary Lyons," Jude said, slipping off his hat. "May I *kumme* in?"

Ach, he's so formal, maybe he'll not attempt a kiss at all . . . She widened the door and returned his serious greeting while Bear made his own welcome.

Jude slipped out of the coat and she noticed that he'd changed into a burgundy-colored shirt which suited his skin and eyes well.

She hung up his coat and hat on the pegs beside the door, then turned, feeling a bit shy. "We have to be quiet," she whispered.

He nodded gravely. "What's your favorite color?"

"What?"

He shrugged. "Mine's green. What's yours?"

She wondered where he was going with the conversation as she indicated with a sweep of her hand that they might sit on the couch.

"Blue," she said softly. "Like your eyes."

"*Danki*, and your favorite season?"

"Summer. Is this a test?"

"*Jah*," he answered. "I also need your darkest fear and the secret you have that no one else knows . . ."

He gave her an expectant look and she stared at him, feeling at a loss. "Well, I . . ."

"Go on, *sei se gut*."

Maybe his sugar is low . . . She bit her lip in thought and Jude made a low sound in the back of his throat.

"Don't bite your lip," he half pleaded.

She stopped but then some female instinct made her rub her tongue tip over the part of her lip she'd bitten and she heard his breath catch. Her heart beat faster and she leaned nearer to him, but he had his hands folded in his lap and appeared resolute in keeping them there.

"My darkest fear," she whispered, reaching to run a hand down the hard muscle of his arm. "Let's see . . ." She wanted to spin out her words, like wool on a loom, and wrap him up, cocoon him in heat. "I'm afraid of bats," she confessed, leaning close to the tanned length of his throat. "I've heard they bite." She surprised even herself by taking an experimental taste of his skin, letting her teeth scrape against him, finding him both salty and sweet. He groaned and arched his neck.

"Mary, what are you . . ."

She let her hands splay over the breadth of his

chest, not missing the tension in his body as her fingers found a pin near the center of his shirt and she slowly withdrew it.

"I don't especially like the howl of a wolf . . . not when it's lonely and sad. It makes me hurt inside." Her fingers slid beneath his shirt in the small gap and pinched at the taut skin. "Do you know what I mean?"

She wanted to smile when she saw that he was having difficulty concentrating and that his hands were now white where he clenched them together.

"No . . . yes . . ." he muttered as she found another pin and took it, wriggling her fingers further across his bare skin.

"And should I tell you secrets?" she asked, sliding her hand over the tempting line of his taut rib cage.

He was breathing deeply, his handsome face flushed, and he nodded as if hearing her words from far away.

"Tell me anything you want," he finally gasped, then turned his body to press hers into the soft cushions of the couch.

Jude was amazed at her responsiveness, the yielding of her soft lips, and the hands she used to thread through his hair and down to touch his shoulders. *Right here. Right now . . .*

But his mind intruded where his body held hard attention. He'd probably regret it later, but he had no desire to make love to his wife for the first time half-on and half-off a small couch, with her brothers and father in the next rooms. And she deserved better than some hurried, fully dressed groping . . . He sat up abruptly and dragged her with him.

"Mary—Mary . . . listen. I want . . ."

"*Ach*, I know what you want." He saw her smile in profile as she nuzzled against him.

"Yes . . . I mean, no. Mary . . ." He caught her shoulders in a gentle grasp.

"Look, sweetheart . . ."

She drew back and studied his face. "Wait . . . you mean you're turning away . . . again?" Her voice rose with agitation.

"No, I'm not turning . . . well, I want us to . . . you to . . ."

She flounced out of his hands and leaned back on the couch, crossing her arms.

"Jude Lyons, I do believe you . . . you are a teaser! *Jah*, that's truth."

He winced as her voice increased in volume. "Mary, shh, *sei se gut*."

"*Ach*, don't you use your Penn Dutch with me, *Herr* Teaser. I am done. This courting night is over." She got up and stormed to her bedroom, opening and slamming the door.

Jude looked at Bear. The dog grunted and, almost on cue, Abner's and the boys' doors opened. Jude rolled his eyes and prepared for the onslaught even while he longed to go after his wife.

Abner appeared, easing a suspender up and rubbing his eyes. "What's going on out here?"

Jude got up and walked to the front door. "Courting, Abner . . . your daughter and I are courting!"

He hollered the last word loud enough to be sure Mary had heard, then stepped out into the cold night, closing the door behind him and wondering where he'd gone wrong.

Mary pressed her hands to her hot cheeks in the darkness of her room. She was embarrassed and ashamed of her behavior, but it had also felt *gut* to let go of her temper for once. Yet she must be over-tired to have reacted so angrily when Jude had obviously been thinking—while she'd been . . . She closed her eyes in the dark as her face flamed anew. *What must he think of me? But I didn't plan on behaving that way—he was simply so attractive and* Amisch-*looking and . . . and . . .*

"But I am his wife," she said aloud suddenly. *And I am determined to have a marriage and not simply a wedding, to be a wife and not merely a bride. Grossmuder* May's words rang in her mind: *And that includes more than the bedding . . .*

"*Ach, jah,* it does!" she exclaimed.

And then she laughed and knew instinctively that her behavior of the evening had maybe been exactly what it should have. She couldn't wait to see what Jude would do next.

Chapter Thirty-Four

Jude entered the Umbles' house, feeling both discouraged and frustrated. *Herr Teaser . . . Great, Lyons . . . great.* Now he wanted nothing more than the relative comfort of the Umbles' guest room, where he'd be living for the month.

He moved through the dark kitchen and almost jumped out of his skin when the bishop spoke from the living area.

"Well, that was the shortest courting time on record—did you have a fight?"

Jude caught his breath. "No . . . why are you up? Is that part of the *Amisch* tradition?"

The old man laughed and turned up a kerosene lamp. "*Kumme* and sit for a moment. I couldn't sleep and was thinking on a book I'd read recently. Mr. Ellis, at the bottom of the hill, you know, loans me books now and then."

Jude came with reluctance and found a seat in the warm glow of light. "A Bible translation?" he asked.

"You must think me an entirely boring man—spiritual, but boring. *Nee*, here."

Jude caught the thin paperback easily. He leaned into the light to read the title. "*Shipwreck at the Bottom of the World—The Extraordinary True Story of Shackleton and the Endurance.* This is what you read?"

"*Jah,* it's about Ernest Shackleton's exploration attempt in Antarctica."

"I know the story somewhat."

The bishop nodded. "But do you know about what they call now the Third Man factor?"

"Are you allowed to be reading this stuff?"

"Answer my question."

Jude settled more comfortably in his chair. "*Nee,* I don't know it."

"They say it's when those in dire peril of their lives have felt a sudden presence at their side, inspiring them to hang on and to survive. Shackleton and the two men who hiked out felt it, said it always felt like 'a fourth man' walked with them, kept them going. Another fellow hiking Mount Everest thought the presence was so real, he offered to share a snack, and another—"

"Wait a minute. I know this!" Jude couldn't keep the excitement from his voice. "I had the same experience."

The bishop raised a shaggy eyebrow at him.

"No, really. Right when Mary and I were leaving Ice Mountain, we stopped at the Ice Mine and I fell in. I saw the shadow of another man who helped Mary pull me up and out. I wouldn't have survived without that . . . presence. And when I think back to it, I feel this tremendous feeling of peace and hope when I consider that . . . other man."

"Very strange," the bishop mused. "I could not

sleep tonight because of the desire to tell you about this book. I wonder if it's a message for you from *Derr Herr*? Do you know, there's an another man story in the Bible?"

Jude shook his head. "No, I don't."

"Then I'll sum it up for you—wouldn't want you to be bored . . . A king insisted all men worship his golden idol. Three young Hebrews refused to worship any but *Derr Herr.* The king had them thrown in a fire so hot, it killed the guards who did the throwing. Then, while the king and his court watched, the three young men walked around in the fire, but the Presence of a fourth man could be seen walking with them through the flames."

"What happened then?" Jude was surprised to discover he was genuinely curious.

"*Ach,* the three men came out unharmed, even their clothes not burned. And the king worshipped *Derr Herr.* Maybe he figured a God who walks with you through life's fires—or ice—is better than no god at all."

Jude knew a strange conviction in his heart at the old man's words. How had he been living lately? In truth, feeling like he'd lost his home in Atlanta, but maybe this Presence, the one at the Ice Mine, the one he'd discovered here, in this place, could give him a new home and a new beginning . . . and could help him find his way with Mary.

He met the wise old eyes of Bishop Umble and smiled. "*Danki.*"

"Anytime, *sohn.* Anytime."

* * *

Isaac Mast was buried the following day, ten days before Thanksgiving. Mary dressed all in black, as was the custom, for the sober affair. She kept her eyes downcast as she filed past the wooden coffin, glancing only briefly at Isaac's still face through the glass top third of the coffin. The mountain *Amisch* cemetery was on the lonely side of a shadowy hill, and she was glad of Jude's arm as she navigated the slippery ground. The graveside words of Bishop Umble were brief, and soon the community was headed back to the horses and sleds.

Jude hadn't spoken to her about the night before. In truth, there was no time to speak about much of anything as Joseph took her arm to help her into the sled beneath the pile of quilts. She worried that she wouldn't be able to talk with Jude at all until he leaned over the edge of the sled and bent as if to brush something from her cheek.

"I'll be over tonight. Is that all right?"

She couldn't suppress the flush of pleasure at his request and gave a demure nod, though inside, she was brimming with happiness. *And I know exactly what we'll do . . .*

Jude hadn't realized, when he'd spent the summer researching, how much hard physical work was involved in keeping a fair-sized farm running, but the bishop seemed determined that he learn. Bishop Umble and his wife kept cattle as well as a good-sized garden. But Jude discovered that the cattle feed yard, where the big animals were moved off the pastures, was the place much of his day was spent. He privately vowed never to own cattle, which raised the question in his mind as to whether or not he'd be happy simply farming on the mountain.

A young calf jolted him back to the present with a knock on the hip.

"Taking *gut* care of these cattle means hard work in the winter and also *gut* concentration," the bishop said as Jude rubbed at his side. "It's not snowing today, so you can go and scrape the manure from the pens and put it into the fertilizer pile. The cattle need pens that are kept clean for good living."

"Right," Jude muttered, adjusting his *Amisch* hat and heading off for the pens. *Goat milk, and we'll be vegetarians . . . no cattle.*

Twenty-four pens and six back-breaking hours later, Jude went to his room to grab a set of clean clothes. He blew past Martha and didn't miss the downward tilt of her nose at his smell.

"Going to the creek, Martha. I'll be back." He grabbed a bar of homemade soap from the kitchen sink as he hurried through.

"Jude, you will freeze," she protested. "I will heat water."

"Nope." He started to whistle a few notes and slung a towel over his shoulder and picked up a lantern. "I'll be fine."

I am going to freeze to death . . . He was shivering so badly in the frigid, ice-crusted water that he could barely manage to hang on to the soap, but he was determined to be clean to court Mary. He knew the *Amisch* didn't bathe every day, but hours in the manure pens surely required drastic measures. He managed to wash his hair, jumped out to towel off for a few mind-numbing seconds, then dressed and drew on Henry's Sunday coat and even cleaned the boots Ben Kauffman had given him with mud and snow, then rinsed them in the creek. By then, his fingers were so cold, he decided he wouldn't be able to manage the reins on the sled and knew that a brisk jog would probably be a better way to get to Mary.

He hurried back to the Umbles' with his things and Martha greeted him at the door.

"See, you're freezing," the old woman declared, hands on hips.

"*N-nee.*" Jude shivered as he spoke. "Invigorated, Martha. Ready to court."

"You're not supposed to tell anyone," she scolded.

He smiled at her, then bent to give her a spontaneous kiss on the cheek. "Don't tell, then, Martha," he whispered.

She actually giggled like a girl and he laughed until she took his things and shooed him back out the door with her apron. He took a deep breath of the cold air, then plunged into his jog, deciding that life was all right for the moment.

Chapter Thirty-Five

Mary adjusted her apron and quietly began to assemble the light corn syrup, powdered sugar, marshmallows, and shortening. She was about to measure the popcorn kernels when she heard Jude's knock at the front door.

She drew a deep breath, then eased the door open, surprised when he half jogged past her and continued moving around before stopping at the woodstove and holding out his hands. He took his hat off as an apparent afterthought and held it out to her.

"Are you cold?" she asked with concern.

He shook his head and blew out a frosty breath. Then she noticed his damp hair. "Jude Lyons! Did you come over here after a bath? You're freezing."

She lowered her voice and took a step nearer him, reaching up to touch his head. "Your hair's still wet. You'll catch your death."

"Wives' tale," he muttered, rubbing his hands together.

She smiled. "What did Martha say about heating water for a bath at the start of the week?"

"She offered . . . I chose the creek instead."

Mary stared at him, dismay filling her chest. "Ach, Jude . . . you are going to be sick. The creek is too cold."

"Don't fuss. I'm fine."

She noticed him rub at his right hip beneath his long black coat.

"Fine, hmm? And what about your hip?"

"It's nothing. One of the cattle bumped into me."

"Lie down on the couch," she ordered, hastening to the medicine closet.

"Not that I mind the suggestion, but why lie down?"

She was rummaging between bottles and found what she sought. "Lie down, take off your coat and shirt, and lower your suspender on that sore side. I've got some *gut* liniment."

He grinned at her. "I'm game, but remember that it's you who's telling me to undress . . . I'm not the one who's teasing."

She flushed a bit and clutched the liniment bottle with determination. "Go on. Hurry up."

She tried not to watch him as he slipped off the heavy coat and put it over a chair, but he was an enticing sight for any bride. He eased out of his suspenders and blue shirt and stood holding it, still shivering.

"*Kumme* on," she urged, fascinated by the play of lantern light and shadow across his bare skin.

He dropped the shirt on top of the coat, and then reached to rub at his hip again. "It is sore."

"Go lie down."

He obeyed, trying to fit most of his big body onto the couch as he got situated on his left side. He made an effort to reach for the waist of his pants and she shooed his hand away. He sighed and stretched out, so she couldn't help but see the light brown thatch of hair under his arm.

She felt rather giddy and slid his pants down an inch from his lean waist, exposing the top of his hip. Then she gasped aloud. "Jude, you're badly bruised."

"It's nothing."

She bit her lip and eased his pants an inch farther, seeing that the bruising extended beyond where she could comfortably undress him. She murmured to herself and poured the tea tree liniment into her hand, the overwhelming scent filling the room. She put the bottle on the floor and knelt by the edge of the couch, then tipped her hand.

The liniment ran in seductive wet rivulets over the line of his hip, and she heard his breath catch. She slid her hand through the moisture and pressed hard against the bruising, angling her arm to get closer. She felt his body arch into her hand, then felt him relax as she began rhythmic circular motions.

"Oh, Mary," he whispered. "That feels so good."

She glanced up the line of his body and pressed harder. He shifted his lower legs and she continued until she was surprised by the sound of his heavy, slow breathing. He'd fallen asleep to her ministrations. *He must be exhausted.*

She finished her rubbing, eased his waistband back up and drew a quilt from the back of the couch over his bare shoulders and chest. Then she recorked the liniment and went with stealthy movements back to the kitchen to wash her hands.

Bear had wandered from his place by the woodstove to jump up on top of Jude's legs and she was surprised when he didn't wake but slid over as if familiar with making room for the big animal. Mary added more wood to the stove and dropped into a chair opposite the couch. She wondered how long he'd sleep, then found herself lulled by the warmth of the woodstove and the tingling of her hand where she'd touched him. She felt her eyes drifting closed and decided a catnap would not hurt her either.

Jude glanced over his bare shoulder at Mary as she began to stir, and he shook the lid and kettle full of popping corn harder.

"Hello, sweetheart," he whispered when she blinked at him and gave a gentle stretch.

He watched her rise from her chair and wander over to him, still looking sleepy. She put out a hand, almost as if she were in the middle of a dream, and brushed his ribs with the backs of her fingers.

"Mmm," she said aloud as if she'd felt something pleasant.

He stopped shaking the pan and turned to her, catching her close in his arms. He bent his head and forgot everything for the moment as he kissed the honeyed slant of her mouth, gently edging the tip of his tongue against her closed lips.

Open, he heard himself beg in his head. *Open for me, please . . .*

And she did, with a tiny breathy sound, so that he could taste the sweetness of her mouth like sugared candy to a boy longing for a treat. He tilted his head to deepen the kiss, aware that her hands roved in fluttery, anxious movements across his chest.

He tore his mouth away once to gasp for breath and caught the smell of burning popcorn. He grabbed a pot holder and the pan and moved to dump the whole lot outdoors into the snow, then returned to where she stood, as if dazed.

"Mary, sweetheart?"

She lifted a hand to her lips as if trying to recapture the sensations of the kiss and he inched close to her, anxious to repeat the experience. But she looked up at him, owl-eyed. "I'm sorry, Jude. I think I was half-asleep."

"I like you half-asleep," he confided, bending to nuzzle the juncture of her dress and neck.

"*Nee*, I mean, I had plans for tonight."

"Okay, let's keep planning." He smiled, his mouth on her skin.

But she took a step back, out of his arms, and he stared at her in consternation. "Mary, what . . ."

"We're going to make popcorn balls," she announced, straightening her apron and moving away from him to take another pan off a nail on the wall.

He struggled to keep up with the situation. "Popcorn balls, right . . . I was making the popcorn. But then I thought we could . . . we were . . ."

She shook her head in determination. "Popcorn balls. A great treat." She landed a lump of butter in the kettle and added a measure of kernels.

"Mary, wait. I don't get it. We were kissing."

She arched a delicate brow at him. "*Ach*, that was more than kissing. Even when we . . . made out, you didn't kiss like that."

He had to chuckle. "Oh, you mean my tongue."

She blushed to the top of her *kapp* and he hooked his fingers in the waistband of his pants and took a step closer to her. "Or I guess I should say *our* tongues—touching, exploring, wet, wanting . . ."

He leveled each word at her with a deliberate seductiveness and she increased her shaking of the kettle to a furious speed. He reached out a hand to brush down the length of her moving sleeve and was pleased to feel her tremble.

"Mary, that's a perfectly normal way to kiss. It simulates what the man wants to do with his body, with the woman's body, together."

She stopped shaking the kettle and stared at him. "*Ach* . . . I never thought . . . so you want to . . ."

"Very much," he spoke softly. "I want very much to make love to you, to use my body to please you, but I can't bring myself to do it here, with your *dat* snoring in the next room. So we'll have to wait until this month's over and I can take you home to our cabin."

"*Ach* . . ." she said again.

He laughed gently. "Yes, *ach* . . . but that doesn't mean that we can't kiss and talk and kiss and make popcorn balls . . . what do you think?"

He watched her search visibly for a reply; then she lowered her lashes. "I think a month will never seem so long."

"Gut." He caught her against his chest, stretching to put his hands over hers to start the kettle moving again. "That's very *gut.*" And he bit lightly at the back of her neck, finding a sensitive spot and making her jump until he'd soothed her with his mouth once more.

Chapter Thirty-Six

"When do you think you can start?" Mary asked, excitement in her voice as she watched her older *bruder* look over the sketches she'd drawn.

"If the weather still holds, I can start tomorrow," Joseph answered, making notes on her drawings with a pencil nub.

Mary knew that Joseph was skilled at carpentry, and he was willing to help her surprise Jude. She'd stayed up half the night after Jude had gone back to the Umbles', working on sketches of how she would love their cabin to be—or Jude's old research cabin from the summer.

She'd drawn two extra rooms on the back, a place for indoor plumbing instead of the outhouse, and had reshaped the roof, which badly needed to be patched.

"And *Dat* owns that land, so we can always keep adding on once the *kinner* . . ."

She trailed off at Joseph's appraising look.

"Nee," she snapped. "There are no babies on the way yet."

He laughed. "To think, a few months back, I would have broken your husband's perfect nose over such a remark."

She shoved at him, then put her hands on her hips. "And I might well ask you, Joseph King, when your own *kinner* will start arriving. You're older than I am."

She'd only been kidding, but her *bruder*'s bleak look reminded her of his talk before about not finding a girl on the mountain. "I'm sorry, Joseph," she said contritely. "I was only teasing."

He waved away her words. "It's of no matter . . . I will be the *oncle* who spoils."

She smiled but knew Joseph was unhappy at heart. She realized that being with Jude made her want others around her to have joy as well, and she gave Joseph a quick hug.

"You're a gut big *bruder. Danki* for your help with this."

He nodded and she knew she had temporarily cleared his heart with her words.

Jude's head throbbed as the bishop quizzed him on his Penn Dutch. Even though Jude knew both High and Low German, the dialect spoken by the Mountain *Amisch* was foreign at times to him and was one of the most difficult aspects of his becoming *Amisch.*

"Let's see, how do you say 'the mischievous child'?"

Jude frowned and rolled his eyes. "Nobody says that."

"*Jah*, they do," the bishop countered.

"*Der brat*—how about that?"

"Nope."

"I give up," Jude admitted, rubbing his temple.

"Well, you should get to know the words well. I've spoken to the deacons and we've decided that although it's a bit unusual, you will be the next teacher—*Herr Dokator*—at our local school. Full pay rate . . . Term starts the Monday after Thanksgiving. Rachel Miller's niece was to have come up the mountain to do it, but she decided not to since Rachel died . . . so it's you. Now, what do you think of that?"

Jude found himself smiling in spite of himself. "But I thought the *Amisch* only approved of female teachers?"

"We're Mountain *Amisch, buwe*! And why waste a man who's *schmart* in the head, hmm? Now, the mischievous child . . ."

Jude's head cleared and his concerns about farming for a living drifted away. "*Der schnickelfritz.*"

Mary looked up from stuffing an orange with cloves when her *fater* came in the front door with a blast of cold air.

"*Ach*, Mary, I saw Jude at Ben Kauffman's store a bit ago. He was there on an errand for the bishop. He asked if he might take you sledding this evening—says he's got a surprise for ya. I told him he's not supposed to ask me but you."

"*Dat* . . ." Mary began to protest.

Her *fater* raised his hand. "But I told him I'd deliver the message, seeing that you are married."

She kissed his weathered cheek at his teasing. *"Danki, Dat."*

"*Ach,* and Jude also sent word that Martha and Bishop Umble have invited us to their home for Thanksgiving."

Mary clapped her hands. "*Wunderbaar!* I was hoping we could get together, but I know the Umbles usually invite those families who have had a difficult year in some way."

Her *fater* stroked his beard. "Well, we almost lost you, and Jude's grandfather passed on, and his parents . . ."

Mary fingered a clove absently. *It's true. It's been a hard year for Jude—his job, his father, his book, and—marrying me.*

She pushed away the doubts she had and went to serve lunch to her father and brothers. They took up a debate as to what kind of pie she should make to take to the Umbles' for the upcoming holiday.

"Raisin," her father prompted.

"Blueberry," Joseph and Edward agreed.

And then Mary had an idea. "No pie," she announced.

"What?" the men cried in unison.

She smiled a secret smile. "I'll make pineapple upside-down cake instead."

Jude put aside his fascinating and sad study of the *Amisch Book of Martyrs* and ambled down the steps to catch the bishop after supper.

The old man usually took up residence on the couch with a book, *The Budget,* or his Bible, and Jude wanted to get to him before he became engrossed in reading.

"So—" Jude settled into the chair opposite the couch where the bishop was already seated. Martha was drying dishes quietly in the kitchen and the soft, homey clinks were soothing to Jude's ears.

"So? How did you find your study of the *Amisch Book of Martyrs*?"

"Painful to read. Some of the tortures and persecutions suffered by the followers of Jacob Amman are unbelievable—but I know they're true."

"Faith costs. Being different costs," the bishop observed. "Now you too join to pay that price."

Jude thought of the prejudices against the *Amisch* in the modern day and understood that Bishop Umble was calling him to a higher thinking, a feeling of being part of a legacy of endurance and hope. He was silent with his thoughts for a moment, then asked about his new position at the school.

"By my calculations from the summer, there are about nineteen children on the mountain of school age. Does that sound about right?"

"Yep." The older man nodded. "And they might give you a fair run too, or they might be in awe of you as a male."

"Do you think they'd respect a female more?"

The bishop stroked his beard. "Respect is returned in the way that it's given."

"I understand that. I've always been respectful with my students. I wondered about cultural differences, I guess."

"You'll do fine, *sohn*. And I'll tell you what—you can take a break from the feed yard tomorrow to go over to the school and see the lay of the land. Get any supplies you want over at Kauffman's. Ben donates whatever we need. And take Mary along with you to tidy up the place. It'll give you a chance to be alone together too."

Yeah . . . like I need that. Jude cleared his throat. "You know, December fourteenth is a month."

"Counting the days, are you?"

Jude shot a glance over his shoulder at Martha and leaned forward. "I think you'd be counting too, if you were my age."

"Ha! I'd count them now, *buwe.* I'd count them now."

Chapter Thirty-Seven

Mary glanced at the long wooden sled with some trepidation. "I thought when you asked *Dat* about sledding, we'd be going in a sled . . . with a horse."

Jude laughed out loud in the clear moonlit air "*Nee,* my delicious *frau,* the thought of you in a cutter sled with me, together under quilts . . ." He broke off and shook his head. "I can't. Besides, this will be fun."

Mary glanced down the snowy hill behind the cemetery. It seemed a long way down and she hadn't sledded, really sledded, since she was a girl.

"*Dat* said you had a surprise for me," she improvised, trying to stall for time. But Jude was already looping the sled rope around his arm and gloved hand.

He dropped his big frame down onto the sled and scrunched back to make room for her. "*Kumme* here. Bundle up your skirts and sit between my legs."

She obeyed with reluctance.

When she was ensconced between his bent knees, he leaned forward to whisper in her ear. "Say hello to the new school teacher on Ice Mountain—*Herr Dokator*—your husband."

She half turned in surprise and he pushed the sled off. She looked forward again quickly and started to scream and laugh at the same time.

The whole descent was terrifying and exhilarating and she was amazed when he guided the sled to a staggering stop at the bottom of the hill. She rolled off and lay back in the soft snow, staring up at the stars and breathing hard.

She felt the weight of his body as he half leaned over her, his eyes very blue in the moonglow of the snow. His hat had blown off somewhere and he looked young and carefree. She reached a hand up to stroke his scruffy cheek with tenderness.

He turned his mouth into her palm, then shook his head. "Oh, no, Mrs. Lyons . . . no temptation tonight. Only good old exercise and exhaustion." He got up and hauled her to her feet. "*Kumme* on."

"Where?"

"Back up the hill."

"Up? There?"

"You're younger than I am. You can do it."

He pulled her hand and caught up the sled rope, then led her trudging back up the steep slope. Mary collapsed on her damp mound of skirts at the top.

"You—go ahead," she gasped.

He sat down beside her. "I'll wait until you catch your breath. You want to know the last time I was sledding—I mean, like this?"

"When?"

"When I was ten. My grandfather took me and held me in front of him. We took a family trip to

Vermont and I remember how fast and free and safe it felt to be in his arms and racing down that hill."

"It's like the snow globe of Ice Mountain I left behind when I . . ." She trailed off.

"Yeah. I never told you, but my father smashed it—threw it against the wall."

"What? I'm so sorry. I know how much that connected you to your grandfather. You miss him a great deal, don't you?"

Jude sighed aloud. "Yeah . . . I do. He tried to teach me what it meant to have a father—a real one. And he was kind . . . a rare person."

Mary thought about Jude's dad, his anger and bitterness, and listened to the wind whisper softly through the surrounding pines.

"You know," she ventured softly, "you might not want to know it, but the Bible says that God puts us in families."

She sensed him stiffen beside her. "No, I guess I don't want to know that . . . except that he put me with you."

"That's true and I am so happy about that, but your dad . . ."

He reached out and gave her his hand. "Let's forget about my father for a while. I'd rather kiss your hand again at the bottom of the hill."

She had to smile and agree.

"I'll pick you up tomorrow morning to go to the school—with a sled and horse. It's a short ride," Jude promised as he gave her a quick kiss on the cheek at her door. *So I should be able to keep my hands off you . . .*

He turned onto the moonlit snow path, dragging the sled behind him. He'd promised to return it to Ben Kauffman's the next day. As he walked, he thought about his time with Mary and what she'd tentatively said back on the hill: *God puts us in families.* It was almost too much to swallow. He'd written to his mother since she'd told him about the divorce, of course, but he'd had no word from his father—nor did he expect to.

He became aware of a rustling in the bushes along the path and looked up alertly, the idea of a rogue bear denning late foremost in his mind. But to his surprise, another *Amisch* man, in dark coat and hat, stepped from the underbrush.

"Mahlon Mast?" Jude asked, feeling relieved.

"Lyons," the older man grunted.

"How are you?"

"It's none of your business."

"Fine." Jude started to walk on.

"Hey," Mast called.

Jude paused. "What?"

"You tell Joseph King he's making a racket pretty late at your place. I got kids who can hear the hammering and can't sleep."

Jude stared at him, trying to piece together what the man had said.

"Joseph . . . my place? You mean my old cabin?"

"Yeah, real *schmart* in the head you are. I heard the deacons voted you in to teacher—a woman's job."

Jude shrugged. "Whatever, Mast. But I have three

of your *kinner* on my roster, so I expect to see them when school starts."

"Remember what I say about your *bruder*-in-law. Working that late means there's more chances than not for an accident to happen to a man."

"Is that some kind of a threat?"

Mast grunted at him and slipped back into the underbrush, leaving Jude with the distinct feeling that it was growing colder and darker. He set off for the Umbles' with a faster step.

Jude's dreams that night were vivid and erotic. He jerked awake on his narrow bed in the bishop's spare room to find himself wet with sweat and pulsing with desire for his wife. He pushed the covers away and went to stand barefoot in his black *Amisch* pants near the window he opened. He stared out moodily at the crust of snow on the ground and gave serious consideration to sneaking out and going to see Mary in her bedroom. *But that wouldn't be very* Amisch *of me, or very honorable . . .*

He sighed and grabbed his white shirt from a peg on the wall, deciding to go downstairs and have something to drink.

"Can't sleep, *sohn*?" the bishop asked when Jude paused on the darkened bottom step to the kitchen.

Jude jumped in spite of himself. "What—do you sit around waiting to startle me when I least expect it?"

The old man laughed and turned up a lantern at the kitchen table. "What troubles you this night?"

Well, I want to have sex with my wife and you are keeping me penned like a . . .

"Aha!" The bishop smiled in the mellow light. "It's counting the days, is it?"

Jude would not give a reply and went to the icebox to find the pitcher of milk. He'd grown used to the taste of raw milk over the summer and poured himself a glass, halfway wishing it was something stronger.

He sat down at the table with reluctance. He wasn't in the mood to talk, but the bishop seemed a determined man.

"How was the sledding?"

"Fine."

"And Mary this evening?"

"Equally fine." *I sound like an errant schoolkid giving up zero information to a parent's request about my day . . .*

"Uh-huh," the bishop mused. "And you're so jumpy—why? Not only the counting of the days, I'd imagine?"

"I saw Mahlon Mast tonight coming home," Jude admitted.

"I hear he's taken to roaming the woods since Isaac passed. Says he cannot sleep."

"Well, he gave me a scare and he seemed to be threatening Joseph—Mary's brother. Something about hammering going on late at my old cabin?"

Jude caught the look in the bishop's eyes as he ducked his head.

"What?" Jude asked. "Tell me, *sei se gut.*"

The bishop spread his aged hands. "It's to be a surprise for you. Mary's planning, you know? She's got Joseph and Edward and a few others over there expanding the place, getting it ready to be a proper home for the two of you."

"What? I never thought . . ." Jude groaned in dismay. "That should be my job."

"Your job is becoming *Amisch.* It doesn't hurt that Mary wanted a surprise for you. And you're not to go over there or speak of it . . . agreed?"

Jude took a swig of milk. "Yeah or *jah* . . . all right."

The bishop laughed. "Something that you should learn about wives, *sohn*—a *gut* one will always be full of surprises!"

Chapter Thirty-Eight

"Well, you're looking fair this morning, Mary," Abner King said with a sigh. "Much like yer *mamm*."

Mary came and looped an arm around her *dat*. "She must have been especially beautiful, then, when she was waiting to see you."

She was pleased to see his face redden. "*Ach* . . . Mary. *Jah,* I forgot you're waiting for Jude. It's the look of love you wear."

Now it was she who blushed. She gave her *fater* another quick squeeze, then went to put on her bonnet and cloak. She'd loaded a work bucket with pine oil, a brush, and some rags, in case the schoolhouse needed a *gut* scrubbing.

Bear began to bark and she went to the window to see Jude pulling one of the bishop's horses and a cutter sled up to the front of the cabin. *Together . . . under the quilts* . . . She shivered in anticipation and bid farewell to her father as she went out the door. She left behind a disappointed Bear but didn't want to risk the dog running about quite yet.

"I would have come in for you." Jude smiled, hopping down to help her in.

"I'm full of energy this morning," she confided, handing him the scrub bucket. He fit it in the back of the sled, then climbed in beside her. She delighted in the press of his hard, lean body as he settled the quilts about her.

"I have a plan for today," he whispered and her heart began to beat faster. "I'm practicing self-discipline."

"*Ach* . . ." she murmured, disappointed.

"*Nee* . . . I mean . . . if you'll agree, I'm allowing myself, er, us, three kisses today. Only three. Is that all right?"

She considered the possibilities. "Anytime?" she breathed. "Anywhere?"

He swallowed and nodded. "Yep."

"Then I agree." She settled back in the comfort of the sled with a smile playing about her lips.

Jude stood inside the doorway of the schoolhouse and surveyed the large, long room. He stepped aside to make room for Mary, who swung her work bucket with a vengeance.

"Cobwebs . . . There hasn't been a term since spring ended. I think squirrels have been nesting in the corner," she sniffed.

But to Jude, it was beautiful. "Still smells like a classroom, though," he said cheerfully, taking in the old-fashioned blackboards and the wooden student desks.

He bent and placed a hard, purposeful kiss on

her surprised mouth. "That's one, sweetheart, because I am so happy to have found something to do for a living on this mountain."

He watched her take a moment to recover from the surprise of the kiss; then she nudged him with a small elbow. "We could have farmed."

He laughed out loud and walked over to the large teacher's desk, then ran a finger over the lectern. "I'd make a bad farmer, Mary. I don't think I have the patience."

She gestured to the empty desks. "Yet you'll grow a crop of *kinner* here and have the patience to help them learn."

"I never thought of it like that . . . you'd make an excellent teacher yourself."

He watched her put down the bucket and walk to sit in one of the student desks. "*Ach, nee* . . . I'd rather be your willing pupil, Professor Lyons."

He felt his body's response as her voice lowered. *How I love to play with her . . . and what I'd love to teach her . . .*

Mingled intimate thoughts drifted across his mind as he adjusted his glasses and leaned an elbow on the lectern.

"Is that so, *Frau* Lyons?"

She nodded, letting her sooty lashes fall against the cream of her cheeks.

He cleared his throat and assumed his most professional manner. *Remember . . . self-discipline. Two kisses left . . . only two.*

"Perhaps you might benefit from some private instruction," he murmured, considering. "But recite for me first what it is that you already know about . . . a kiss."

She lifted her head and her beautiful hazel eyes took on a luminous faraway look. "A kiss can be as warm as the summer sun, reaching through your dress to heat your skin and leaving you breathless and in need—of cooling."

Wow . . . I didn't expect that. Her words made his mouth sting with sensation and he shifted his weight. *Hold it together, Lyons . . .*

"Anything else?" He managed to keep his voice level.

"I'm afraid I need more experience in the matter," she said with a demure look.

"Yes, well . . . you will step forward, please."

She came on light feet to stand before the lectern and he saw the soft glow in her eyes, a sleepy sensuality that made him wonder with sudden jealousy if she'd ever kissed anyone but him before.

"And the experience you have had . . . was it . . . with more than one man?" he asked gruffly.

She eyed him with open innocence and he had his answer and felt satisfied and moved at the same time.

"Never mind . . . close your eyes. And keep them closed."

She squeezed her eyes shut tight like a little girl and he came around the lectern to inch her backward a few steps.

"Relax," he bent forward to whisper and she stopped squeezing her eyelids and biting her lip. "Now," he said as if conveying a weighty lecture, "a touch can be a prelude to a kiss. For example . . ."

He moved to stand behind her and put a finger on the nape of her neck. "If I trail my hand down the curve of your back and . . . perhaps a bit lower . . . it could mean that I want to touch you with my mouth as well."

"And do you?" Her voice came out high and breathless as he matched the movement of his hand with his words.

"Ah, patience, Mary . . . you must learn that keeping still and waiting can add to the experience of a kiss. But to answer your question . . ." He dipped his head to breathe in her ear. "*Jah*, I do."

He smiled when she leaned into his body, clearly expecting that he would close his mouth on the tempting tiny lobe of her ear. But he drew himself up sharply and walked in front of her instead.

"You're too eager," he scolded, brushing the back of his hand across the midline of her breasts. "Are you wanting, Mary?"

He watched the pretty flush his touch produced and let his hand slide downward a bit to touch the slight curve of her belly. "Do you feel funny in here? Maybe half pleasure—half pain?"

"*J-jah*," she whispered and put her hands out to come in contact with his chest.

"Ahhh . . . no touching, please. Hands behind your back. Good girl."

He ran his hand back up her body and put one fingertip to her parted pink lips. "You're very responsive, and that bodes well for future education, but for now . . ." He tapped her lips. "Open, please, and . . . suck . . . hard."

I am going to die, he thought when she obeyed

instantly. Her small tongue and mouth drew earnestly on his finger until he had to pull away.

"Good," he choked. "Very good. I think you've earned . . . something to bolster your practice. You may open your eyes and you may kiss me . . . but," he used his damp finger to lift her chin, "if you cannot make me respond to your mouth, we may have to devise a suitable punishment. So, kiss well . . . but only once."

Mary drew a deep breath and stood on her tiptoes, balancing with her hands still behind her back. He looked so stern, so professor-like, but she saw the sleepy warmth of his blue eyes before he lowered his thick lashes.

One kiss . . . one kiss to make him respond. It was a bold challenge, and she focused with determination on his mouth. She realized that he didn't give instruction on how long the kiss could be and decided to use that omission to her advantage. Then she stared up at him and considered . . . *He expects me to be soft and gentle, but what if I kiss him like he's kissed me—deep and hard?* The thought was heady and made that funny ache he'd described in her belly burn more fiercely. She slammed her mouth into his, causing him to start backward, but she followed, not breaking contact with the firm line of his lips. She slanted her head and increased the pressure, running the tip of her tongue against his closed mouth back and forth, again and again, until, with a hoarse sound from the back of his throat, he opened his lips to her, as if against his will. She kissed him with triumph, a long, sultry play that melted his composure and had him gasping as if he'd run a mile in a snow-filled field. When she had to stop to breathe, she stepped back, her heart pounding, and she knew she had succeeded. Whatever he'd experienced in the past, whether with Carol or whoever, she doubted he'd been as undone by a kiss as he was now.

"How was that, Professor Lyons?" she purred in low tones.

He glared at her fiercely, then straightened his glasses and gasped for breath, his pupils large and dilated. Then he gave her a wicked smile and bowed his head in acknowledgment. "A-plus, *Frau* Lyons. An A-plus in oral deportment."

Mary pulled her hands from behind her back and resisted the urge to clap. Instead, she turned, then flung him a saucy look over her shoulder as she picked up her wash bucket. "We'd better hurry, Jude. We can't spend all day kissing when you've got a school to prepare."

She laughed out loud and ducked when he threw an eraser her way, then started busily on wiping down the desks, a song in her heart.

Jude could barely think straight. He felt as though he was moving outside of himself, watching his body sweep and mend and clean the schoolroom—and the feeling had nothing to do with his sugar levels. He wished it did, though, so that he could get over the strange sensation that he was powerless when his wife chose to kiss him the way she had.

"I think we need a coat of paint on this back wall," he said aloud, abruptly breaking into his own thoughts and startling Mary as she was washing the blackboards. "Yes, paint," he went on. "Yellow."

"All right."

She was looking at him as if he'd gone off the deep end. *But if I don't get out of this torture chamber with her, our first time is going to be on a dusty wood plank floor, and I'll never be able to teach here without thinking of her and . . .*

"Let's go." He dropped the broom he held with a clatter and scooped up her bonnet, handing it to her. "We'll go to Ben Kauffman's; he's sure to have paint. And yellow is cheerful, right?"

He hustled her out to the sled, untied the bishop's horse, and set the cutter into quick motion.

"Are you all right?" he heard her venture when he'd started to whistle to distract himself from her delicate scent.

No . . . not all right. Three kisses . . . one more to go. How exactly did I think this was self-discipline? How am I supposed to get through another kiss like the last one?

He stopped whistling. "I'm fine, really." *Liar . . .*

He couldn't think of anything sensible to say, so he was silent with his thoughts until they arrived at Ben's store. The front of the building was crowded, as usual, and he found a length of post to tie up the horse and then reached to swing Mary out of the sled.

Do it now, his mind whispered. *Right . . . one kiss . . . in public . . . no problem.* He let her slight form slide against his as he eased her to the ground, then bent his head to kiss her. He was unprepared for the gentle arms that twined about his neck in response and the soft sound she made when his lips touched hers. He groaned against her mouth and forgot that they were standing in front of a busy store. His hands found the curve of her back of their own accord and he rocked his weight against her so that they were pressed against the side of the sled. He felt her push her hips against him and everything was lost.

"Don't," he moaned softly. "Dear *Gott*, don't move, Mary."

"But I can't help it," she breathed.

He caught the ridge of the sled with his bare hands, gripping it painfully hard. "Oh, Mary . . . I want . . . do you think . . ."

"Hey, not in front of my store, you two!"

Jude felt as if he'd been doused in a bucket of ice water as the sound of Ben Kauffman's cheerful voice broke the moments of intimacy with his wife. Jude lifted his head slowly to see Ben grinning at him from the porch of the store. Then he realized that interested faces were pressed against the front glass windows and he shielded Mary with his body and rolled his eyes.

"What do the *Englischers* say?" Ben laughed. "Get a room? *Ach*, but you two are still courting . . . I must say I've never seen it done that way before."

Jude threw him a sour look and found his voice. "We've come for yellow paint."

"Uh-huh," Ben called. "You've come for something."

Jude straightened Mary's bonnet and decorously offered her his arm. She took it and he was happy to see that she looked flushed but amused by the whole scene.

Then he led her up the steps and past the jovial storekeeper and myriad smiles and whispers of customers as he found his way, mercifully, to the paint section.

"Professor Lyons, wait!" One of Ben Kauffman's sons, Daniel, who made the run to the bottom of the mountain for the mail every few days, caught up with them breathlessly as they finally left the crowded store.

"A letter for you."

"*Danki*, Dan." Jude took the envelope, recognizing his mother's handwriting.

He smiled at the boy and turned to tuck Mary into the cutter. Then he decided on impulse to open the letter instead of waiting until later. He read the brief missive with increasing surprise, then turned to Mary.

"What's wrong?" she asked.

"Nothing . . . maybe everything." He turned the letter over to look at the postmark and groaned aloud. "My mother will be at the bottom of the mountain—tomorrow. She's decided to come for Thanksgiving."

"*Ach*, that's *wunderbaar*," Mary exclaimed, genuine enthusiasm in her voice.

Jude turned to look at her. "Can you picture my mother hiking up this mountain? And where will she stay?"

"Joseph can sleep on the couch—she can have his room."

"How nice for Joseph."

"It'll be an experience." Mary patted his hand reassuringly.

Jude nodded in grim agreement. "That's what I'm afraid of."

Chapter Thirty-Nine

"Everything is simply charming, Mary. And I do appreciate your brother giving up his room—Joseph, is it? Yes, well, and your father is wonderfully amusing with his harrumphing around, rather like one of those old elephants in *The Jungle Book*, don't you think?"

Mary smiled, enjoying her mother-in-law's chatter as she changed the bedding in Joseph's room with a light heart. The *gut* weather had held and Jude and her *bruders* had set out earlier that morning to fetch Mrs. Lyons. Mary had hoped that the older woman would be able to make it up the mountain, having forgotten that Jude's mother played tennis and jogged in Georgia, so the *buwes* had actually tired out more quickly.

Now Mary spread a blue hued Nine Patch quilt on the bed and Mrs. Lyons exclaimed in pleasure. "I suppose you made this, darling?"

Mary gave a shy nod as something tender crossed the other woman's face.

"Look at how close together these stitches are—

you have so much patience. I suppose you'll make a wonderful mother."

"I—uh . . ."

"Oh, forgive me, honey. I know you Amish are shy, right? And I do understand that you're doing this strange month-long abstinence thing to practice courting or something that Jude was explaining to me on the way up here. Whatever—as long as you're both happy. You are happy with my son, aren't you, Mary?"

"*Ach, jah* . . . I cannot begin to explain how much I . . ."

Lydia waved her hand, visible tears in her eyes, and Mary stumbled to a stop.

"I want Jude to have a marriage—a life—like I didn't have with Ted. Do you know he's actually come round several times to the house I inherited from my father? He says he's changed—that he loves me, but I know him—he wants what he cannot have. But for Jude, I want so much more, and you, with all of your Amish culture and fascination and heart, are exactly what I want for my son—I can feel it."

"Thank you," Mary said gravely. She wished she might ask more about Jude's father but it didn't seem an appropriate time so she stood, fingering the quilt and waiting for Mrs. Lyons to compose herself.

Instead, Mrs. Lyons gave a huge sneeze and then sought her pocket for a tissue. "Oh, my sinuses . . . I could feel them getting worse the whole trip up here. I do hope I'm well for Thanksgiving."

Mary gave her a sympathetic look. "If you'd like,

we could go see *Grossmuder* May . . . she'll help you, I'm sure."

"Ah—ahchoo! Well, is that the local doctor?" Lydia sniffed.

"Sort of . . . she's more of a healer. We have to leave the mountain for really serious things."

"Oh, a naturalist! I'd love to go, if we can get an appointment."

Mary smiled with confidence. "I'm sure we can."

Jude invited Joseph and Edward to the bishop's house for coffee after seeing his mother safely ensconced with Mary. But Edward made an excuse and slipped away, leaving Jude and Joseph alone while Bishop Umble and his wife were out on a call.

Jude brought the coffeepot to the table and offered Joseph a mug. It was the first time he'd really talked alone with his *bruder*-in-law and he felt a bit awkward. Joseph, like many *Amisch* men, appeared to be a very private person. Jude wanted to thank him for the secret work he knew was being done on his cabin, but he'd given his word to keep Mary's surprise intact.

"What's it like out there?" Joseph asked, so abruptly that Jude nearly burned his mouth on his sip of coffee.

"Out there?"

Joseph shrugged his broad shoulders. "You know, out in the real world."

"I guess I think this world is real enough," Jude said, his mind on the fulfilling lives the Mountain

Amisch led, but then he saw the bleakness in Joseph's eyes. "What do you want to know?"

Joseph sighed. "Truth to tell, I get restless lately. I—I see you and Mary together, how happy she is, and I feel lonely. I've tried to pray on it, but nothing new ever seems to happen here."

"Have you ever been off the mountain?"

"Twice . . . once when I broke my arm and had to go to the hospital, and another time when we took a family trip to Cape May, New Jersey. I was about six . . . *Mamm* hadn't had Mary yet."

Jude was surprised at how sheltered a life the other man had led. *But what is he really missing? Traffic and stress and bad television . . .*

"I should be married already, as the eldest, but all the girls here . . . well, I either grew up with them or they've, well, turned to someone else." His tone lowered as if in despair.

"Joseph, was there a girl here that you . . ."

Jude watched him run a hand across the back of his neck as if it pained him. "It don't matter now."

"Sure it does—if you got hurt, no wonder you want to get away." Jude tried to put heart into his voice, wanting badly to cheer up this new member of his family.

Joseph took a long drink of his coffee, then set the mug back on the table and got up to reach for his coat. "*Danki* for listening, Professor."

Jude wanted to say more but was hesitant to break the new confidence that Joseph had shared. *Maybe he'll talk again sometime . . .* "Hey, Joe—anytime. All right? Anytime at all."

Joseph nodded and slipped out the front door, leaving Jude alone to consider the conversation.

The path curved up a small hill laden with wintergreen berries and holly. Somehow, *Grossmuder* May's cabin always seemed inviting, no matter the season. An old hound dog, Rusty Joe, bayed out a welcome from the front porch and the door opened as Mary put her foot on the first of the steps.

"Well, child, have you brought another *Englischer* to your heart this season?"

Mary couldn't contain the blush that stained her cheeks as she remembered the seemingly long-ago blessing of her marriage bed. She hastened to offer Mrs. Lyons a hand up the steps when she sneezed again and Mary avoided *Grossmuder* May's direct gaze.

"*Nee* . . . er . . . I mean . . . This is Jude's *mamm*, *Frau* Lyons. She's come for the Thanksgiving holiday but is having a bit of trouble with her nose."

Lydia smiled, then blew her nose. "Oh, Miss May, I'd shake your hand but I think it would be rude to possibly infect you with my germs."

Grossmuder May gave a grave nod, then held the wooden door wide. "*Kumme. Kumme* in, mother of Jude, and we'll see what ails you."

Mary followed, ducking under the dried herbs and flowers that hung from the cabin's interior rafters, and took a deep breath in appreciation. The delicious smell of cinnamon and other spices came from a black cast-iron pot boiling cheerfully over an open fire in the stone fireplace. And two chairs were drawn up in a cozy fashion near the warm flames.

Mary could remember feeling enveloped in all her senses when she'd come here for healing as a child. It was no less welcoming a home now, and she was glad when Mrs. Lyons took one of the seats near the fire and *Grossmuder* May bent close to examine the woman. Mary sat down at the simply carved wooden table and let her eyes wander over the many shelves filled with boxes and bottles and the occasional seashell—all tokens of a long life well lived by the old *Amisch* woman.

"Yer sinus cavities are draining like a swollen creek," *Grossmuder* May pronounced after a few moments.

"And I never thought to get my prescription allergy meds filled," Mrs. Lyons groaned.

"Ha! You need a poultice and some herbals and you'll be right as rain, or at least your nose will be. Now, let me see . . ."

Mary caught the look her mother-in-law threw her after *Grossmuder* May spoke, and Mary shrugged.

"Uh, Miss May . . . excuse me, but what do you mean, at least my nose will be? What else do you think is wrong with me?" Lydia asked.

Grossmuder May snorted. "Hmmm . . . well, yer heart's broke." The old woman drew a bundle of herbs down.

Mary watched Mrs. Lyons put a hand to her chest in alarm and felt a vague shadow of fear herself.

Grossmuder May waved her hand. "Not yer real ticker, yer heart in your mind, in your soul."

Mary struggled to grasp what the healer was getting at, then noticed that Lydia had bowed her head and her shoulders were shaking with sobs.

Mary rose in confusion and dismay, wanting to go to the other woman.

"Sit, child," *Grossmuder* May snapped.

Mary sat.

Grossmuder May went to Jude's mother and put an aged hand on her shoulder.

"Oh, Miss May . . . you are so astute. My heart is broken—I do so miss my father," Lydia cried.

"Him too," *Grossmuder* May agreed.

Lydia Lyons stopped crying and lifted her head. Mary saw her stare up at the other woman, a grim expression coming over her face.

"Yes," she said quietly after a moment. "I miss Ted. I miss the man I married—everything I hoped for and dreamed of and believed in . . . but I lost him long ago."

Grossmuder May nodded. "And it might be that yer cryin' now because you never mourned those losses. He hurt yer heart."

"Yes."

Mary watched the strange tableau being played out before the fire and thought how sad it was that Jude's *fater* could not or would not change. *But some people, even with much prayer, never change.* She knew in her heart that Jude had not mourned for the father he'd never had and wondered at the pain he seemed to be able to carry so well. But perhaps it was all beneath the surface, like his mother's . . .

She sighed to herself and was glad when *Grossmuder* May offered them both some spiced cider and the tension in the old cabin lifted.

Chapter Forty

The days before Thanksgiving flew by in a flurry of food preparation, and Mary was happy to see the holiday dawn bright and clear. It was unusual on the mountain to have such fine weather at this time of year, but she was grateful for it all the same. She knew her *bruders* and their friends were making fine progress on the cabin, and she hoped to somehow still keep it a secret from Jude until it was completed.

In her mind's eye she already could see how she would simply decorate the cabin and hear Jude's praise about how grateful he was after a hard day of teaching to enter their warm and cozy home. There'd be chicken 'n' dumplings simmering on the stove and homemade apple crisp for dessert to add to the sweetness of their love. Then he'd sweep her into his strong arms, showering her with warm kisses, growing more demanding until she'd surrender, feigning helplessness while he taught her the ways of love. Her heart skittered with anticipation. *Ach* . . . daydreaming wouldn't get the cake baked, and she did want it to be perfect for their first Thanksgiving together.

"So, who else is coming today?" Jude asked idly as he helped the bishop split firewood for the holiday.

Bishop Umble shot him a quick glance. "You all . . . and the Mast family."

Jude raised the axe, then froze in mid-swing. He slowly lowered the tool and stared at the older man. "You mean Mahlon Mast's family. Are you *narrisch*?"

The bishop gave him a dry smile. "*Amisch* rule 101, *buwe*, don't ask your bishop if he's crazy . . . And *nee*, I'm not. Martha and I always make it a point to invite those to Thanksgiving who have suffered particular loss over the year and also those who must come to some mutual accord. If you want to know the truth, it does bother me that Mahlon seems to hold a grudge against both you and Mary—I would like to see it resolved. And breaking bread with a man can lead to peace."

Jude blew out a breath, realizing that there was truth in the wise man's words. "All right. I don't know how Mary will feel, but I need to get to know his children for school. Maybe this will be a *gut* opportunity."

Bishop Umble clapped him on the shoulder. "A nice and very *Amisch* answer, *sohn*. I think your studies are coming along."

Jude couldn't help but smile at the praise.

* * *

Mary remembered her decision to choose to forgive when she walked into the Umbles' and saw Mahlon Mast's family assembled there. She smiled at them all and handed over the cake she carried to Jude, who came forward to meet her.

"What's under the foil?" he wanted to know, trying to take a peek as he took it from her hands.

She slapped his arm playfully. "*Ach*, one of your favorites, I think . . . pineapple upside-down cake."

She caught a quick glimpse of the flash in his blue eyes and had to look away. Her pulse quickened and her thoughts drifted again to her daydreaming earlier. Soon, very soon, her dreaming would be a reality, and she could hardly wait until they were truly man and wife.

She peeked at Jude one more time, seeing his eyes smolder at her even as he greeted his mother, then forced herself to concentrate on setting the table with the bishop's wife, Martha, and Mahlon Mast's quiet wife, Anne. She wanted to say something about missing Isaac to his *mamm*, but Anne Mast, like her husband, seemed to offer little opening for conversation. And besides, the three younger Mast children literally clung to their mother's skirt so that Mary had a hard time picking out who was who.

She placed the last fork, then went to where Sarah Mast, a girl her own age, and her *bruder* Edward were talking at the sink. Mary had never noticed before what a pretty girl Sarah was, and she had the distinct impression that she might be interrupting something romantic when Sarah stopped talking and Edward sent a faint frown in Mary's direction when she approached. Quick to take the hint, Mary went back to the table as the bishop invited everyone to find a seat on the long benches there.

The Mast family inevitably huddled close together, except Sarah, who sat next to Edward, much to the open annoyance of both fathers present. Bishop Umble was seated at the head of the table with his wife to his right, while Abner and Joseph occupied the opposite end and Jude and Mary and Lydia Lyons were rather squeezed in the middle.

Mary couldn't help but notice that even Lydia Lyons was awkwardly silent after the bishop asked everyone to bow for a minute of silent grace. The normal homey chatter of goodwill was certainly missing from this gathering, Mary observed sadly to herself. Then Jude spoke up in a clear voice.

"*Kumme*, let's all go around the table and each person say what he or she is thankful for this day."

Mary turned to smile at her husband. She knew he would never allow awkward silence in his classroom or at a holiday dinner.

"I'll start," Jude said in a serious tone. He was discreetly studying Mahlon Mast's three youngest children, who appeared to be about five, seven, and ten. He decided that they could probably use a good laugh, so he paused dramatically in his words. "I am thankful for . . . the stripes on skunks."

Jude had the satisfaction of gaining everyone's attention and saw a surprised look in the youngest child's eyes. "I'm also thankful for . . . grumpy old men, too-tight suspenders, my boots, my wife, my wife's boots, ladder-back chairs, soap, *Grossmuder*

May's garlic poultices, our dog Bear—who eats bears—and the dust balls behind every couch."

Mrs. Umble looked so affronted at this last outlandish comment that he almost laughed out loud, but he held his composure and was rewarded with faint smiles from all three Mast children. He turned to his wife.

"Mary," he asked like a game show host. "What are you thankful for?" He delighted in the sparkle in her eyes and knew he wouldn't play alone for long.

"Pink reindeer, Aunti Maude's bunions, onions, bunions on onions, yellow paint, strange happenings, the rabbit's cotton tail, and goat's milk." Mary concluded her thanks with a demure nod and Jude had to smile.

The bishop cleared his throat, eyeing his wife with a grin. "What did you put in this turkey? Ahem . . . let's see, not to be outdone or underdone, as the case may be, I am thankful for . . . rats' toes, my nose, the wild fern that grows, small *kinner*, big *kinner*, *Englischers*, and my long underwear."

"Mercy!" *Frau* Umble exclaimed.

Jude looked down the table at Abner, who was laughing and who seemed about to speak when Mahlon Mast cut in angrily.

"Bishop, *Frau* Umble, *danki* for the *gut* meal. But this . . . foolishness is too close and ready to Isaac's death to be decent. You'll have to excuse us. We're leaving." He jerked his chin at his wife, who hurried to gather the children as Jude threw down his napkin.

"Mast, you've got four other *kinner* here that I see,

people who might need a little joy. Can you spare any?"

Jude watched the older man spin back on his heel. "*Nee,*" he growled. "There is none to spare." And the whole Mast clan shuffled out with their plates left full.

The door slammed and Lydia Lyons blew her nose delicately. "My, what a cheerless man . . . and those poor children, and his wife! Mercy, indeed."

But Jude had his head down. "I'm sorry," he muttered to the table at large. "I wanted to please the kids and I guess I . . ."

The bishop laid his hand down on the table with a firm slap. "Enough, *sohn.* You were earnest and true in spirit." His voice softened. "Jude, we tried."

Jude nodded and was truly thankful for Mary's hand placed softly over his. He squeezed her fingers and attempted to smile. "Yeah, we tried."

Chapter Forty-One

Jude knew he wasn't being much of a courting companion that night, but he still felt bad about dinner at the bishop's. He paced the confines of Abner's cabin living area, aware that Mary watched him with worried eyes.

"Maybe he reminds you of your *fater*," she said into the silence.

"What? Who?"

"Mahlon Mast."

He wanted to reject the thought, but he knew she was right. *Mast is a cheerless, joy-stealing individual. Those qualities do resonate with me on many levels . . .*

He sighed and sank down onto the couch next to her. "I suppose you're right. I was that unsmiling kid when I was young. My grandfather provided the diversions that saved me."

"And you simply tried to repeat that today. Is that so wrong?"

"*Nee* . . . but . . ."

"Jude," she said gently, "maybe what really troubles you is the fact that you couldn't control your *fater*'s reaction to you any more than you can control Mahlon's."

He swallowed hard. "You know me well, I guess." He turned to look at her and gathered her close for a hug. "Thank you." He was about to kiss her when Bear made a strange, strangled sound.

"What is wrong with that dog?" Jude asked in exasperation. "That's the third time in a row that he's howled. Maybe there's someone outside. I'd better take a look around—it's really late."

He went and opened the front door, and the distinctive smell of smoke wafted in on the cold night air. Bear tore out the door, barking fiercely, and Jude spotted an ominous glow in the sky behind some distant trees.

"Fire!" Jude exclaimed. "Where is that?" He was pulling on his coat as he spoke and Mary turned from running to wake her *dat* and *bruders.*

"That's our cabin, Jude," she wailed. "I'm sure of it."

"Our cabin?" And then he blinked and ran out into the night, following the eerie glow and the trail of smoke in the sky.

He ran through the paths and sometimes cut through the trees, finally approaching the cabin he'd used the previous summer. He could tell, even with the engulfing flames, how much larger it had been made, and he stared at the burning wood in dismay. Then he realized that Bear had cornered someone who was yelling for help.

"Call it off! Call off your dog!"

Jude gave a sharp whistle and Bear backed away but kept low on his haunches. In the light of the flames, Jude recognized Mahlon Mast, and something clicked in his brain. *A man could have an easy accident that time of night . . .*

"You!" Jude exclaimed. "You set this fire!"

"I did not!" Mahlon screeched. "I saw the light and came to help put it out."

"I should let Bear have at you."

"Nee, nee." Mahlon held his hands up in front of him. "I'm telling the truth."

"Yeah, right. I'm going to . . ." One of the taller side walls of the cabin collapsed and fell outward, sending sparks drifting toward the tall pines and coming dangerously close to the two men. Bear yelped as Jude automatically pushed Mahlon out of harm's way. Both men slipped and fell in the snow as Bear circled around them, barking.

"The trees," Mahlon cried out. "If the fire spreads, it could take the whole mountaintop!"

Jude scrambled to his feet as Mast did the same. "How do we put it out?"

"Others will come soon. We need a bucket line from the creek."

"We can start with snow," Jude yelled. He ran to the small shed and grabbed two buckets, tossing one back to Mast. Then they began to scoop up snow and throw it at the ever-consuming fire.

Soon Jude became aware that many men, women, and teenagers were there—practically the whole community—and orderly bucket lines were formed from the creek to the burning cabin. He got a glimpse of his mother in one of the lines, wearing a large black *Amisch* man's coat, and then his eyes sought the crowd for Mary.

He saw her, small but sturdily trudging with a

bucket toward the secret home she'd planned for him, even though it was apparent that all was lost. He thought about how she must be feeling, and then he knew the familiar, engulfing blackness of his lowered blood sugar and he collapsed, helpless to do otherwise, on the wet and muddy ground.

"How long has he been doing this?"

The white-coated doctor's tone was brisk and Mary looked quickly across the emergency room bed at Lydia Lyons's sooty, tearful face.

"Since he was a teenager," Jude's *mamm* answered. "But he's been to the best endocrinologist in Atlanta."

"When was his last appointment?" the doctor questioned dryly.

"He does this often, er, over the last few months," Mary supplied.

"Well, it's no longer something he can manage alone. I need to check his labs." The doctor gave a brief nod and slipped outside the yellow curtain.

A rotund, motherly-looking nurse entered. "There are some forms that need to be filled out."

Mary looked doubtfully at her mother-in-law. "I'll do it," Lydia said. "You stay here with him, Mary."

Jude began to stir a few moments later, then opened his blue eyes to peer owl-like up at her. "I can't see very well," he complained.

"Your glasses got broken when you fell," she said softly, trying to hold back tears. She hated to see him look so pale and confused.

He peered around the room. "Where am I?"

"The Coudersport Hospital emergency room."

He half tried to sit up and she pushed him back. "Please, Jude."

"What? Well, how in the world did I get here? It's twenty miles from Ice Mountain . . ."

"I know . . . my *bruders* and Mahlon Mast got you down the mountain on a sled and Mr. Ellis drove us the rest of the way."

"Mast? The fire . . ." She felt him search her face frantically. "I think Mast started the fire."

Mary shook her head. "*Nee.* Joseph says one of the younger *buwes* left some kerosene and matches where some raccoons had a bit of a play. The fire was an accident."

"How long have I been out?" he asked.

"Too long." The doctor had reappeared and gave Jude a stern look. "Your blood sugar is out of control, Professor."

Jude frowned. "I've been to the best endo—"

"I know." The doctor held up a hand. "Five years ago. Things have gotten worse since then it seems."

"I want to get up."

"You'll stop scaring your pretty wife and lie right there . . . and forgive me, I'm Dr. McCaully. Luke, actually. And before you question my diagnosis, I'm Harvard trained."

Jude lay back and visibly relaxed. "What are you doing in Coudersport, Pennsylvania?"

"I could ask you the same thing." The doctor's brown eyes twinkled at Mary. "But I think I can guess. In any case, I'm going to give you a prescription. You can fill it here. We need to get your sugar regulated. I'll see you off that mountain in my office in a month, and I want you to rest for a few days."

Mary knew what her husband was going to say before he said it. *Like an old married couple . . .* The thought made her smile.

"I can't rest for long. I start a new job on Monday."

"I'm sure the bishop will make an allowance," Mary said.

"Yeah . . . well . . ."

"Gut," the doctor quipped in perfect Penn Dutch. "Very *gut.*"

Chapter Forty-Two

"I feel fine," Jude snapped to the bishop on Saturday morning. "And where are you going, anyway?"

"Out," Bishop Umble returned in a mild tone. "And so is my *frau*—we'll be gone the whole day. You, *Herr Dokator*, behave, stay on that couch, and I'll see about having Mary drop by to visit. Besides, you can't see anyway without your glasses, and Daniel isn't running down to Mr. Ellis until this afternoon to get your new ones. So sit still."

Jude scowled and laid his head back after the Umbles had gone. He felt restless but, he had to admit, not quite himself. The medication would take some adjusting to; it made him drowsy, but he wasn't good at waiting . . . *except when it comes to my wife.* He smiled and drifted off into a pleasant lassitude.

Mary entered the Umble house on quiet feet. She knew where everyone was going that day, but she had no desire for Jude to guess, so she decided to keep his mind—*and maybe his hands*—occupied.

But when she saw his big body sprawled on the Umbles' small couch, a crocheted afghan tangled around his waist and his white *Amisch* shirt half-undone, she knew that she'd truly have to focus to achieve her goal and not be swept up by emotion . . . or sensation . . . herself.

She approached the couch and knelt down by his outstretched arm. He was obviously dreaming of something enjoyable because a half smile played about his perfect lips and there was a heady flush on his handsome cheeks as he moved slightly, arching his back.

She put out a finger and trailed it across his large hand. His nails were neat and short, as always, and she tested the calluses that had formed across the pads of his palm, reveling in his strength but also seeing the fragility of life in his relaxed grip. He was only man, only flesh and blood and bone, and she'd been so worried about him the night they took him to the hospital. She realized that she couldn't imagine her life now without him, and the thought shook her. She bit her lip and looked up to find his blue eyes open and sleepy . . . and heated.

"Dreaming about you," he slurred with a smile.

"What about?"

He shook his head. "Mmm . . . can't tell."

"*Jah*, you can," she whispered, liking to see him so relaxed yet obviously aroused.

"We were on a beach alone. You were on my lap with the water all around us . . . it was so nice, so wet." He sighed and closed his eyes, nestling his head deeper into his pillow.

She touched his arm after his breathing evened out. "Jude?"

She smiled when he didn't answer, then got up to pull a chair close to him, content to watch him dream.

By Monday morning, Jude insisted on being up. Even Mary's pleas fell on deaf ears as he pulled on his heavy coat. The bishop and his wife were gone from the house once more, as they'd been on Saturday, and Jude felt the curious sensation that he was missing out on something.

He adjusted his new glasses and handed Mary her cloak. "Let's go for a walk. Only a short one," he amended when she began to protest. "We'll go over to the store. I need some exercise, Mary, especially if I'm going to open school Wednesday."

She agreed reluctantly, fidgeting with the closure on her cloak. He reached down to do it for her and lifted her chin with his fingertips. "Why are you so nervous?"

She avoided his eyes. "I . . . um . . . we're alone. Do you want to make out?"

He smiled, mystified. "Normally I'd be jumping at that offer, Mrs. Lyons, but something tells me I shouldn't. Now let's go, woman."

She took his hand with a sigh and let him lead her out the door. As they walked, he enjoyed the mountain smell of the brisk, cold air and kept up a pleasant conversation that left little room for Mary to try to dissuade him from going to Ben's store.

But to his amazement, when they arrived at the Kauffmans', the store was marked with a large Closed sign on the front window.

"Closed? On a Monday . . . it is Monday, right?" He turned to look at Mary, who was biting her lip again.

"*Jah*, it's Monday," she murmured.

He put his hands on his hips. "All right, sweetheart, what's going on? Is the community having a vote to kick me out or something?"

"*Nee, ach, nee*—it's nothing like that, really."

"Uh-huh . . . then tell me what's going on, *sei se gut*."

She gave a frustrated sigh. "*Ach*, I was supposed to keep you occupied."

"Mary, *kumme* on."

"All right, I'll show you, but we'll have to go through the trees and we cannot let anyone see us."

"Okaay . . . is it some strange *Amisch* ritual I don't know about where *Grossmuder* May dresses up like a cat and dances in a hexagon?"

She laughed. "*Nee*."

"*Gut* . . . I don't want to find out I've joined a bunch of crazies even if the rest of the *Amisch* world finds you mountain people to be odd."

She smiled up at him, displaying perfect, white teeth. "Am I odd?"

He bent and kissed her nose. "You're beautiful . . . now, let's go." He gave her a playful swat on her bottom and she squeaked, then took off toward the woods. He had to hurry to catch up with her.

Mary had only ever seen one barn raising in her lifetime, but many cabins had been built by the community. Still, as she pressed down the snow-crusted branches of an old pine and peered at the industry of her people, moving in masterful unison, her heart was struck by the beauty and symmetry of the working men. And the women worked together too, preparing food over open fires and stirring brews of hot cider and hot chocolate while laughing and talking. She could even see Jude's *mamm* carrying a tray of mugs while looking pretty in a white outfit with a fur-edged vest.

Mary heard Jude's breath behind her and pushed the branches down another inch so that he might see better.

"They're rebuilding our cabin," he said in hoarse wonder.

Mary nodded, feeling tears fill her eyes at the emotion in his voice. "It was to have been a surprise . . ."

She felt him slide his hands around her waist, lacing them in front of her belly as he leaned his chin on top of her bonnet. "I'm sorry I pestered it out of you, sweetheart . . . I can't believe . . . I've never had a whole community come together like this . . . for me . . . for us."

She smiled. "That's what it is to be *Amisch.*"

"Well, it's not *Amisch* to be sneaking around while men are trying to work," a low voice growled, and Mary moved in Jude's arms to see Mahlon Mast standing behind them in the trees.

Jude turned around to slowly face Mast, easing Mary tight against his side. The other man wore no hat and had on a work apron filled with tools; he also carried a hammer.

"Why are you here?" Jude asked, keeping his voice low and level.

"Why do you think I'm here? Can't you see with them glasses? I'm helpin' build your cabin."

"But why?" Jude asked again. "And why, even after I blamed you for the fire, did you help get me down the mountain the night I went to the hospital?"

Mast gave a sullen shrug. "Stupid *Englischer*. What else was I to do?"

Something about being called stupid and being reminded that he was the outsider struck Jude hard and he swallowed as a terrible rage swept through him.

"You know, Mast, I've known one other man like you in my life—my father. He too can't forgive, can't forget. He hates because that's all he knows inside—he wants what he cannot have and has what he does not want . . . And I don't care if you don't want me here, I'm here. I'm alive and it's too bad that I didn't die, it's too bad that I'm not what you want . . . what you'll ever accept . . ." Jude became aware that he was yelling and that Mary was pulling on his sleeve. He felt a wave of nauseous dizziness and started to tilt forward, realizing he was screaming at Mast as if he were his father. It was too much, and he gave in to the swamping desire to collapse, but felt Mahlon Mast's arms catch and hold him from the ground. He heard Mary's frightened cry and then Mast leaned close to him and spoke in a choked whisper. "I'm sorry—Jude."

Chapter Forty-Three

For the second time in less than five days, Jude woke, not sure exactly where he was. Then he recognized the Umbles' afghan and sighed aloud as remnants of his fit with Mahlon Mast came back to him.

"Jude?"

He turned to peer up at Mary. "We have to stop meeting like this."

"You—have to stop scaring me like this!" Her voice broke and Jude caught her hand, drawing it to his lips.

"I'm sorry, sweetheart."

"As you should be."

Jude couldn't believe his ears. He blinked and stared around Mary's waist to see Mahlon Mast sitting in a chair beside the couch. The older man looked red-faced and harassed, but there was something different in his eyes, something calm, that gave Jude pause.

Mary let go of his hand and stepped away, and

Jude swallowed hard. "I guess I owe you an apology, Mast."

"Mahlon," the older man corrected him absently.

"Mahlon." Jude found it wasn't so hard to say once he'd let go of a little pride. "I'm sorry. I, uh, have some problems with my father. And I suppose he's about your age, so for whatever reason, I . . ."

Mahlon shook his head. "Don't need to explain. My *fater* too was a . . . hard man. Broke my spirit long ago, but you still got some left, *buwe.* Hang on to it." He drew out a red handkerchief and blew his nose fiercely.

Jude was quiet. Hearing the years of abuse that had probably been heaped on the other man as it had been piled on him—it gave him a strange feeling of kinship with Mahlon, as if he were a stranger no longer.

"Well," Mahlon said, slapping his hands to his knees. "I'd best git back to yer cabin. We should have it done by tomorrow. And . . . my *kinner* will see you Wednesday, if yer up to it to be teaching."

Jude extended his hand and Mahlon took it in a fierce grip, then stomped away and out the door.

Mary wiped her eyes and stepped back in Jude's line of vision after Mahlon had gone.

"That was . . . odd," Jude said, a half smile on his lips.

"But I think it was *Gott*'s plan." She handed him his glasses.

He slid them on and nodded. "I suppose—and at least it showed me how much anger and hurt I have in regard to my father. I wonder if you ever get over something like that or if it keeps on hurting forever?"

She felt her eyes well with tears again. "I don't like the thought of you hurting forever—I believe when *Gott* says He can make all things new—not that you'll ever have a relationship with your *fater*, but maybe that *Derr Herr* can make your heart new, your thoughts and feelings new."

"My wise *Amisch frau* . . ." He held out a hand to her and she took it, letting him pull her down to sit on him sideways as he reclined on the couch. He reached up to thumb his way across her cheek, making her feel fragile as she leaned into his hand. "Do you know how many days are left until you can become my wife in every sense of the word?"

She shook her head. "I forgot to count."

He bounced his hips a bit, jiggling her. "Shame on you . . . Well, I know—after today, it'll be twelve."

She mentally counted, then giggled when she lost track. "Almost two weeks. What are you going to do to—discipline yourself until then?"

He stretched beneath her. "Oh, I don't know. Teach . . . bathe in the creek . . . court and bathe in the creek . . . learn my Penn Dutch and . . ."

"Bathe in the creek?" she questioned, leaning over to put her weight on his chest.

"Yep."

She bent to kiss him, slow and deep, until he arched against her, all hard pressure and leashed power. She ran her hands across his chest. "I love you, Jude Lyons."

"And I love you, Mary Lyons . . . Now, how about that suggestion of making out?"

She bounced off him abruptly.

"Hey," he groaned. "*Kumme* back."

"*Nee.*" She shook her head. "My offer to make out was simply to divert you, nothing else."

"Now who's *Frau* Teaser?"

"Me," she laughed, then turned to go to the kitchen to get him his medicine.

Early Wednesday morning, Jude hugged his mother in a tight grip. "Be careful going down, all right? Tell the driver to be careful on these mountain roads. And, Mom, thanks for all you've done here. I'm really proud to have you visit—anytime."

"Anytime," Mary echoed, enjoying the embrace of the older woman.

"You're darlings, both of you." Lydia smiled, her eyes shining with happy tears. "And remember, after this whole courting thing—well, I'll expect the grandchildren to come for Christmas with you now and then."

Jude smiled at Mary's flustered response and then watched Joseph and Edward head off down the mountain with his mom walking easily in between.

"She's different," he said once they were out of sight. "More fun and relaxed." He didn't add the reason . . . Mary understood it well enough.

He cleared his throat. "Want to come to the Umbles' for breakfast? The bishop says he's got some tips for me before I start teaching today . . . it ought to be interesting."

"I'd like to, but the women and I are having a paint frolic today at our cabin, remember?"

He reached down to pull her close. "Are you using yellow paint, by any chance?"

"*Nee*—light blue."

"Hmmm . . . very *Amisch.*" He nuzzled her neck.

"I hope you'll like it."

"I'd like you."

"I know," she whispered, hiding her face for a moment in his dark coat.

He smiled and squeezed her tight. "Have fun, then."

She nodded and he watched her walk off, Bear tagging behind, and then he turned back to the Umbles'.

"I'm not saying it has to be a big production." The bishop waved his piece of toast like a conductor. "Something small is *gut*, but fun . . . everyone expects some fun."

Jude took a bite of his scrambled eggs and tried to control the rising panic he felt inside. "You mean to tell me that I start teaching today and there's a community school Christmas program on the twentieth? That's two weeks to get nineteen kids into some sort of holiday theme—it is not a recipe for fun, I'll tell you that. You're going to get recitations and 'Silent Night' and that's about all."

"*Ach*, well . . ." Bishop Umble shook his head regretfully. "I thought you were made of sterner stuff."

Jude knew he was rising to the bait but he didn't care. "Do you remember my idea of fun at Thanksgiving? That went over well."

The bishop laughed. "Mahlon likes you now."

"Yeah . . . right."

"*Kumme* on, *buwe.* Buck up! How hard can it be for a wise professor like yourself to get nineteen kids in order in two weeks' time? It'll be no problem."

Jude chewed his eggs. *Yeah . . . no problem.*

Mary wielded the paintbrush with an expert hand. She loved to paint, and having the other women of the community laughing and talking throughout the cabin made the work all the more fun. She turned to the paint bucket and dipped her brush in at the same time as someone else. She looked up with a smile to see Sarah Mast, the girl she'd thought Edward might be interested in at Thanksgiving.

Sarah looked even paler than usual and Mary caught her hand, drawing the brush from the other girl's grip. "Sarah, let's walk outside for a breath of fresh air. These paint fumes are heavy."

Sarah agreed with visible reluctance and Mary hurried her out, grabbing their cloaks as she went. They walked a bit away from the new cabin, beyond the happy couplets of women laughing while they worked washing windows. Mary impulsively put a hand on Sarah's arm when they were out of earshot of any potential listeners.

"Sarah, forgive me if I'm wrong, but I saw you and Edward at the Umbles' at Thanksgiving, and I thought—well, I—he seemed to like you."

Sarah paled even further. "*Jah,* we've been seeing each other."

"But that's *gut,* right?" Mary asked, not understanding the strange expression on the other girl's face.

Sarah's blue eyes welled with sudden tears. "*Jah,* it would be, but—but—he's leaving."

Mary stared at her in consternation. "What do you mean—leaving?"

"He's leaving after the holidays to go work the Marcellus Shale rigs. He wants to make money so we can get married, but I fear that it will change him to leave the mountain."

Mary tried to picture Edward out on the gas rigs . . . She knew it was hard labor and that the *Englisch* men might be even harder, but Edward was strong. Yet she couldn't imagine life without her middle *bruder.*

"*Sei se gut,* don't tell anyone, Mary. Edward did not want me to speak of it—no one knows we're even courting, of course."

Mary caught her hand. "Of course I won't—though I might tell Jude. He won't say anything, and perhaps he can talk to Edward . . . see if there's some other way around this idea of making money to marry."

"I've tried to talk him out of it, but . . . he, well, he doesn't get on well with my *fater,* and he wants to be independent."

"Of course," Mary agreed. They turned in mutual accord to walk back to the cabin, but the day had lost some of its fun as Mary considered her *bruder*'s decision.

* * *

Jude gazed at the students of all ages staring back at him and knew he'd never been as nervous, even teaching at the university level. There were all grades represented, from first through eighth . . . and probably one or two younger than first who'd been sent along by their *mamms* for good measure.

"Herr Dokator?" One little boy raised a thin hand.

I might as well start where I mean to begin . . . Jude shook his head slightly. "Let's all work on speaking English, shall we? The bishop told me that was his wish this morning. So, you may call me Professor Lyons."

The little boy tried again. "Professor Lyons?"

"*Ja*—yes?"

"Mother says I have an awful nervous stomach, and there was something funny tasting about that scrapple we ate this morning—I think I'm going to . . ."

Jude moved fast with the waste can, but not fast enough. He got his boots splattered in the unfortunate process and sent the boy outside to clean up at the pump.

Later, he'd consider it the highlight of the day because everything went downhill from there. Girls cried over his being a male teacher, boys looked disgusted, got bored, and had to be restrained from wrestling, and the scrapple from breakfast made a second visit to the classroom. Jude, opening the windows and taking slow breaths, decided he'd well earn his pay and thought with brief longing of the steers in the Umbles' feed yard.

Chapter Forty-Four

Mary stroked Jude's hair as he lay with his head buried in his arms at her *dat*'s kitchen table. It was late Wednesday and she knew that he was tired as well as discouraged.

"Was it really that bad?" she asked softly.

"Worse," he mumbled, not lifting his head. "And I've got to get that rabble organized for the whole community to see. I'm used to talking to college kids, and besides, the littlest ones are terrified of me, I think."

Mary sighed. "The bishop didn't tell you that the last teacher left, did he?"

Jude turned his head to open one eye at her. "What? Why?"

"Well, *Amisch* schools are usually very ordered and the children extremely well-behaved. But the *kinner* here on the mountain have run a bit wild and are probably spoiled to some extent. Teachers have come and gone, and past Christmas programs have not been . . . all that *wunderbaar*."

He lifted his head. "Really?"

"Jah."

"I guess I've been setting it up in my mind as this big thing that I have to do to prove myself to the community."

"But, Jude," she answered gently. "You don't have to seek approval . . . you're accepted here—you're part of us. The *Amisch* talk of community sometimes as grains of wheat being sifted together to make a single batch of bread—each one contributes what he or she can, and all work together to create something nourishing."

He adjusted his glasses and thought for a minute. "Yeah . . . but we both know that *Amisch* communities aren't perfect. They're idealized, certainly, but people are people, with all of their flaws and shortcomings, *Amisch* or *Englisch.*"

Mary nodded in agreement. "I know, but maybe you can trust that the *Amisch* do have a corner on community."

He thought of the myriad subdivisions he knew where neighbors two or three doors down never spoke to each other, simply pulled their expensive cars in and out of their garages, closing their doors, closing their lives . . .

He reached over and took her hand. "All right, sweetheart. Thank you—I've got trust issues when it comes to being accepted."

"I'll always accept you," she said solemnly.

It was a simple declaration, given with ease and love, yet it shook him to the core. He turned to gather her close in his arms, pressing his lips against her forehead in a fervent kiss. *Thank God for her . . . thank You, God . . .*

* * *

"Professor Lyons?" The little boy who'd baptized the floor his first day of school raised his hand and Jude automatically grabbed the waste can.

"Yes, Rob? Are you sick?"

"No, sir. I wanted to ask if we could make some decorations for the Christmas program. My *mamm*—uh, mother said she'd make some raisin-filled cookies to bring if I do a good job."

There were some murmurs from other students, citing their own mothers' promises for snacks, and Jude considered the idea of decorations. *I need my mother here, and her interior design people . . .*

One of the older girls, Tabitha, raised her hand and he called on her. "I know how to make garland out of construction paper, and we could do red Christmas roses out of tissue—if we had some. And, Professor, what are we actually going to be doing?"

The oldest boy, Daniel, who fetched the mail, raised a hand with some hesitancy. "Uh, my dad always says to come get what we need from the store . . . I've been working on carving a crèche with him and some of the other fellas—maybe we can display that at the program."

Jude smiled. "That's great, Dan. Yes, as a matter of fact, I'll stop by your dad's store on my way home tonight and get everything we need. Tabitha, make a list please. And I'll—uh—have what we're going to do for the program ready for you tomorrow." *And I'll persuade my wife to help me figure that out.*

He watched as even the older children gathered around Tabby and offered suggestions for her to write down, and then he remembered Mary's description of the wheat kernels and the bread. The small community of his classroom was beautifully proving her analogy. He decided that maybe being the schoolteacher might not be so bad after all.

Jude was on his way to Mary's for a night of courting and classroom planning when he met Joseph along the moonlit trail. Joseph carried a lantern, which he swung in a disconsolate manner that caught Jude's attention.

"What's up, Joe?"

Joseph sighed and turned to walk with him slowly, back toward Abner's home. "Edward is leaving to work on the rigs."

"Mary told me. I've been looking for a chance to talk to him, but nothing's come up. He's elusive at times."

"*Jah* . . . he is that. I've decided with *Dat* that I can't let him go off alone. I'm worried that he'd be too easily influenced by the outside world, and he's moody enough to get himself into trouble working with *Englischers*—no offense meant."

"None taken." Jude smiled. "I'm becoming *Amisch*, remember?"

"Sorry, I know."

Jude thought as they walked. "So, are you really going for Edward, or is this a *gut* way for you to escape the mountain too?"

Joseph half laughed. "Mary says you're smart . . . it's both reasons, I guess."

"And you're afraid that it's you who might not want to come back?"

"Right . . . what happens if I go out there and find that it's better for me?"

Jude stopped and Joseph paused with him, staring down at the ground.

"Look, Joe, I am not great at understanding and knowing all the faith stuff yet, but aren't we supposed to believe that *Gott* leads us, gives us direction and has an individual purpose for our lives?"

"You've been studying to some purpose, I'd say . . . *Jah*, you're right. *Danki* for the reminder."

Jude laughed ruefully as they walked on. "Believe me, it's something I need to learn better myself."

Joseph clapped him on the shoulder. "Well, whatever the plan, I'm glad that you were brought here to be my *bruder*-in-law."

"You have no idea how much that means to me. Thanks, Joe."

They walked on in silent accord until the lights from the cabin came into view.

Mary was pleased to see Jude and Joseph enter the cabin together. She hoped that Jude had been able to give her *bruder* some advice since her family had finally discovered Edward's plan and Joseph's idea to go with him.

Joseph put his lantern on the table and nodded

at her. "I'll be going to bed to leave you two to your courting."

Mary looked at Jude when her brother had gone. "Did you talk?"

Jude turned from hanging up his coat and hat. "Yep. I think it's a good thing for Joseph to go, Mary."

"I don't know what *Dat* will do."

"He can live with us—we've got two extra rooms."

Mary smiled with pleasure at his easy thoughtfulness. "*Nee, danki,* Jude. I know you mean it, but even though I'm concerned about my *fater,* I have to admit that a newly married couple needs time alone for—well, time alone." She paused awkwardly and he came forward to take her into his arms.

"Time alone? Tell me what you expect from that time alone, *Frau* Lyons."

She smiled up at him, then shook her head and buried her face in his shirt, loving the fresh smell of him—like summer and pine and the outdoors.

"*Kumme* on, sweetheart. You're talking to a man who has to do some persuading tonight with you, and I need a few ideas."

She lifted her face. "Why do I need to be persuaded?"

"To help me plan the Christmas program . . . nothing big, only some ideas."

She stretched on tiptoe to reach his mouth. "My price is one kiss per idea," she breathed against his lips.

He bent his head and complied with eager warmth.

Chapter Forty-Five

One Saturday morning, Jude slept late only to wake and remember that it was December fourteenth. He could hardly believe how fast time had gone by—he had been so busy with his teaching and so exhausted by nightfall as he adjusted to the medication he'd been prescribed. *But today, I will finally make love to my wife.* He had the vague feeling that it was like Christmas morning to a child prepared to open a wonderful gift, and he had to restrain himself from laughing out loud in pure joy as he hurriedly dressed in the Umbles' spare room.

But his steps slowed as he made his way down to the kitchen. *I don't want to seem like some overeager idiot . . . maybe she'll want to simply spend some time getting to know our new home . . .* The thought dampened his spirits somewhat, but he knew that the prize was well worth the wait.

Bishop Umble greeted him with an uncharacteristic grunt and Jude raised an eyebrow in question to *Frau* Umble, who simply shrugged and carried the laundry basket out of the room.

"What's the matter?" Jude asked finally, after moments of silence, fearing there would be some new time constraint put upon him.

"If you must know," the old man sniffed, "I am going to miss you."

"Oh . . . oh, really? Wow!"

"I don't think 'wow' is in the Penn Dutch dictionary."

"It should be. Thank you—I mean, *danki.* I'll miss you too." *And I will . . . he's taught me so much . . .*

"Well." The bishop straightened his suspenders as if preparing for a big talk. "I know you might think it's not my business, but I . . ." He lowered his voice, glancing over his shoulder and back to Jude. "I wonder if you need any advice on the wedding night, since it seems that you haven't—er, didn't . . ."

Jude tried hard to keep a straight face, but then he laughed. Bishop Umble shot him a scowl, looking like he was going to erupt, then burst out laughing too. "All right, Jude, you're on your own."

"*Gut,* but really . . ." He reached across the table and grasped the old hand nearest him. "Thank you for helping me learn how to live. I won't ever forget."

"Anytime, *sohn.*"

Jude nodded and wiped the tears from his own eyes even as he smiled.

Mary paced the spacious living area of the new cabin, admiring the cheerful painting and the mermaid *fraktur* that Rachel Miller had given them as their wedding gift. Jude had brought it over the day before. Low bookshelves had been built into one wall, and Jude's books as well as her mother's Bible, cookbook, and *Wuthering Heights* were all in their proper places. Furniture had been donated by many, and the rooms were beautiful and comfortable looking, as several families had given of the best they had in antique wood pieces.

Mary couldn't help stealing a glance into the bedroom at the pristine block quilt and large log bed. Snow-white pillow shams finished off the look while her and Jude's clothes were already hung neatly on pegs on each side of the bed.

She nearly jumped when she heard the front door open with a friendly creak and turned to face Jude, who had his hat in his hands.

"Mary." His voice was low, caressing, but she sensed hesitancy in his stance. She took his coat and hat and hung them up while he worked off his boots, then went to stand before the open hearth fireplace, his broad back to her in his light blue shirt, long black pants, and dark socks.

"Are you biting your lip?" he asked without turning around.

She stopped biting her lip and choked on a giggle. "*Nee* . . . is everything all right?"

He nodded but still didn't turn to her. She wanted to move him somehow, shake him out of his reserved composure. "Are you going to make love to me in broad daylight?" *I cannot believe I said that* . . . but he'd turned and was watching her with a speculative gaze.

"Do you want me to?" he whispered.

"Do you want to?" She bit her lip again and he

crossed the room in two long strides, caught her in his arms, and bent to take her mouth with a fierce pressure that left her in little doubt of his wanting.

He carried her easily to the big bed, not breaking contact with her mouth, and she shivered in delight when he laid her on her back and started to work frantically at his suspenders and shirt with one hand. She reached to help him and he finally broke the kiss to step back and rid himself of the garment, then came back to her mouth with a hoarse sound of pleasure.

He'd meant to go slow, had rehearsed some of it in his mind both for practice and pleasure, but nothing turned out the way he planned when she spanned his bare chest with inquisitive hands. *Say something romantic, you idiot* . . . But he was tossed in a kaleidoscope of tangled clothing, ravaging heat, and soft, feminine sounds of approval.

"I don't want to hurt you," he gasped at the last possible second, holding himself poised over her, an iron rein on his need.

"You won't," she breathed.

I won't . . . He lunged, his teeth bared in his desire, and then he heard her sharp cry. He tried to stop, tried to think, and then bit out a sobbing breath as his body found the release it sought even though his mind registered that she was not with him in the pleasure.

He lay still against her for a moment, then pulled back to stare down at her. Her beautiful face was flushed, and two tiny tears stole their way down her cheeks. "O, *Gott*, Mary, I'm so sorry . . . I wanted . . ."

She reached up to press her fingers against his lips and smiled at him. "It only hurt for a moment, Jude. I'm sorry to be such a *boppli* . . . I knew there was to be some pain." She moved her hips suggestively. "But there is to be pleasure too, in the marriage bed, isn't that right?"

He kissed the two tears away and shook his head. "From now on, for always."

"Can you show me?" she asked, touching his damp hair.

Her question, one of complete trust, made him feel powerful and vulnerable at the same time, and he diligently showed her all that she wished to know and feel.

Mary stretched lazily in the big bed as she listened to the sound of her husband knocking icicles off the porch roof edge to fill the bathtub for her. She heard him haul the heavy tub indoors, then slide it into position in front of the open fire to heat. Then he came back into the bedroom.

He looked distinctly and wonderfully rumpled, his shirt half-open, his suspenders slung over the waist of his pants, and his hair, usually so perfect, stuck up on one side. But she felt his shining blue eyes, behind the dark-rimmed glasses, drink her in with a clarity that made her toes dance beneath the bed sheet that she held to her breast.

He leaned his hip against one of the end bedposts and smiled at her, a smile she recognized as both satisfied and expectant.

"Shall I play lady's maid for you, my beautiful *frau*?" he asked low.

She felt her heart begin to pound, wondering if he'd want to play after so much . . . play. The thought made her blush but she still kept her gaze level.

"Are you asking to serve me?" She raised her eyebrows and gave a haughty toss of her hair.

He grinned, then quickly lowered his lashes and dipped his head. "Yes, please. If my lady will have me . . . I'll do anything you like."

"Anything?" She kept her tone dubious.

"Yes," he whispered. "Please."

She tilted her head, considering his lean frame, then gave a brief nod, extending her hand. "You may try to please me, sir. But I must warn you that I am quite particular. I like my bath exactly right."

He reached for his shirt, shrugging it off, then moving forward with his head down to take her hand. "I'll do everything I can."

And, she thought a sated hour later, *he did* . . .

Chapter Forty-Six

"Oh," he groaned, haphazardly dressing on Monday morning. "I'm going to be late."

"Yes, Professor, you are," she purred, stretching back against the pillows.

"Minx!" He grinned at her as he snapped on his suspenders.

He started to leave the room, then had to go back to the warm bed for one last, lingering kiss.

He hustled down the path to the schoolhouse, feeling a renewed vigor about life and teaching. But when he opened the door to the cloakroom, he found it to be too quiet and he glanced around the brief partition, feeling suddenly worried.

He saw every student sitting perfectly still while the bishop sat behind the teacher's desk, accompanied by two other men he recognized as deacons.

Great . . . the school board comes to visit on the day I'm home . . . well, it was worth it.

With this pleasurable thought in mind, he walked

in with more confidence and nodded to his guests. "Bishop Umble, *Herr* Keim, *Herr* Lapp, thank you for coming. Forgive my tardiness. What would you like to know or see from the classes?"

Herr Lapp, who was a tall, ruddy, red-haired man in his mid-forties, stood with his arms crossed. Jude saw Lucy Lapp's seven-year-old legs swinging nervously at her desk. He shot her a faint smile, then returned his gaze to her father.

"It seems a teacher should be on time," *Herr* Lapp commented drily.

Jude shrugged good-naturedly. "Again, forgive me. I was kissing my wife good-bye." *Like you probably did once upon a time.* He vowed to himself right then to always kiss Mary good-bye.

Deacon Keim, a jolly fellow, choked on a sudden cough as Deacon Lapp's face reddened beneath the fall of his red hair and some of the students giggled. Jude thought he saw the bishop wink, but it could have been a trick of the morning light.

"So, gentlemen, a recitation perhaps?" Jude asked. "We've been discussing American history to an extent . . . maybe Daniel Kauffman could . . ."

"How is the Christmas program shaping up?" Deacon Lapp interrupted, obviously trying to regain level ground.

Jude smiled but felt a prick of irritation, which goaded his answer. "Given the fact that your last teacher left and I've heard that other programs have been—shall we say—not as organized as they might have been, I'd have to tell you that this group of students will give you the best program Ice Mountain has ever seen."

That's great, Lyons . . . Open your big mouth . . .

Jude avoided the bishop's sudden smile and Deacon Keim laughed out loud a bit nervously. "Well, you've got four more days to prepare. I'm sure it will go well."

"It had better," Deacon Lapp declared. "And seeing as the bishop here has laryngitis, it'll be you, Professor, who'll be giving the main address. We thought you'd want to know."

Jude's gaze swiveled to Bishop Umble, who gave a dry croak of a cough and shrugged innocently.

"Uh . . . the main address?"

"Jah." Deacon Lapp clapped his hat on his head. "And try not to be kissing your wife *kumme* this Friday, Professor. The community might grow weary waiting. Good day."

The men filed out and silence still reigned in the classroom after the back door closed. Jude walked slowly to his desk and sank into his chair, feeling deflated and worse. "Rob," he said, after a moment.

"Yes, sir?" the little boy replied.

"I think I need the waste can . . ."

Mary found that the blessing of her new home continued that week, as many different women of the community arrived with a variety of delicious foods as well as a sometimes cheeky remark or well wishing for a happy home full of children. Her people definitely subscribed to the *Amisch* proverb, "Blessed is the lap that is full of *kinner.*"

Grossmuder May brought cinnamon rolls, with her

well-known hand-rolled dough that dripped with sticky goodness. "No time for baking now, I'd imagine, child. Making *kinner* takes hard work."

Mary caught herself from disagreeing about the work aspect and took the buns with a blushing smile. "*Danki, Grossmuder*, and thank you for your blessings."

Ben Kauffman's wife, Emma, came next, her demeanor practical and helpful after having six children of her own and with another one on the way. "It's a cornbread casserole, Mary. Heat and eat . . . and enjoy this time alone with your husband."

"Well, I surely am, Emma. How are you feeling?"

"Great," the other woman assured her as they embraced. "And rest assured that you can come to me for any everyday advice that might be needed—I feel like I've felt it all."

Mary laughed, treasuring this offer, and saw her to the door.

Esther Miller came next with a whole baked ham, molasses baked beans, and an apple streusel pie. The older woman piled everything on the table and gave Mary a faint look of apology. "I was thinking back to when Henry and I first married and, well . . . I guess I got carried away. This'll keep for a while in the icebox."

Mary accepted the large meal with grace and tried to imagine Esther and Henry young and together . . . it took some thinking, but it was an example to her of how time must go by so quickly when you loved someone.

"Thank you, Esther. Jude will love the pie."

Esther nodded and sniffed as she left. "*Jah*, so does Henry."

By the late afternoon, Mary had managed to put away everything that was brought and plan out how she'd use each gift for meals during the coming week. Then she sat down in a rocking chair by the fire with Bear beside her and found herself drowsy as she waited for Jude to come home, grateful for all that she been given in life.

Jude came home late because he'd lost track of the time grading some work, and then needed to stop by the store for some more paper that the students had wanted. It grew dark on the mountain early in winter, and he hurried along the path toward the cabin, his head down against the wind, with hands in his pockets. He was preoccupied with the idea of speaking at the Christmas program but also with pleasant thoughts of Mary, so that he barely noticed when he bumped into another *Amisch* man in the shadows.

"Whoa, sorry," Jude called, steadying himself.

"How are you doing, Jude?"

He recognized Mahlon Mast's voice and smiled at the man's use of his first name. "All right, I guess, Mahlon. Do you—want to come in for a bit?" *Don't come in . . . I want to hold my wife.*

"*Nee*, my wife, Anne, sent a raisin pie is all—for your new home. Here."

Jude took the pie thrust at him. "*Danki*." He was about to walk on when he sensed that Mahlon wanted to say something more, so he rocked back on his heels in the cold air and waited for a moment.

Finally, the older man spoke. "I, uh, heard that Lapp was over at the schoolhouse today. Don't pay him no mind. He's all bluster and blow. You'll do fine at the Christmas thing, ain't no reason for worrying none."

Jude stood up straighter, feeling a bit relieved. "Thank you, Mahlon. That means a lot."*I mean it.*

"*Jah*, well, I'd best go on. My *kinner* say you're the best teacher what they've had . . . So, *gut nacht*."

Jude watched him turn and stomp off in the wind and smiled to himself. There was no doubt that Mahlon Mast had become a source of unexpected support in his life, and he never could have imagined that happening. He started to whistle, holding the warm pie close, and went indoors to his wife.

Chapter Forty-Seven

Mary woke before Jude the morning of the Christmas program. It was only first light outside, but she could see the heavy flakes of snow falling and filling the windowsills outside. She turned on her side to study Jude as he slept, hating to wake him.

Her eyes drank in his tousled hair, the heavy fall of his eyelashes against his cheeks, and the strength of his bare throat and chest. He was so generous when he loved her, she thought with a delighted shiver, remembering the previous night. And he made her want to give to him all the more—of her body, mind, and heart.

She bit her lip and eased carefully atop him, loving the moment when his blue eyes opened, still drugged with sleep. His mouth curved in a faint smile as she felt him lift his hands to her hips.

"Mmm," he murmured. "This is a nice way to wake up."

"Is it?" She shifted slightly against him and watched him arch his throat with a sharp, indrawn cry.

"Jah," he gasped.

She bent to kiss him deeply, savoring the taste and feel of him, and relishing the fact that she'd started his potentially difficult day with pleasure.

Jude was thankful that Ben Kauffman had instructed Daniel to shovel the steps and start the fire in the woodstove early at school. The boy had then returned home for breakfast, leaving Jude plenty of time to set out the folding wooden chairs he'd found in a side closet and to pray that all would go well that day.

For some reason, as he stood, taking in the cheerful decorations and the beautifully carved crèche, he thought of his book and all the ambitions he'd had a year ago. Yet here he was, in the middle of a schoolroom out of the nineteenth century, his feet planted firmly on the uneven hardwoods, feeling like he was as centered as he'd ever been in his life. It was a momentary flash, a granted personal insight, but it sustained him as the students began to arrive, followed by the adult members of the community.

Jude nodded encouragingly to the class of five first graders who were to sing the *Englisch* version of "Away in a Manger."

He had to smile to himself as Mahlon Mast's son puffed out his chest and belted the carol with operatic intent, despite all of their practice. His co-choir frowned and struggled along, but Samuel carried the tune and ended a good twenty seconds before the others.

As expected, there was no applause—only some laughter from the crowd. The *Amisch* liked to hold their clapping until the end of things and only showed approval if it was well deserved.

Daniel Kauffman and the other boys who'd carved the crèche got up to tell individual parts of the Christmas story, then surprised Jude by giving an impromptu lesson in woodworking when describing how they'd turned the cows' legs on the lathe.

Tabitha held Lucy Lapp's hand and joined some other girls in reciting bits of poetry they'd written about God's creation of winter and what He must have been thinking.

And Rob rounded things off by singing a sweet medley of catchy *Englisch* carol refrains, while Jude held the waste can close by.

Then the whole class sang a verse of "We Wish You a Merry Christmas" and Jude rose to his feet.

He stepped in front of the lectern and his eyes swept the crowded schoolroom until he found Mary's eager face and shining eyes. He adjusted his glasses and cleared his throat.

"I think there's no reason to guard against vanity today, as the *kinner* here have done such a *wunderbaar* job." He lifted his hands to clap and was pleased by the resounding echo that came from the community.

When the room quieted, he tried to marshal his thoughts and found he had no idea what to say.

Please Gott, *help me out . . .* His eyes drifted to Mahlon Mast's steady face, and something shifted in his heart. He grasped the lectern and began to speak.

"As you all know, Bishop Umble's got a bad throat, but he let me know that he wanted me to speak, so here we go. I know it may seem strange to talk about something other than the Christmas story, but you each have given me part of Christmas every day here on Ice Mountain. You've all helped me to find true joy and true peace.

"But most importantly," he continued, "you've taught me what it means to be a father, to have a father, and to understand *Gott* as my Father. In learning this, I—I've discovered that I am able to feel forgiveness for my earthly father and to accept that we may never have the relationship that I've wanted for nearly all my life." He paused to open Mary's Bible in front of him. "I won't read it word for word, but in here, I've learned that it is my privilege, but also my right, to call God—Abba—which in Aramaic means Daddy—*Der Daadi*. I could never say this as a child to my own father—it never fit."

Jude paused and swallowed when he saw Mahlon Mast take out a blue handkerchief and wipe at his eyes while his wife patted his arm.

"It never fit . . . and maybe it didn't or doesn't for some of you, but it always fits with God. And, I'll close by saying that someone very wise and dear once told me that God puts us in families. I realize now that she was right, and if I hadn't experienced the loss of having the father I wanted, I could never appreciate in truth the One I have today. Thank you all."

He sat down at his desk in the still silence, wondering if he'd said too much or too little when the community burst into thunderous applause. Jude knew it was both acknowledgment of his words and, more importantly, praise for the Father above, and his heart was glad.

Mary caught him in her arms afterward, careless of who saw or watched.

"*Ach*, Jude, it was so *wunderbaar*, really."

She felt him smile against her mouth as he swung her around once. Then he bent to whisper in her ear. "I'm so glad it's over because I have plans for you, Mrs. Lyons, my dutiful student . . ."

She laughed out loud and met his gaze with a bold one of her own. "Always and willing, sir."

He grinned and took her hand. *"Gut."*

Then she joined him in a round of Christmas cookies and hot apple cider as they bid farewell to the students and families for the upcoming holiday break.

Chapter Forty-Eight

Late that night, Jude shivered in pleasure and spread the fall of her hair across his chest. "You know, before my grandfather died, he told me not to believe you about something . . . what do you think he meant by that?"

She played with clever fingers at his waist and shrugged. "He must have known the truth somehow."

"The . . . truth?" he managed to say.

"That from the beginning, I've wanted a marriage with you, not simply a wedding. I've wanted to be a wife, not—not merely a bride."

"And you are my wife in truth." He shifted his hips. "Not only the wife of my body, but of my heart and my mind, and my soul . . . the wife of all that I have to give and to learn and to be."

"And that response deserves a gift," she said.

"What is it?" he asked with a smile and genuine curiosity as she padded back to their bed with a small package.

"Henry Miller found it when he was going through Rachel's things . . . I guess I must have mentioned it to him, but . . ."

She paused as he unrolled the brown paper and pulled out an exact replica of the Ice Mine snow globe that his grandfather had once had.

"Oh, Mary," he whispered, shaking the dome so that the gentle snow fell inside the little world. "I never expected to find another of these, but maybe Henry would like to keep . . ."

"Henry gave it to me, and I am giving it to you—so that you'll always remember Ice Mountain and the bride you found there."

"So that I'll always remember that true love makes all things new." He put the globe down on the floor and pulled her close.

And she reveled in his fervent touch as he began the art of lovemaking once more . . .

Epilogue

On the first clear Sunday of spring, Jude lit the lamp in the Ice Mine and lifted it high to shine on the walls now forming their seasonal coating of ice. He kept a hand on Mary's arm, holding her far back from the edge of the deep mine, and smiled down at her when she would have protested.

"No chances of any kind," he said, his voice echoing softly in the cave.

"You know Dr. McCaully says that everything is going well, and the first trimester is up in a few weeks," she reminded him.

He put his arm around her and pulled her close, letting his hand stay still against her fragile rib cage. "I won't relax until the last day of this pregnancy is up."

"You'd think you would be more excited about the bishop's approval of your self-publishing your book."

He bent and nuzzled her throat against the top of her cape. "No, sweetheart, there will never be anything more important to me than you, our baby, and the world here on Ice Mountain."

He lifted his head as a shadow fell across the opening to the mine. Joseph appeared, looking both nervous and excited. "The driver's here to take me and Edward. I guess we'd better say *macht-gut.*"

Jude helped Mary walk out into the damp sunlight, blinking at the baby green color that had started to infuse the mountains surrounding them. He watched his wife hug her *bruders,* and then he too embraced each one.

Edward walked to the car, visibly anxious to get going, but Joseph lingered for a moment.

"I'll be back soon," he said finally, then turned to get in the gas company car and waved as they drove off.

Jude looked down as Mary nestled close to him.

"Why does Joseph sound like he's trying to convince himself?" she asked.

Jude smiled at her. "Because I think he is trying." Then he pulled her nearer and laid his hand on her stomach. "But this place changes a man and I don't think anyone can truly leave it, even if they're a world away."

She put her arms around his neck and he responded with a tender kiss on her mouth, tasting her warmth and the resonance of his words in her heart.

You can visit the *Amisch* of Ice Mountain
again next May with
AN AMISH MAN OF ICE MOUNTAIN.

He worked from dark to dark; four weeks on, two weeks off. The work was exhausting—mentally, physically, and spiritually, but twenty-three-year-old *Amisch* Joseph King was used to hard living. More than anything though, he was driven by the need to keep his younger *bruder*, Edward, safe from the world's influence, and if that meant being a roughneck on a gas rig in the middle of nowhere, then so be it.

"I don't see that you clocked out yet, Aim-ish! You still belong to me for the next three minutes unless you'd like to go back to mucking manure!" The resonating scream of the shift's "Push," Edmunds, the man who was paid to keep the fellas moving, startled Joseph despite the man's continual yelling. He tried to catch himself on the icy single support bar of the metal walkway in the unseasonable sleet. But he lost his footing and his big body went down hard, slamming his right cheekbone into the muddy slush at his superior's booted feet.

Edmunds and the crew nearby roared with echoing laughter as Joseph got up.

"You can add another minute onto my time, Mr. Edmunds," Joseph said evenly, wiping at his face with the long sleeve of his coveralls and pushing his dark hair back beneath his hard hat. He resisted the urge to glance in Edward's direction. His *bruder* would probably be looking as shamed as Joseph should feel, but he'd learned, since coming to the rigs, to let a lot roll off his back. *This time it happens to be sleet* . . . He edged past Edmunds and the few other men gathered and made his way down the catwalk, looking at gauges, until he reached his younger *bruder*, who was leaning near a steam heater, with a dangerous look of apathy on his twenty-one-year-old face.

"What are you doing?" Joseph snapped. "Straighten up. You know how easy it is to get too comfortable around this equipment. Do you want to get burned?"

"At least I'm not falling on my face," Edward drawled, half joking, the overhead lights playing on his blue eyes and fair hair. *They were complete opposites*, Joseph thought with sudden insight. Edward as fair as he was dark, and his brother's disposition was carefree while he . . .

The shift whistle blew, and Joseph frowned, staring out into the dark fields beyond the artificially lit rig. His brother's insolence didn't hurt half as much as the discord and loneliness he felt whenever their two weeks off came up. It was too long a drive to go home to Ice Mountain—not that he would ever drive, of course. But he also knew that getting a ride would make it even more difficult to come back. It was enough, he supposed, that Bishop Umble hadn't suggested they be shunned for doing such work—yet.

He sighed aloud and couldn't wait for the luxury of a hot bath and dry clothes, which he knew he could get at the Bear Claw Inn, four miles from the site. Joseph much preferred the Inn for time off than the so-called "man camps" that were on the drilling site itself. Even though the man camps had catered food and the opportunity to have laundry done, there was too much alcohol about for Joseph and his *Amisch* upbringing, though it didn't seem to bother Edward—which was exactly why it troubled Joseph. His younger *bruder* fell too easily into drinking and playing cards during off time.

Now, they climbed down from the rig and Joseph clambered wearily into the cab of the company truck, pushing aside beer cans and potato chip bags from beneath his feet to make room for Edward beside him. Big Moe, a Texan roughneck, was driving.

"Whoo-ee! You boys stink to high heaven—sweat and wet dog got nuthin' on you two."

"Thanks, Moe," Joseph muttered dryly. He was trying to control the shivering that was part and parcel of twelve hours of standing in the sleet.

"So, y'all been here for two months thereabouts—you ready to go home yet?"

Edward grunted, "I don't quit," and Joseph elbowed him, knowing Big Moe was trying to make conversation.

"Ahh, I used to feel like that myself some 'til my girls came along." Moe smiled. "Now I'd do anything to be home with my wife and daughters, but there don't seem a better way to make money. Those young'uns go through clothes faster than a weevil through wheat and it's my job to take care of them."

"'So *Gott* made a roughneck . . .'" Joseph murmured.

"What's that, Joe?" the Texan asked, pausing to let another company truck ease out in front of him.

"*Ach*, nothing. Well, something I read actually—about how God made a roughneck."

"You read too much," Edward sighed.

"How's it go?" Moe asked, interested.

"I can't remember the whole thing, but it was something like . . . "God said, 'I need somebody who understands the dignity of work—work that isn't pleasant or easy, but is rewarding, who takes pride in what they do, for they know that the work they do will . . . help others'—so God made a roughneck.'"

The truck bumped along and Joseph listened to the sudden silence in the cab until Moe cleared his throat. "That's right pretty like. Makes a man feel he can hang on awhile if he knows God's behind him—thanks, Joe."

Joseph nodded, glancing sideways at his *bruder*, who appeared to have fallen asleep. *Maybe I do read too much* . . . He sighed to himself and concentrated on the welcoming bright lights of the inn up ahead.

Mary "Mama" Malizza ran the Bear Claw Inn with a soft heart and an iron hand. She knew how to handle rough men and understood that most of the time, roughness was a necessary guard against homesickness, weariness, and loneliness.

But the beautiful red-haired slip of a girl who stood before her desk now proved as tenacious as the most moody of her male customers, and Mary was uncertain exactly how to proceed.

"You say you're twenty-one?" Mary asked again, buying time. *The kid looks about seventeen . . . maybe I'm getting old.*

"Yes." The girl's voice was melodic and soft, maybe too soft for her to be any kind of a waitress at the inn, but there was something about the girl's blue eyes that made Mary think of a proud, starving cat. And besides, she liked gumption when she saw it.

"You got a man?"

There, that made Miss Red-Head flinch . . . But Mary had the distinctly uncomfortable feeling that she'd touched a painful nerve from the way the girl straightened her shoulders even more.

"No, no—man."

There was something wry about the way the girl said it that made Mary decide to leave the subject alone.

"Well, I run a clean place, as far as can be, and I won't harbor no runaways. I ran away when I was about your age and nearly killed my Ma, and I won't . . ."

"My mother's already dead."

"Oh," Mary said, deflated. "Well . . . we'll give it a week's trial and no hard feelings if it don't work. You can start tonight because I'm short-handed. But those trays are heavy and the men are hungry, and some might be hungry for a pretty little thing like you. Most ain't seen so much as a hair of a woman for a long month's time."

"I understand," the girl said, visibly relieved now that the brief interview was over.

Mary thought of something as she looked down at the sketchily filled in application in front of her. "Hey, you don't list an address. I don't have any rooms open for board."

The girl flushed a bit but lifted her chin. "I wasn't certain of the last digit of the zip code. I have an apartment down the road but I moved only this week. I'll get the information for you tomorrow. Do you mind if I run out to my car for a minute?"

"Sure, but I don't hold with smoking—from the workers or the men on premises. I got asthma."

The girl shook her head. "I'm sorry. I don't smoke."

Mary nodded, half satisfied, then peered again at the application. "I can't make it out. How'd you spell your name? I need it for your waitress tag."

"Oh, it's Priscilla." The girl gave the appropriate spelling, then slipped out of the office.

Mary shook her head. *The kid won't last a week . . .*